THE WIDOW MAKER

"Can't you at least leave him here so I can bury him proper?" she asked.

"Hell, no," he replied with a smirk. "That would cost me two hundred dollars." His smile widened when he added, "I expect that's a lot more than he was worth when he was still kickin'." He hesitated a moment longer, grinning at the grieving widow before giving his horse a nudge. "Well," he slurred sarcastically, "sorry I can't stay to supper with you, but I'd best get ol' Grady here back to Bismarck before he starts to stink."

"Goddamn you to hell, you filthy son of a bitch!" she suddenly shouted after him.

It was all the warning he needed. His pistol already drawn, he wheeled in the saddle and fired three times before she had time to raise her pistol and aim. Killed almost instantly, Ruby Crowder crumpled to the ground amid the screams of her terrified daughter.

"I can't abide a foulmouthed woman," Slocum calmly stated, and holstered his pistol.

EVIL BREED

———※———

Charles G. West

A SIGNET BOOK

SIGNET
Published by New American Library, a division of
Penguin Group (USA) Inc., 375 Hudson Street,
New York, New York 10014, U.S.A.
Penguin Books Ltd, 80 Strand,
London WC2R 0RL, England
Penguin Books Australia Ltd, 250 Camberwell Road,
Camberwell, Victoria 3124, Australia
Penguin Books Canada Ltd, 10 Alcorn Avenue,
Toronto, Ontario, Canada M4V 3B2
Penguin Books (N.Z.) Ltd, Cnr Rosedale and Airborne Roads,
Albany, Auckland 1310, New Zealand

Penguin Books Ltd, Registered Offices:
80 Strand, London WC2R 0RL, England

First published by Signet, an imprint of New American Library,
a division of Penguin Group (USA) Inc.

First Printing, October 2003
10 9 8 7 6 5 4 3 2 1

For Ronda

Chapter 1

"Hello, there, little missy. Is your daddy home?"

The thin little girl seated in the soft dirt of the creek bank craned her neck to look up at the huge man riding the iron-gray stallion. Absorbed in her play with the rag doll in her lap, she had not heard the stranger approaching until he spoke. Startled at first to discover the horse and rider right behind her, she quickly felt a feeling of dread as she looked up into the cruel face hovering over her. Although his greeting had sounded friendly enough, the words did not flow naturally from his lips. There was no hint of kindness in that face, a face half covered with heavy black whiskers with one long jagged scar that ran from his left eye to his chin. Annie was at once frightened by the inherent evil she saw in the deep-set eyes that appeared to penetrate the mind of the nine-year-old child.

"Is your daddy down at the house?" Slocum

asked again when there was no immediate response from the frightened youngster. He was accustomed to this response from small children, even amused by it. "How about your mama? Is she in the house?" He glanced in the direction of the rudely constructed dwelling, built almost entirely of blocks of mud and straw. It was typical of so many prairie houses, commonly referred to as soddies. "Where's your papa?" Slocum pressed, his glance still focusing on the soddy some forty or fifty yards from where he now sat his horse. There was no sign of anyone in the pitiful garden plot beside the house or in the corral, where a pair of mules and one saddle horse stood gazing in his direction.

Finding her voice at last, Annie answered, barely above a whisper, "Papa's not home. He's gone after the cow." She hoped that now the sinister stranger would go away, but the narrowing of his eyes and his impatient frown told her that he was not satisfied with her answer.

Without another glance at the child, he turned his horse and moved off down the creek at a slow walk, eyeing the sod house cautiously. When he reached a point directly behind the house, he rode up from the creek and walked the gray up close to the back of the crude structure. Without consciously thinking about it, he reached down and eased his Colt .45 up a little to make sure it was sitting lightly in the holster. Then he dismounted and dropped the reins. Pausing a moment to listen, he then moved quietly around the side of the dwelling to a window.

Making no attempt to be secretive or hide himself, he peered into the open window. *Huh,* he thought silently when he saw the woman. Naked from the waist up, she presented a bony back to him as she scrubbed the grimy garden soil from her neck and arms, using a cloth soaked in soapy gray water from the basin on the table. She was not aware of her visitor even though the bright afternoon sun cast his shadow across her pale shoulders. He watched with amused interest for a few moments before moving toward the door. Slocum seldom had thoughts of lust, so he was not distracted from his primary mission by the sight of a woman's bare flesh.

Without bothering to announce his presence beforehand, he walked through the open door and was standing before the startled woman. Terrified when she turned to discover him, she shrieked as if in pain and frantically clutched her bodice to her breast in an effort to cover herself.

Slocum sneered at her modesty. "Don't trouble yourself, lady. I've seen bigger tits on a bird dog."

Horrified, she took a few stumbling steps backward, certain that she was about to be struck down by the fearsome brute. Slocum merely grunted his amusement and looked around at the squalor that was home to this woman and her family. Bringing his accusing gaze back to focus on the cowering woman, he snapped, "I reckon you'd be Mrs. Crowder." She didn't respond. "Where's Grady?" Again she made no reply. Her eyes wide with fright, she shook her head slowly, still unable to find her voice. His patience already exhausted, he suddenly grabbed a handful of her hair and pulled her up close to his face. "I ain't got no time to waste on your scrawny ass. Your little brat said Grady went to get the cow. Went where?" he demanded, yanking hard on her hair.

She cried out again, flinching from his other hand that was poised above her face, threatening to backhand her. "I don't know," she said in a whimper. "The cow got out. Grady went looking for her."

"Which way?" he demanded, raising his hand, still threatening to strike her.

"Yonder way!" she cried, pointing toward a low rise on the other side of the creek.

He hesitated a moment, looking in the direction indicated before releasing her to drop to the dirt floor at his feet. Then he took another look around the room to make sure there was no rifle propped in a corner somewhere that she might grab as soon as he showed her his back. Taking note of the obvious poverty she lived in, he smirked. "Grady weren't much better at farming than he was at robbing banks, was he?"

Outside the door, he encountered little Annie, who had run to the house, fearful that her mother might be in danger. She backed away immediately to put a safe distance between herself and the dark monster. Slocum favored her with a crooked grin as he strode past her and stepped up into the saddle. The child was terrified after having peeked through the open door to see the abuse of her mother. He gazed at her a moment longer before turning his horse toward the rise on the opposite side of the creek. She would soon be without a father. Slocum didn't give a damn.

Grady Crowder cursed the obstinate milk cow as she watched him approach. Taking slow, deliberate steps in an effort not to startle her, he got within ten yards of her before she turned and trotted off again. "Damn you!" Grady spat. He wished then that he had taken the time to slip a bridle on his horse. At least he wasn't wearing his gun. He might have been tempted to shoot the ornery beast. Still cursing under his breath, he started to run after her again, almost stumbling on the rough prairie ground. This time she stopped after increasing the distance between them to only thirty yards. Maybe she was getting tired of playing this game, he thought, and stopped running. Evidently he was right, because she now chose to ignore him and started grazing on the thin prairie grass.

Unaware of the dingy gray horse slowly topping the rise behind him, or the dark sinister figure deliberately drawing a rifle from the saddle sling, Grady approached his disobedient milk cow. His curses now converted to words of calm, he reached down to pick up the rope trailing behind her. He never heard the bark of the rifle as he stood up again and was suddenly knocked to his knees by the solid impact of the .45 bullet between his shoulder blades. Stunned, he wasn't even sure what had happened as a veil of darkness descended over his eyes and he suddenly lost all control of his body. Consciousness slipped away and he fell facedown on the prairie.

Slocum didn't move for a few moments, his rifle still raised and aimed in Grady's direction. When it became obvious that a second bullet was unnecessary, he replaced the weapon in the sling and nudged the gray with his knees. Approaching his victim slowly, his hand resting on the handle of his pistol in case Grady might not be as dead as he appeared to be, Slocum pulled up beside the body.

"You sure don't look like you're worth two hundred dollars," he said, looking down at the last member of the five-man gang that had made an unsuccessful attempt to rob the First Citizens' Bank in Bismarck. The bounty was one thousand dollars for all five. Grady Crowder had been the hardest to find, but Slocum eventually found every man he started out after. He dismounted and tied a rope around Grady's ankles.

*   *   *

Back at the house, a worried Ruby Crowder uttered an involuntary cry of alarm when she heard the single rifle shot. She had lived in fear that someone would come looking for her husband ever since he had agreed to go along with Rafe Wilson and his brothers. Grady hadn't even gone inside the bank. He just held the horses while the Wilsons went inside. It was bad luck that the sheriff was in the bank at the time. The Wilson brothers were caught by surprise and had to shoot their way out. Rafe and one of his brothers were wounded in the gun battle, and all five were lucky to escape, even though they left without one penny of the bank's money.

Grady had assured her that the law wouldn't likely come this far to look for him. The bank hadn't lost any money, he reasoned, and this territory wasn't even in the sheriff's jurisdiction. It was Indian territory. But the day she feared had come. Grady hadn't counted on a bounty hunter.

There had been only one shot, and Grady didn't have his gun with him. Maybe the shot she heard had been a warning shot. What should she do? She had to help her husband. Annie, standing beside her, began to cry. Ruby pulled the child close to her and tried to tell her not to be afraid. But Ruby was afraid as well. The menacing brute who had surprised her at her bath looked to be capable of any amount of evil. Determined that she must be prepared to protect herself, she took Grady's pistol out of the bureau drawer and stationed herself by the window.

Her wait was not long. She saw his head first, when it appeared above the rise, with his flat-crowned, wide-brimmed hat pulled low over his eyes. Trembling with fear, she tried to steady the hand that held the heavy pistol as she stared at the emerging specter from below the rise. Like an evil sun rising on the horizon, he emerged: head, shoulders, massive trunk, until the man and his horse both topped the rise. But there was no sign of her husband. At once her heart beat with excitement. *Maybe Grady got away!* But then another thought invaded her mind. *Grady may be dead!* Maybe that was what the shot had meant. Afraid to take her thoughts any further, she told herself that surely the man would be aiming to capture her husband in order to take him back for trial. Then she caught sight of the rope stretched taut behind the saddle, seconds before her husband's body bounced over the top of the rise, raising a cloud of dust as Slocum dragged it down toward the creek.

Crying out in stunned despair, she ran from the house in an effort to reach her husband's body before Slocum dragged it through the creek. She was too late. Driving his horse right by her, Slocum didn't stop until he was at the corral.

"I reckon I'm gonna need that horse," he said, nodding toward the one saddle horse in the corral. "I don't wanna drag his sorry ass all the way to Bismarck—too hard on my horse." It didn't escape his eye that she was holding a pistol in her hand. "Your cow's likely down by the creek, if you're of a mind to go get her." He watched her carefully, waiting for her response. She seemed to be in a trance. Her eyes, devoid of tears, were staring wide in shocked disbelief, seeing nothing, the pistol in her hand forgotten. She was seemingly unaware of her daughter, who had run from the house and had now clamped both arms around her mother's leg.

Slocum, indifferent to her grief, shrugged his shoulders and dismounted. Wasting no more time, he pulled out the two poles that served as a gate for the corral and bridled Grady's horse. With a cautious eye still on the devastated widow, he picked up Grady's body and, in one motion, slung it across the horse's back. In motions practiced countless times, he quickly took the rope tied around Grady's ankles, looped it around the horse's belly a couple of times and knotted the loose end around Grady's wrists. That done, he grabbed the seat of Grady's pants and tugged a couple of times to make sure the corpse was secure.

"That oughta do just fine," he said, one corner of his mouth raised in a crooked grin as he cocked his head toward Grady's wife. Still the woman stood transfixed in a state of shock that served to paralyze her entire body. Her demeanor was a curiosity to Slocum. Most wives screamed and fought in similar situations. This one acted as if she'd been hit in the head. He shrugged and stepped up into the saddle.

"He didn't even go in the bank," she said, surprising him with the plaintive utterance.

"Ain't for me to say, lady," he replied, turning his horse's head toward the east. "I just go get 'em."

"Can't you at least leave him here so I can bury him proper?" she asked.

"Hell, no," he replied with a smirk. "That would cost me two hundred dollars." His smile widened when he added, "I expect that's a lot more than he was worth when he was still kickin'." The slight narrowing of her eyes and a sudden tremble in the hand that still held the pistol were enough to alert him to watch himself. He hesitated a moment longer, grinning at the grieving widow before giving his horse a nudge. "Well," he slurred sarcastically, "sorry I can't stay to supper with you, but I'd best get ol' Grady here back to Bismarck before he starts to stink."

"Goddamn you to hell, you filthy son of a bitch!" she suddenly shouted after him, his sarcasm serving to shake her from her trance.

It was all the warning he needed. His pistol already drawn, he wheeled in the saddle and fired three times before she had time to raise her pistol and aim. Killed almost instantly, Ruby Crowder crumpled to the ground amid the screams of her terrified daughter.

"I can't abide a foulmouthed woman," Slocum calmly stated, and holstered his pistol. He started out again, then pulled up on the reins. Looking back at the sobbing child trying to get her mother to speak to her, he said, "I expect you'd best head for the settlement. Salt Springs is thataway." He pointed toward the distant horizon to the east. "You oughta be old enough to put a bridle on one of them mules." Satisfied that he had done more than he felt obligated to do, he kicked his horse to a fast walk.

He had gotten no farther than the edge of the yard when he heard the shot, and a bullet whistled harmlessly off to his right. Turning to look back at Annie, who was now terrified that she had missed, he threw back his head and laughed. "Not bad," he said. "That's about the age I first took a shot at a man." The memory of that incident forced a smile to his face. It was the last time his pa had ever whipped him, and his ma never forgave him for making her a widow. He hadn't thought about that in a long time. In fact, he had no idea if his mother was still living or not. He and his twin brother had left home right after that. His brother was the only other person he had any use for. It was natural, he reckoned, since they were identical twins. But the two of them had parted not long after leaving home together. The last Slocum had heard of his brother, he was looking for gold in Montana territory.

Bringing his mind back to the present, he

turned to look again at Annie Crowder. The child's efforts to shoot him tickled him. "Yessir, not bad. Hell, I believe you've got enough sand to make it."

She could still hear him laughing as he led her father's horse along the far edge of the garden.

Chapter 2

Sheriff Sam Hewitt looked up from his plate when the lone rider leading a horse passed in front of the window. Though he only caught sight of him out of the corner of his eye, there was no mistaking the massive figure of the despised bounty hunter Slocum. Sheriff Hewitt took supper in the hotel dining room every night. Slocum knew that, so Hewitt knew the surly bounty hunter would turn around and come back to the hotel when he found the jail locked. *Might as well go on down there*, he thought, pushing his plate away. *Seeing him takes my appetite, anyway.*

Slocum was already back in the saddle when he saw the sheriff walking from the hotel. He dismounted again, stepped back up on the walkway, and waited by the office door. "Evenin', Sheriff," Slocum said as Hewitt approached.

"Slocum," Hewitt acknowledged. He stopped and stood on the walkway, working a toothpick around in his mouth as he gazed at the stiffened corpse draped across the extra horse. "I reckon that would be Crowder," he stated.

"Yep, that's him," Slocum replied, grinning. "That's all five of 'em," he reminded the sheriff. There was no love lost between the two men, and Slocum knew it. For that reason he enjoyed Hewitt's irritation when he brought a man in dead. The notice said "Dead or Alive," so Slocum figured, why bother with nursemaiding them?

Hewitt stepped down from the walk to take a closer look at the corpse, which exhibited a great deal of trauma as a result of being dragged over a quarter mile of rough prairie and through a rocky creek. He didn't make any comment at once, taking his time to determine if the body was indeed that of Grady Crowder. Crowder was not well known around town, and Hewitt did not put it past Slocum to substitute any corpse and claim it was Crowder. When he decided it was probably the fifth member of the gang of would-be bank robbers, he finally spoke. "What in hell happened to him? Half the skin's scraped off him."

"He put up a fight," Slocum replied casually.

Hewitt stared at the huge man for a few seconds, considering his reply. "He did, huh?" He pulled the blood-encrusted shirt away from Grady's back. "Shot him in the back, just like two of the others you brought in," he said accusingly.

"He run," was Slocum's simple explanation.

"He ran," Hewitt repeated, disgusted, "and you just happened to shoot him in the back."

Slocum's grin returned. "Like I said, he run. If he'da run backward, then I reckon I'da shot him in the chest."

Hewitt shook his head, perplexed. He didn't like bounty hunters in general, and Slocum was the worst of them. But there was nothing he could do but apply for the reward money for the obstinate brute. "All right, dammit. I'll accept the body, and you'll get your blood money."

"Thank you kindly," Slocum said with a touch of sarcasm.

"You know, if you were the sheriff here, there wouldn't be no need to have a jail. All we'd need is the graveyard."

Slocum laughed. "I'll be back for my money in a week or two." He untied Grady's body and slid it off on his shoulder. " 'Scuse me, Sheriff," he said as he stepped up on the walk in front of Hewitt. With effortless strength, he carried the body over and deposited it beside the office door. With a satisfied grin for the sheriff, he proceeded to mount up and turned to leave.

"What about that horse?" Hewitt asked, indicating Grady Crowder's chestnut and knowing what the answer would be.

"That's my horse," Slocum replied. "Grady musta sold his." He gave the gray his heels, leaving the sheriff to grumble alone as he led Grady's chestnut mare behind him.

* * *

True to his word, Slocum showed up before two weeks had passed. Sheriff Hewitt looked up from his desk when the light from the doorway was suddenly blocked out as the hulking man stepped inside. Hewitt reached in his desk drawer and took out an envelope. He tossed it on the desk, and Slocum quickly snatched it up. The crooked grin that Hewitt had come to despise appeared immediately as Slocum tore into the envelope and started counting the money.

"It's all there," Hewitt growled, making no attempt to hide the contempt he felt.

"Why, I'm sure it is," Slocum retorted, enjoying Hewitt's discomfort. "I just like to count it." When he finished counting, he flashed his grin again and said, "Come on down to the saloon with me, and I'll buy you a drink."

"Thanks just the same," Hewitt replied dryly. He remained seated at his desk while Slocum stuffed the envelope inside the waistband of his trousers and turned toward the door. The sheriff was tempted to hold his tongue and let the contemptible bully walk out. However, he had promised to deliver a message to Slocum, so he stopped him before he closed the door. "I've got a message for you from over at the fort," he called out.

His hand on the doorknob, Slocum paused. "Is that a fact?" Suspicious at once, he quickly thought back over his movements during the past few months. He couldn't think of any point at which he might have done anything to rile the military's anger. Still cautious, he asked, "What in hell's the army want with me?"

"They might have a job for you." He wrote a name on a piece of paper and slid it across his desk. "Go see this captain in the adjutant's office."

Slocum picked up the piece of paper and stared stupidly at it. "You know, Sheriff, I ain't never took the time to learn to read. Ain't never needed to."

Hewitt favored him with a tired expression, then said, "Captain Boyd."

"Captain Boyd." Slocum repeated the name, then looked up at Hewitt. "Where do I find him? I ain't spent much time at Fort Lincoln."

"Hell, I don't know," Hewitt replied impatiently. Slocum's visit had already extended far beyond the sheriff's tolerance. "He's with the infantry detachment up on the bluff, is all I can tell you. You fancy yourself a tracker. You find him."

Slocum's grin slowly crept back into place. "That I will, Sheriff. Much obliged."

Captain Thomas Boyd glanced up at the young private standing in the door. "Sir, there's somebody out here says you wanted to see him."

"Who is it?" Boyd asked. He couldn't recall recently ordering anyone to report to him.

"Civilian, sir—looks like a scout or something—says his name's Slocum."

"Slocum." Boyd pronounced the name slowly,

not recalling immediately. Then he remembered his conversation with the sheriff in Bismarck, and the sheriff's description of the bounty hunter. "Slocum," he repeated. "Big, nasty-looking fellow?" The private grinned and nodded his head. "Send him in," Boyd said.

In spite of Sheriff Hewitt's description of the man, Captain Boyd was still taken aback by the appearance of the brute who crossed his threshold on that morning. Boyd was taller than average. Still the bounty hunter towered over him, with shoulders as wide as the doorway and arms like hams that threatened to split the sleeves of his woolsey shirt. It was the face that caused a man to draw a sudden breath, however. In describing the man to a fellow officer afterward, Boyd likened that face to an artist's rendering of evil in its purest form. Coarse black hair forced its way from under a flat-crowned hat, the broad brim of which drooped low over his face and the back of his neck. His face was covered by a heavy beard, except for a long, jagged scar on the left side where no beard would grow. At once repelled by the man's ghastly appearance, Boyd realized that this just might be the perfect candidate for the job he had in mind.

"I'm Captain Boyd," he said, starting to extend his hand, then deciding against it. Slocum noticed, but couldn't care less. "Sheriff Hewitt tells me you might be the man I need to do a job for the army. I need a good tracker."

"That so?" Slocum replied, showing no interest. "What about all them redskin scouts you got hanging around here? Ain't they supposed to be good trackers?"

"They are," Boyd said. "But I expect most of them will be going on an expedition to the Black Hills with the post commander in a couple of weeks. Besides, this job isn't suited for an Indian scout. It may take some time, and you may have to hunt him in towns and forts, as well as in the hills. An Indian scout couldn't very well do that, and it's too far to send a cavalry patrol out looking for him."

"Who are you looking for?" Slocum asked, only mildly interested. He had just cashed in on a big payday, and he felt no urgency to take to the wilds again.

"A fugitive. James Ryman Culver is his name."

"What did he do?"

"He murdered an officer in the United States Army." Boyd had been there when Lieutenant Ebersole shot at young Jim Culver on his father's farm in Virginia, then paid for his bad aim with his life. Perhaps it was more self-defense than murder, but Boyd felt justified in calling it the latter. The army could not tolerate the killing of an officer by a civilian. He went on to give Slocum a description of Jim Culver and where he had last been seen.

"Hell, there's a lot of fellers that look like that."

"He'll be the only one carrying one of those

new Winchester seventy-threes with his initials, J.R.C., carved in the stock. He rides a big bay Morgan with a white star on its face, and he calls it Toby.'' Boyd paused to try to remember anything else that would help identify Jim Culver. "He's pretty handy with a rawhide whip. He used it on an officer in Fredericksburg, so he's probably carrying it on his saddle.

"He fled Virginia and came west. The last report we had was from Fort Laramie. He showed up with a young woman at the sutler's store just before winter set in. They said he left Laramie to go over South Pass with a man carrying a wagonload of supplies to a little settlement called Canyon Creek." He paused to judge Slocum's interest, but the passive giant's expression offered no clue. "I'm authorized to pay you five dollars a day, but you'll have to stand the cost of all your supplies and ammunition."

Slocum's only response was a slight narrowing of his eyes as he added up the possible total in his mind. He preferred to work on his own time and collect a lump sum, but this wasn't a bad deal when he realized the length of time a job like that would require. Maybe it might be the start of some regular work for the army. "That's five dollars a day, starting from the day I leave here?" Slocum asked.

"That's right."

"Fort Laramie's a hell of a piece from here— take me close to two weeks to get there to even start lookin' for this feller."

"More like a week and a half, but I don't care if you have to follow him to Oregon. I want this man brought to trial."

"There's a heap of Injuns between here and there that would love to catch a lone white man traveling across that country."

"Granted," Boyd replied. "That's why I sent for you. Sheriff Hewitt said you traveled in Indian territory all the time."

"All right," Slocum decided. "I'll get him for you."

"Good. We've got a deal. But I've been told a little about your reputation. I want you to understand one thing for certain. I want him brought back alive. It's important that we try this man for murder. Folks have to know they can't kill an officer of the U.S. Army and get away with it."

This caused Slocum to cock his head back a notch. "Alive?" he exclaimed. "What if he puts up a fight? What if I *have* to kill him?"

"No deal, that's what." The captain was adamant. "You don't get paid for a dead man. Wounded, if you've got no choice, but the army doesn't want to try a corpse. If you get the job done in a month's time, you'll receive a two-hundred-dollar bonus."

This raised his interest considerably, but the insistence that Culver had to be alive didn't sit well with Slocum. He never thought much of bothering with a prisoner. It was just a lot more efficient to shoot the son of a bitch and carry the meat home—just like any other kind of hunting. He was almost of a mind to turn the deal down, but decided the potential for additional jobs for the army might be worth the extra trouble. "All right then," he said. "I'm gonna need me a night in town first. I'll set out for Fort Laramie tomorrow morning."

Chapter 3

Far west of Fort Lincoln, beyond South Pass and the southern slopes of the Wind River Mountains, Jim Culver stood on a massive outcropping of rock and looked toward the southern end of a valley. Long and narrow, the valley extended far beyond his eyesight. The settlement below him had been named Canyon Creek by the handful of immigrants who had first discovered the upper part of the valley. They were good people, these settlers who had built cabins and cleared land for crops. Hardworking and proper Christians, they asked for nothing more than to be allowed to live in peace, working the land. It was a quality Jim applauded, but knew was not ingrained in his soul. Like his brother Clay, Jim was hard put to stay in one place for very long.

Unaware that anyone back east still had reason to look for him, he decided that it was time to see what was on the far side of the mountains that surrounded Canyon Creek. There were some things that troubled his mind, and he needed room to sort out his feelings. The past few months had been some of the best of his life. He had to admit that. Getting reacquainted with his older brother, Clay, was well worth the time spent helping him build a new cabin for Katie Mashburn. They had built it about one hundred yards from the ashes of the original cabin, a little closer to the river. It was a sight bigger than the one Katie's father and late husband had built. Lettie Henderson, the young girl whom Jim had met on the trail west from St. Louis, had decided to stay on in Canyon Creek after the winter instead of returning to St. Louis, and Katie had invited her to move in with her. It had been a decision that pleased Jim, although he was reluctant to admit it, even to himself.

As soon as the cabin had been completed, Clay had left. He had obligated himself to scout for the army at Fort Laramie, and was already late in reporting. Jim had taken on the responsibility of helping Katie and Lettie move in and get settled. He had plenty of help from Luke Kendall, a young half-breed boy Katie had more or less adopted. Now that they were situated comfortably, Jim felt free to go in search of his medicine, as Clay had expressed it. And that could best be found in the high mountains, where a man was a notch closer to his maker.

Once he admitted it to himself, he realized the biggest thing that troubled his mind was what to do about Lettie Henderson. No more than a slip of a girl, she had taken over a sizable portion of his mind. There was no denying he had feelings for her, but he wasn't really sure what they meant. He wouldn't admit to being sweet on her. It was just that whenever she was away from him, he always seemed to catch himself wondering when she was coming back. She had feelings for him, too. There was little doubt of that. A shiver ran the length of Jim's spine when he thought of comments Clay had made. *That little gal's already got a rope on you. She's just giving you plenty of slack right now. When she's ready, she'll start drawing you in.* Jim was sure he wasn't cut out to be a farmer. And it bothered him that he couldn't help worrying about those two women alone in the cabin, trying to work that little farm. They had Luke there to help them now, but how long would he stay? *Hell, he's half Shoshoni. How the hell is Katie gonna make a farmer outta him?*

Jim guessed he must have the same blood coursing through his veins as Clay. For, like his brother, he needed solitude to examine his feelings, and maybe sort out a path for his life to follow. Being around people, especially Lettie, clouded his thinking. Even as a boy, back home in Virginia, he had been more at peace in the woods.

Thinking of Virginia, he knew he could never be satisfied going back there after seeing the Rockies. His father's health had been failing when Jim left, leaving Jim's two brothers to do the brunt of the work. They were capable. He was confident of their ability to take care of the farm. And after that incident with the soldiers by the Rapidan River, it might not be wise to ever return to his boyhood home anyway.

It had been self-defense, pure and simple. That hotheaded lieutenant had taken a shot at him. Jim had had little choice but to shoot back. It had just been bad luck for the lieutenant that Jim usually hit what he aimed at, even in a split second, as that had been. The captain knew his officer had fired first. There were four more soldiers as well as the sheriff who had witnessed the killing. Still, Jim had decided not to risk hanging around to see what a military court might decide on the issue. Surely, he felt, the whole incident would have been forgotten after this much time had passed. He sure as hell wasn't the first man to leave his past in the east and head west with a clean slate.

Now he couldn't help but feel he was running again, only this time he was running from himself. With the completion of the cabin, the talk had turned to planting this field and that one—what crops to try on that piece above the old homeplace, whether or not the garden could be extended to take in one corner of the old cornfield. He admitted that he had probably panicked, but he had to get away from such talk. He could feel the noose tightening around his neck, and he couldn't forget the worried look in

Lettie's eyes when he had ridden out that morning. He couldn't help but wonder if it had been a coincidence that she had put on a dress that morning, instead of the shirt and pants she had been wearing to work on the cabin. There was no doubt that the transformation had had the proper effect on him, for she had implanted an image in his mind that he was not likely to forget. He wanted to leave and he wanted to stay. He knew he had to get away to think things out.

Now, as he put a foot in the stirrup and climbed aboard Toby, he tried to put those thoughts out of his mind. As he crossed over the first ridge, it didn't take long before the excitement of seeing country he had never seen before took hold of him. For the rest of that day and most of the next, he pushed deeper and deeper into the rugged mountains.

Following an old game trail that led down through a thick belt of arrow-straight pines that towered high over his head, he suddenly emerged to find himself in a lush green meadow dotted profusely with tall buttercups and blue flag. All thoughts of Virginia and Lettie Henderson were immediately forgotten for the moment, banished from his conscious mind by the sheer beauty of the vista before him. He did not consider himself to be an emotional person, but he could not deny the involuntary shiver that touched his entire body as he pulled his horse up to take it all in. It was too much for the mind to contain. He gazed up at the snow-covered peaks above him. Tall and unyielding, they stood like silent symbols of immortality, reminding him that his time on earth held no more significance than that of the deer fly buzzing around his head. And yet he felt a part of it—the rocky cliffs, the trees, the steep meadows sloping steeply away from him, and the intense blue of the sky overhead—and he had a sense of coming home. Farther down the mountain, the slope of the meadow gradually lessened until it finally came to rest at the edge of an emerald lake that filled the narrow valley. On the far shore, an elk bugled his lovesick call and disappeared into the trees that lined the water. God had outdone Himself. There could be no place on Earth that matched it.

Jim made his camp by the water's edge and hobbled Toby close by to graze in the lush grass. Toby didn't like hobbles, and probably wouldn't have strayed far anyway, but Jim decided it was best to take precautions. Clay had cautioned him to be careful. It was Indian territory, either Shoshoni or Crow, depending upon how far north he had traveled. In spite of this, he felt at home in this country. He wondered if the horse felt it, too. Toby seemed content enough, even with the hobbles.

He spent three days camped by the lake. He rigged up a fishing line, he listened to the elks bugle, and he watched the slow, lazy wheeling of hawks high over the valley. And he spent a lot of hours peering up into the starry heavens each night, desperately searching for insights to the life path he should follow. It was to no avail, however. He was still undecided, and he didn't have a clue as far as what his *medicine* might be. Maybe that kind of thing worked only for Indians. Maybe white men didn't have any special medicine. Maybe it was because he didn't go on a fast. Clay said Indian warriors fasted for several days before attaining their vision. Jim couldn't see the sense in that.

"Ah, to hell with it," he finally exclaimed to Toby on the morning of the fourth day. In spite of his fascination with the country, he was disappointed to realize that he had been unsuccessful in ridding his mind of Lettie Henderson. "Dammit! I ain't ready to tie my ass to a plow," he complained loudly. Toby flicked his ears and snorted. *Now I've got both of us confused,* Jim thought, taking note of the horse's reaction. He picked up his bedroll and tied it on behind the saddle. It was time to leave this perfect spot and move on, but he burned the location deep into his memory, knowing he would return one day.

As much as the land tempted him to wander, with the snowy peaks in the distance summoning him like pale sirens, still he knew he could not afford to roam aimlessly. Basic supplies and cartridges for his rifle didn't grow on trees. Seeking a purpose, he made up his mind to ride to Fort Laramie. Maybe he could sign on as a scout, like Clay. That would do for a while until he discovered something else to do.

Backtracking to pick up the old game trail he had followed into the valley, he stopped to take one last look at the shimmering lake behind him before nudging Toby onward once more. Even though he had decided on a destination, there was no need to hurry. He could take the time to explore the lofty mountain range between him and South Pass.

Working his way around a towering peak, Jim climbed as high up the mountain as he could before Toby began to have trouble finding solid footing. Sidling across an area of loose shale, his horse labored to reach an outcropping of solid rock that would give Jim an uninterrupted view of the southern end of the range.

Once he reached the outcropping, he dismounted to rest his horse. Toby gazed at him as if saying, *This damn sure had better be worth that climb.* It was. He was not close to the peak; a horse couldn't make that climb. But he was high enough to command a view of the rugged slopes around him that only hawks and mountain goats had witnessed. The experience had a profound effect upon him, and he knew then that he would always yearn to breathe in the clear mountain air and let his heart soar where the hawks and eagles flew.

Man and horse remained on their lofty perch until the sun began to sink toward the distant peaks, the man contemplating his place in God's plan, the horse content to rest and graze in the sparse patches of bear grass. Realizing late that he had waited too long before starting back down the steep slope, Jim resigned himself to spend the night there. The thought caused no great concern. There was nothing to use to build a fire, however, but he could chew on some dried venison for his supper and he could share his canteen with Toby. So he settled in for the night, watching a glorious sunset of scarlet and gold before a sudden impenetrable darkness settled upon him like a silent shroud.

Morning found him stiff and shivering from the cold as a gray dawn gradually awakened the mountain range. Though eager to descend to more comfortable climes, he had to wait for the sun to climb high enough to light the dark pockets below him, lest Toby make a misstep and send them both tumbling down the steep mountainside.

When at last the first golden rays of the morning sun found their way through the narrow gaps of the upper ridges, Jim walked to the edge of the rocky precipice to experience one last look at the rugged expanse below him. Raising his rifle in both hands, he stretched his arms high overhead in an effort to relieve some of the stiffness in his shoulders. With his toes right at the edge of the rock, he glanced straight down at the ledges below him.

Startled, he almost staggered. Directly under him, some fifty feet at most, he was astonished to discover a lone Indian warrior. Unaware of

Jim above him, the man was kneeling, facing the sun, his arms outstretched as if he were performing some sort of ritual. On reflex, Jim immediately dropped his arms, holding his rifle in a ready position, but made no other move or sound. Fascinated by the unlikely presence of the Indian, Jim continued to watch. The man was wearing no more than a loincloth and moccasins, with nothing but one blanket to protect him from the morning cold. Jim was reminded of Clay's comments about seeking his *medicine*, and he felt certain that this was what the Indian was attempting. Judging by the Indian's lack of clothes to make his body suffer, and the fact the man had no weapon other than a knife, it was apparent that Jim had guessed correctly.

War Ax ended his prayer to the Great Spirit. He felt his medicine was strong. He had spent three days and nights on the rocky ledge with no food and only a few mouthfuls of water. On the last night he had dreamed of slaughtering many enemies that had surrounded him in a fierce battle, and this was indeed a strong sign that he would remain a mighty war chief.

He had not come to this place since discovering it while a boy, searching for his medicine. It was a good place, for he had been successful in finding his path of life, an important undertaking for every Blackfoot warrior. Now it provided a renewal of his strength for the coming raids on his enemies, the Crow.

Ready to return to his village now, he rose to his feet, pulling the blanket around his shoulders to ward off the morning chill. Suddenly his senses warned him of danger, and he looked up above him. *A white man!* Standing on a ledge overhead, a white man, holding a rifle, looked down at him impassively. Ordinarily quick to react, War Ax stood, gazing up at Jim, unsure whether he was looking at a vision or a real man. Neither man uttered a sound as their eyes locked upon each other. When the vision did not go away or even fade, War Ax realized that it was a real man who stood over him. The realization also struck him that the white man had stood watching him as he made his prayer to the sun, helpless to defend himself. But the white man did not kill him. *Why?* War Ax could not explain.

Several long minutes passed. Still the white man and the Indian stood transfixed, gazing at each other. Finally Jim raised his rifle slightly in a simple salute and turned away. War Ax, below him, nodded in brief response, and turned away as well. Both men prepared to descend from the mountain, each going down a different side.

It was toward the middle of the afternoon when Jim guided Toby down the side of a wide ravine to a trail that appeared to offer a passage to the foothills beyond. He had already spent a good portion of the morning backtracking from previous attempts to find a trail down from the steep slopes of the mountain he had chosen to cross. Although he was keeping a sharp eye for any sign of the warrior he had seen that morning, he had seen nothing. The Indian was almost forgotten by the time Jim found a trail that showed promise of a way out. There were a good many tracks of unshod horses on the trail, which told him that it was commonly used.

"It's a good thing I ain't in a hurry to get to Laramie," he confided to Toby. "I wonder if the army will hire a scout who can't find his way to the fort." He was about to laugh at his own joke when he was startled by the sudden crack of a pistol and the sound of cracking limbs as the bullet ripped through the pines right behind him. Toby jumped at the sudden report, and Jim, ducking instinctively, let the startled horse have his head.

After lying low on Toby's neck for about fifty yards until the trail took a sharp turn, Jim drew the horse up to a stop, figuring he had ample cover to try to determine who was shooting at him. His first thought was of the Indian back on the mountaintop. Drawing his rifle, he dismounted quickly and moved back to the point where the trail had taken a turn. Kneeling there, he slowly scanned the trees up the side of the ravine and back down. There was no sign of anyone.

Leaving Toby tied to a low tree limb, he climbed up above the narrow trail and made his way back, weaving through the lodgepole pines that covered the slope. He was close to the point where he had heard the shot when he detected the faint sound of someone calling out. He stopped to listen. There it was again! The sound was muffled, as if someone were shouting from inside a cave. He worked his way closer, stopping to listen each time the call was repeated, until he crossed over the trail and continued to move down the slope. Finally he realized he was almost on top of the source, because the call rang out again, and this time he could hear the words distinctly. "Come back, Gawdammit!"

Jim carefully pulled a laurel branch aside and discovered that he was on the edge of a deep gully. Peering over the rim, he was amazed to find a horse at the bottom with a man seated in the saddle, facing away from him. It was a strange sight, and one that puzzled Jim, for it appeared that the horse and rider were jammed into the narrow end of the gully between two rock sides, waiting there for no apparent reason. At that moment the rider, a young man with long black hair, worn in two braids, Indian-fashion, threw back his head and yelled, "Help! Dammit."

"I can hear you," Jim replied.

Startled, the young man twisted around in an effort to see who had spoken. Relieved that the reply had been in English, he was further gratified to discover that Jim was alone. "I heard you ride off. I thought you weren't coming to help me."

"I thought you shot at me," Jim calmly replied. "You didn't miss by much." Satisfied that he was no longer in danger of being shot, he pushed through the laurel bushes, walked around to a point above and beside the man, and squatted on his heels while he studied the problem.

"Sorry," the rider said, "but my yelling didn't seem to be doing no good." He threw up his hands in a helpless gesture. "I could hear your horse, but I wasn't sure you could hear me."

Jim nodded slowly while he considered that, then said, "Why don't you get off that horse and climb outta there? He looks like he's dead."

Speaking with the forced patience of a man who had long since run out of it, the dark-haired young man replied, "Mister, that's a God-given fact. He's dead, all right—broke his neck when the damn-fool nag fell in this gully. Got spooked by a damn groundhog or something, I never did see what it was. He jumped off the trail up yonder, and before I knew what was happening, there wasn't no ground under us. And I promise you, I'da climbed outta here except for a little matter of having my leg jammed up against the side of this hole."

Jim took a moment to consider this, looking the young man's situation over for himself. He was in a fix, all right. The horse's body held the man's leg pinned against the side of the hard dirt bank—a foot farther and his leg would have been jammed against solid rock. Jim could see where the man had been trying to pick a hole in the dirt with his knife, but he had made very little progress. The problem didn't appear to be the dirt bank itself, but more specifically a root the size of a man's arm that crossed over his leg just above his ankle. The trapped rider had succeeded in digging out enough dirt to expose a portion of the root.

Seeing the job to be done, Jim stood up again. "Well, I expect it'll take you the better part of a month to saw through that root with your knife. I've got a hand ax in my pack that might speed things up a bit. I'll be right back." He turned to leave.

"Much obliged, mister. I'm damn glad you happened along. I thought about butchering the damn horse to get loose, but I didn't wanna draw the buzzards and wolves with the smell of raw meat."

"Reckon not," Jim replied. "We'll get you out of there." He started climbing back up the side of the ravine. "I'll be back in a minute."

After bringing Toby to the point where the trapped horse had left the trail, Jim tied a rope to the saddle horn and got his ax from the saddle pack. Making his way back to the gully, he lowered himself down the side until he ended up standing on the horse's rump. "You're lucky your leg ain't jammed up against that rock," he commented. "I've got an ax, but I don't have any dynamite."

The young man laughed and twisted around

to extend his hand. "I'm obliged for the ax," he said. "My name's Johnny Malotte."

"Jim Culver," Jim said, shaking his hand.

Jim made short work of the root, chopping it in two in little more than ten minutes. But it took both men digging and chopping another forty-five minutes before the end of the root could be wrenched from the ground, freeing Johnny's leg. Jim helped him get up from the saddle, carefully pulling the injured leg up from the stirrup. After cautiously testing his foot and ankle, Johnny determined that the leg was not broken, merely bruised and scraped. Relieved to find that he was not seriously injured, he flashed a wide, white-toothed smile at Jim, and shook his hand again, this time with added vigor.

"Yessir," Johnny said, nodding his head for emphasis, "I'm damn lucky you happened along. I ain't sure I coulda got outta here by myself." He steadied himself on the wall of the gully while he tested his injured leg to see if he could put his full weight on it. It was a little awkward with the two men standing on the dead horse, so Jim helped steady him with a hand on his shoulder. "I ain't sure about this," Johnny said. "You might have to help me up."

"Grab hold of the rope, and I'll give you a boost. Toby will do the rest." Jim cupped his hands together, making a stirrup for Johnny. When Johnny had a good grasp on the rope, Jim called out, "Toby, get up, boy." And the horse obediently began to walk up the slope, pulling

Johnny up the steep side of the gully. Once Johnny was safely up and had scrambled over the edge of the chasm, Jim said, "Back him up and throw me the rope."

Johnny stood there brushing the dirt off his trousers for a few moments before flashing his toothy smile at Jim. "I'd love to, friend, but I'm in kind of a hurry. I've got about twelve head of horses that are most likely standing around somewhere at the bottom of this mountain. And the Injuns I stole 'em from might be showing up anytime now. I've already wasted too much time in that damn hole."

"Why, you son of a bitch—" Jim began.

Johnny interrupted before Jim could say more. "Now, no hard feelings, Jim. I'm a fair man. I'm trading you that horse you're standing on—and a damn good saddle—for your horse and saddle, even swap. I wouldn't leave you here to die. You oughta be able to get yourself outta there if you work at it. I coulda got out myself if I hadn't got my leg hung up. It'll just take you a while. I'd love to stay and visit with you some more, but I best be on my way."

In a fit of anger, Jim reached for his pistol, but Johnny ducked back out of sight. Furious and feeling like a damn fool, Jim could hear him laughing as he walked away. Jim yelled for Toby, but the horse was too far up the ravine to realize his master was calling. "Damn you, Toby, you'll let anybody ride you." He stood there, completely at a loss for several minutes, waiting for his blood to cool down, cursing himself for being so trusting of a total stranger. After another minute or two, he eased up on himself a little. *Hell, how could I know? The man was in trouble.* The logic was true, but it didn't make him feel any less the fool. "Johnny Malotte," he pronounced, "you ain't seen the last of me."

He was determined he would track Malotte down and recover his horse and possessions if he had to track him till doomsday. He was mad, madder than when that lieutenant back in Virginia had taken a shot at him. He could understand the lieutenant's motivation. Jim had laid open a few welts on the officer's back with a whip when he caught the lieutenant forcing himself on a young girl. Malotte was different. He had saved Malotte's ass, and this was how he was repaid for his help. The thought of the dark-haired young man sitting astraddle Toby made his blood boil. *Okay*, he told himself, *the first thing I've got to do is cool down and get myself out of this damn hole.*

He immediately began to evaluate his new situation. He still had his ax. He could try to chop handholds in the steep sides of the gully. It would be a lot quicker if he had a rope. As soon as he thought it, it occurred to him to check the saddle he was standing on. Sure enough, there was a coil of rope tied beside the saddle horn. Close beside that he saw the butt of a rifle protruding from a deerskin sling. It was jammed tight between the carcass and the side of the gully, but came out after he gave it a strong tug. An old iron-frame Henry .44, it was a poor swap for his Winchester, but it had a fully loaded magazine. He propped it against the side of the gully and untied the rope.

His first thought was to wonder why Malotte hadn't tried to use the rope. Then he reasoned that he probably would have, but all of his initial effort went toward freeing his leg. Jim wasted no more time on speculation. Untying the rope, he looked overhead, searching for something stout enough to support his weight. His gaze settled upon a couple of saplings, growing together almost on the lip of the gully. They were too tall to try to throw a loop over, so his only option was to try to toss one end of the rope over the saplings near their roots. He looked around for something to use as a weight. There was his ax. He considered that for a moment. *If I throw it up there and it gets hung on something, then I've thrown away the tool to cut toeholds and handholds.* He gave that a moment's thought. *Hell, if it hangs up so tight that I can't pull it down, then it ought to support my weight.*

Knotting the end of the rope as tightly around the head of the ax as he could, he fed out a good twenty feet of slack. Swinging the ax back and forth to test the weight, he steadied himself with one foot on the saddle and the other on the horse's rump, gradually increasing the arc of the swing until he finally heaved it upward.

His aim was to throw it over the two saplings, some fifteen feet above his head, causing the hatchet to drop down on the other side, pulling the rope back down to him. His toss was a few feet short, and the ax caught on the trunk of one of the trees, just as he had suspected might happen. He gave the rope a couple of hard tugs. The ax was lodged tight. Giving it one more tug, he decided it was secure, so he grabbed Malotte's rifle by the barrel and threw it as far as he could to clear the top of the gulch. Then he reached up, took a firm hold, and began pulling himself up hand over hand.

So far, so good, he thought, straining against the rope, his boots trying to find purchase in the hard side of the gully. Halfway up, he felt the rope slipping on the handle of the hatchet. "Oh, shit!" he exclaimed, and tried to climb faster. It was too late. Suddenly the knot slid down the smooth handle, and at once he was dropped back in the gully, landing once again on the carcass of Johnny Malotte's horse. "Dammit to hell!" he cursed, and got to his feet, still holding the rope.

He untied the knot in the end of the rope and looked around for something else to use for a weight. Finding nothing better, he emptied the cartridges from his pistol, pulled the end of the rope through the trigger guard, and knotted it. Hefting it a couple of times, he decided it should be easier to lob over the saplings than the ax had been. The thought proved to be true, but it still took half a dozen attempts before the pistol successfully looped over the trees and dropped back down to him. He knew then he was as good as out. He tied the two ends of the rope together to preclude any danger of losing one end while he pulled himself up. Three minutes later he was out, standing on the edge of the deep slash in the earth. With no time to waste, he looked around to quickly retrieve his ax and the rifle. Then he was off at a trot down the mountain.

Shunning the trail that wound down the mountain, he hurried straight down the slope, making his way through the brush as fast as he could without losing his balance and breaking his neck. His determination fueled by pure anger, he pushed his body relentlessly. He was afraid it had taken him too long to escape from the gully, and his only hope of catching up to Malotte would be if the horses he had mentioned were so scattered that it would take him some time to round them up.

Breathing hard, he came to a small meadow no more than fifty yards from the bottom of the slope. Off to his right he could see where the game trail made one more sharp turn before descending to the rolling hills. There was no sign of Johnny Malotte or any horses. He was too late. Dejected, but still determined, he walked across the meadow, trying to give his breath a chance to catch up. He had to decide which direction to take from the base of the mountain. There had to be enough tracks to point the way.

Just as he left the open meadow and entered the pines that ringed the base of the mountain, he heard voices above him, coming from the trail. Dropping to one knee, he brought the Henry up to rest across his other knee while he listened. It took but a moment to realize that it had to be the Indian war party tracking their stolen horses. There was a decision to be made, and he made it quickly. He was still new to the country, and he didn't know which Indians might be friendly, and which ones viewed any white man as an enemy. He had to consider the possibility that the Indians might mistakenly take him to be the one who stole their horses. Clay had warned him that even those supposedly friendly to the white man might take a lone man's scalp if they caught him in the wrong territory. So until he knew them better, he decided to treat them all as hostile. He couldn't speak in their tongue, anyway. How in hell could he explain he was after the man who stole their horses, the same as they were? Better to keep out of sight, he decided.

Lying flat on his belly behind a rotten log, he waited for the war party to pass by him. Thirteen strong, they filed by—young warriors, painted for the warpath, feathers fluttering in the afternoon breeze, their ponies prancing impatiently as they were held to a walk while sev-

eral of the riders studied the tracks at the bottom
of the slope. Jim could not help but admire the
way the warriors, most of them naked from the
waist up, sat straight and alert on their ponies.
He wondered if they were Sioux, Crow, or Shoshoni. It made him determined to learn to make
the distinction for himself.

He guessed there had to be a confusion of
tracks left by the scattered ponies when they descended the trail unattended. It couldn't have
taken Johnny Malotte long to round them up,
however—to be already out of sight driving a
herd of horses. He probably got lucky, Jim decided, and found them in a bunch at the bottom
of the trail. There was a small branch not far
from the base of the hill. The horses were probably drinking when Johnny had arrived on Toby.
The image of that stirred Jim's anger once more,
and his hand tightened on the stock of the
Henry.

The warriors didn't take long in scouting the
trail. They looked around carefully, then dis-
cussed the sign. In two minutes they agreed on
the direction and set off toward a line of low-
lying hills to the south. Jim counted the war
party as a definite sign of luck for him. He had
no doubt that they would track Johnny Malotte
down. All he had to do was follow the warriors—if he could keep up. With that thought in
mind, he sprang to his feet and gave chase, the
Henry rifle in one hand, the coil of rope in the
other, and the ax stuck in his belt.

Although Jim considered himself a strong runner, he soon found that he was going to be hard-pressed to keep the war party in sight. They were moving fast, and he was already gasping for air. Pretty soon he had to stop for a few moments to catch his breath. His heart pounding in his chest, he looked up at the sun. It was getting low. He wondered if Malotte would stop to make camp before dark. There was not much hope that Jim would be able to follow the tracks after dark. He had to keep the Indians in sight. Taking a deep breath, he started out again, this time at a trot. He had not covered a hundred yards before his breathing became labored again. He pushed on, spurred on by his ire at having been gulled by the smiling Johnny Malotte.

He was breathing so hard that he didn't hear the hoofbeats behind him until the horse nudged him between the shoulder blades. Startled, he leaped aside, stumbling as he did so, causing him to tumble head over heels and wind up on his back, gazing up into the dark eye of a curious paint pony. Jim lay there for a few moments while the pony sniffed his chest and belly, looking for some sign of recognition. He immediately realized that luck had sent him some transportation when he most sorely needed it. Evidently Malotte could not afford the time to round up all his stolen horses, and this one was obviously following the others.

"Easy, boy," Jim cooed, and reached up to

stroke the white face of the paint. The pony accepted the affection and made no attempt to retreat when Jim slowly got to his feet. "Easy, boy," he said again as he stroked the horse's neck. "I believe you're somebody's favorite. You're as tame as a kitten." It was a fine horse and obviously well cared for—no doubt by one angry individual riding in the war party ahead of him. "Well, son, let's go find your papa." He fashioned a bridle by cutting off a length of rope and looping a couple of half hitches around the pony's lower jaw. Then he hopped on its back and set off after the Indians.

Well, looks like you've got your ass in a tight spot again, Jim thought as he knelt on one knee, watching the scene below him. There was his old friend Johnny Malotte, tied to a tree trunk, while off to the side a baker's dozen Indians sat around a fire eating what looked to be deer or possibly antelope. On the other side of a small stream the horses grazed, Toby among them, still saddled. Jim felt a little quiver of relief when he spotted the big horse standing with the smaller Indian ponies. Behind him he heard a low nicker from the paint. Although out of sight behind the hill where Jim knelt, the horse was aware of the other horses across the creek. There was an answering whinny from one of them, but the warriors seated around the fire paid it no mind.

Jim focused his attention upon the hapless

horse thief bound hand and foot to the cotton-wood. Johnny's head was hanging, his chin almost touching his chest, but Jim could still see streaks of drying blood across his face, glistening as they reflected the glow of the firelight. It gave him the eerie appearance of a painted warrior. Judging by the man's sagging body, Jim could guess that Malotte had been severely beaten. It surprised him that he was still alive. As angry as he was at Johnny, he couldn't help but feel a modicum of sympathy for him. *It's his own damn fault,* he told himself. *He dug his own grave. Serves him right.*

Jim gave the situation a great deal of thought. If he went down there to try to reclaim his horse and rifle, there was a pretty good possibility he might wind up tied to the tree next to Johnny. But he knew without doubt that he was damn sure going down there to get his horse.

There was another option. He checked the magazine of Johnny's Henry rifle again. It was loaded. So he had sixteen cartridges, and there weren't but thirteen Indians. The odds were in his favor that he could maybe cut half of them down before they had a chance to protect themselves. But after that he would have a hell of a battle on his hands, one in which he would be outnumbered as much as six to one. Then, too, he really had no reason to attack the Indians. They had done him no harm. They were merely dealing with a horse thief. It was hard to say

what method of execution they planned for
Johnny, but Jim was certain it wasn't going to
be pleasant. *But, hell, it ain't none of my affair.* He
squatted on his heels for a long minute, trying
to decide the best way to approach the group
of Indians. "Hell," he finally concluded, "I aim
to get my horse and rifle back."

Iron Bow held up his hand to silence his com-
rades. The conversation around the campfire
ceased immediately, and the warriors turned to
see what had captured the war chief's attention.
In a few moments they all saw what had caused
him to gesture. As one, they all started to spring
for their weapons, but Iron Bow calmed them
again with no more than a silent signal. "Wait,"
he said. "It is only one man." With moonlight
bathing the clearing before the camp, it was apparent that it was a lone rider approaching the
camp. Seeing no threat from one man, the warriors waited, watching with curiosity, their
weapons ready nonetheless.

Determined to take back that which belonged
to him, Jim sat ramrod straight as he walked the
paint Indian pony slowly toward the middle of
the camp. He held Johnny Malotte's rifle up
over his head, his red bandanna tied around the
barrel. He had nothing white to use as a flag of
peace, but in the light of the moon it was difficult to determine the color, anyway. "I come in
peace," he called out, hoping they understood

English. There was no verbal response, just a puzzled exchange of looks and murmured comments among the warriors standing there.

As Jim entered the circle of firelight, one of the warriors suddenly grabbed a rifle and started toward him. Iron Bow quickly stopped him. The warrior protested. "That is my pony!"

"I see that," Iron Bow replied, never taking his eyes off the white man now practically in their midst. He was fascinated by Jim's boldness against such overwhelming odds and was curious to see what the white man intended to do. "We can easily kill him. Let's see what this white fool is going to do." Wounded Leg obediently stepped back and silently watched with the others.

Without knowing the language, Jim didn't know what had been said, but it was clear to him that Iron Bow was the leader. His bluff had paid off to this point. By boldly riding into camp, he had piqued the warriors' curiosity, and they had not immediately set upon him. He knew what they knew: They could kill him anytime they took a notion. He only hoped that his brazen attitude would gain him enough respect to bluff his way out of there with his horse and rifle.

Barely glancing at the warriors now closing in on either side of him, he pulled the paint up before Iron Bow and dismounted. With exaggerated gestures, he motioned for Iron Bow to follow him, and started walking toward the horses across the stream, leading Wounded Leg's paint behind him. They all followed. Jim didn't even glance at the sagging body of Johnny Malotte as he walked past the tree where he was tied.

Toby raised his head and whinnied softly when Jim crossed over the narrow stream and stopped before him. Jim turned to Iron Bow. He pointed to Toby and then back to himself, pounding his chest with his finger. The Indians dutifully followed his every motion. Jim then pointed beyond them to Johnny Malotte and then back to Toby. He tried to make riding motions to convey to them that Malotte had ridden off with his horse. He could see the puzzled expressions on their faces, so he tried to exaggerate the motions, swinging his hips back and forth in rhythm. This only seemed to confuse them more. Finally Iron Bow's curiosity got the best of him.

"Are you trying to say that man mated with the horse?" Iron Bow asked in almost perfect English.

"No!" Jim shot back. "No. What I'm saying is that man *stole* my horse. I wish I'd known you spoke American. I coulda told you straight out." He nodded his head toward the paint. "This horse belongs to you. I brought him back to trade for my horse. He stole my rifle." He held up the Henry. "This rifle for my rifle." He looked Iron Bow in the eyes. "Give me the things that belong to me, and I'll leave you in peace."

Iron Bow was truly fascinated by the brash young man. He turned to relay what Jim had said to his warriors. Jim couldn't tell from their reactions whether he was in deep trouble or not. There was a great deal of discussion among them, and after some earnest conversation between Iron Bow and one of the warriors, the warrior stepped forward and held out Jim's Winchester. Jim wasted no time taking it, at the same time handing the warrior Johnny's Henry. Looking around him now, he met smiling faces, and he realized that there was going to be no trouble over reclaiming his possessions.

"How are you called?" Iron Bow asked.

"Jim, Jim Culver," he responded.

"I am Iron Bow of the Crows. You must camp here and eat with us tonight. Then you can go on your way in the morning."

Jim accepted graciously. He might have preferred to move on immediately, but he figured he might insult Iron Bow if he refused his hospitality.

Across the stream, Johnny Malotte raised his chin slightly. Having heard the exchange between the Indian and the white man, he prayed there might be hope for him.

"What do you intend to do with him?" Jim asked, gesturing toward Malotte.

"Him?" Iron Bow echoed with an uninterested shrug of his shoulders. "He is a horse thief. We will kill him in the morning."

Jim didn't reply. He turned and took a hard

look at the man bound to the tree. He wondered why the Indians hadn't already killed Malotte—not so much for stealing horses, but merely because he was a white man. *Probably want to let him think about it all night. It ain't my business. Johnny Malotte dug his own grave.* Death was a pretty severe penalty for stealing horses, especially among Indians, who customarily stole horses whenever the opportunity presented itself. Horse thieves were commonly hung by the supposedly civilized whites, but to an Indian it was the natural thing to do. He shrugged. It wasn't his business, he reminded himself.

Iron Bow turned out to be a gracious host. He and his warriors were happy to share their food with Jim. Wounded Leg was especially grateful for the return of his favorite war pony. He had trained the animal from a colt, and he had been crestfallen to discover the paint missing when they caught up with Malotte and the other stolen horses.

Iron Bow told Jim that he and several of the others in his small band had often served as scouts for the soldiers at Fort Laramie. "The Crows have long been friends to the soldiers," he said. When Jim said that his brother sometimes scouted for the soldiers at Fort Laramie as well, Iron Bow asked his brother's name.

"Culver," Jim replied, "Clay Culver."

Iron Bow's eyes lit up. "Ahh, Ghost Wind," he said, nodding his head approvingly. "I have ridden with your brother. He is a mighty warrior."

"Ghost Wind?" Jim asked.

Iron Bow smiled. "That is the name given him by the Crow scouts. When the Hush Wings flies—that is the bird the white man calls an owl—it flies silently, making no sound with its wings. It is said that if you hear the sound of the Hush Wings' flight, it is a Ghost Wind. Your brother moves silently like the Hush Wings. Those who hear him hear the Ghost Wind.

Jim took a minute to think that over. Smiling to himself, he tried to picture his brother Clay as a huge owl, silently flying through the night. *Maybe so,* he allowed. At any rate, he would try to remember to call him Ghost Wind the next time he saw him.

There was such a casual air about the camp of Crow warriors that Jim at times forgot the battered prisoner bound to the cottonwood outside the fire's glow. He might have forgotten him altogether except for a few times during the evening when Malotte tried to get Jim's attention. Each time he did he would receive a beating, administered by one of the warriors with his quirt. Jim did his best to ignore the punishment, but he could not help but feel some compassion for Johnny's fate.

The next morning Jim awoke with the first rays of the sun, feeling that he had not rested at all. His sleep had been a fitful one; he'd awakened often to look around him at the sleeping

Indians. In spite of the warm welcome he had received from Iron Bow and his friends, there remained a wariness that told him to sleep with one eye open. It had been unnecessary caution, apparently, judging by his sleeping hosts. The only one awake other than himself was Johnny Malotte, whose sagging body was hanging to one side of the tree trunk. When Jim got up and began to stir the coals of the campfire, Johnny raised his head and whispered, "Cut me loose, Jim, before they wake up." Jim hesitated. "Come on, Jim, give me a chance to run. They're gonna gut me and leave me to die. You ain't gonna side with a bunch of Injuns, are you?"

Perplexed, Jim turned to face him, but before he could reply to Johnny's pleas, Iron Bow stirred from his blanket and sat up. Jim quickly returned his attention to the fire. To himself, he cursed Johnny Malotte for putting him in the position of making a judgment on his life. The man was a damn horse thief, caught red-handed. He had stolen Toby, for chrissakes. He deserved to be hung. But did anybody deserve to be tortured to death? Iron Bow had assured him that Malotte's death would be slow and painful.

"You rise early," Iron Bow said as he watched Jim place some limbs on the fire.

"Yeah, I expect I'd better get started," Jim replied.

"Don't you want to stay long enough to see the man who stole your horse die?"

"No, I guess not," Jim pronounced slowly, thinking hard on what he was about to propose, and what he was going to do if Iron Bow rejected it. "This man"—he motioned toward Johnny Malotte—"has stolen Crow ponies, and he stole from me. You want him punished. I want him punished. The soldiers have been looking for him for a long time. They want to punish him, too. I think the army would be grateful to you if you turn him over to me and let me take him to Fort Laramie so they can let others like him witness his punishment."

Iron Bow was only mildly interested in the proposition. "You can tell the soldiers that we killed him. Why should you have to bother with him? It's four days from here to Fort Laramie."

"That's true," Jim replied, trying to seem as unconcerned over Malotte's fate as his Crow friend. "I would not trouble myself, but I think the army would like to show other white men what will happen to them if they try to steal horses from our friends the Crows."

Iron Bow paused to consider the wisdom in this. After a few moments' thought, he nodded his head in approval. "This might be a good thing. Maybe what you say would be the right thing to do." The more he thought about it, the more he began to see it as an opportunity to show that the Crows were not the savages most white men thought they were. "It is a good thing," he repeated. "You should take him back to Laramie with you." He hesitated, thinking. "He cannot take one of our ponies, though."

"No," Jim quickly agreed, still surprised that Iron Bow was going to turn Malotte over to him that easily. "I wouldn't let him ride, even if he had a horse."

To Jim's further surprise, the others in Iron Bow's band voiced no opposition to their leader's decision to turn their prisoner over. So, after a breakfast of dried meat, Iron Bow cut the bonds that held Johnny Malotte to the cottonwood. Johnny slumped to the ground, too weak to stand. With his foot, Iron Bow rolled him over onto his back and tied his wrists together. Then he stepped back to let Jim take over.

Johnny Malotte didn't look too good. Jim wondered if he was going to have a dead man on his hands before he had ridden out of sight. He bent low over Johnny while he tied a rope to Johnny's bound wrists. Malotte's eyes, almost closed until that moment, suddenly flickered wide open, and he gazed into Jim's eyes. "I'm fixing to take your sorry ass outta here," Jim whispered. "Can you walk?"

"I'll damn sure walk outta here," Johnny rasped.

The rope secured, Jim pulled his prisoner to his feet. Johnny struggled for a few moments to keep from staggering and took a few shaky steps forward as the group of interested Crow warriors watched. One of them saw fit to administer a stinging swipe across Johnny's back with his quirt. Johnny recoiled with the pain, but managed to stay on his feet. Jim figured he'd better get the beaten man out of there before the Crows changed their minds and decided to whip him to death. With a quick farewell to Iron Bow, he climbed aboard Toby and started out of camp, walking his horse slowly, one end of the lead rope looped around his saddle horn, the other tied to Johnny's wrists.

"Go in peace, Jim Culver," Iron Bow called after him.

Jim never looked back at his stumbling prisoner, staggering drunkenly at the end of the rope, until he had ridden beyond a line of hills that crossed his path. He felt certain that the Indians were watching him. Once he rode out of sight of the camp, he stopped to let Johnny catch up to him. As soon as Johnny was even with his stirrup, Jim handed him his canteen and watched silently as the desperate man gulped the water down. It served to revive him somewhat.

"I'll never forget you for this," Johnny rasped, his voice still hoarse from his long period without water. Holding up his hands, he said, "Here, cut me loose."

Jim didn't say anything while he untied the lead rope from Johnny's wrists. Then he said, "I think I'll leave your hands tied for a while yet."

"Ah, hell," Johnny complained. "Whaddaya

want to do that for? Hell, man, you saved my life back yonder. That makes us the same as blood brothers or something. I knew I had you pegged as a fair man."

Jim straightened up in the saddle, and gazed at him in cool appraisal. "You don't know shit about me," he assured him. "You're the same blood brother that left me down in a hole while you ran off with my horse. I think I'll keep your hands tied for a while."

"You ain't gonna leave me on foot with my hands tied, are you?"

Jim smirked. "Now, what kind of son of a bitch would do something like that?"

"All right, I guess I had that coming. But, dammit, Jim, I'm pretty stove up. Them Injuns beat the hell outta me. That horse of yours is strong as an ox. He could carry double all day and not even know the difference."

"If things aren't to your liking, I guess I could take you back to Iron Bow. His boys would probably throw a party for you."

Johnny realized that it was useless to try to sway Jim, so he reluctantly acknowledged the futility of his position. "All right," he said. "I reckon you're holding all the cards."

Jim studied the plaintive face looking hopefully up at him for a few moments more. He couldn't leave the man on the prairie with his hands tied. *Ah, shit,* he thought, and drew his knife. He reached down and cut the rawhide bonds around Johnny's wrists, then quickly backed Toby away a few yards. "I saved your worthless hide from those Crow Indians, but I damn sure didn't take you to raise. You were on your own before I met up with you, so you're on your own again. The fact that you're on foot is your own doing." He could see the seeds of understanding taking root in Johnny's eyes. But the battered man still attempted to appeal to Jim's conscience.

"Jim, I know I wronged you, and I'm sorry for that, I swear. But I'm stove up pretty bad, and I ain't had food for days. I'm too weak to get very far on foot. Without no gun, I can't even hunt for something to eat. You might as well shoot me right here. I'm as good as dead, anyway."

Jim silently cursed himself for having even the slightest compassion for the man who had stolen his horse. He wasn't softheaded enough to give Johnny a gun, though. He thought it over for a few moments before deciding. "Now, I'll tell you what I'm gonna do," he said, turning in the saddle and pointing toward the southeast. "I'm heading that way, just about on a straight line with that tallest hill you see in the distance. I'm gonna hunt for some fresh meat when I get in those hills. If I'm lucky enough to find some game, I'll share some of it with you. You might be as hungry as you say, but you don't look all that feeble to me. You've been walking pretty good since we got out of sight of those Injuns. I think you ought to make it to those hills by nightfall. You can eat what I leave on top of that highest one." That said, he wheeled Toby and rode off, leaving a disillusioned Johnny Malotte standing there staring after him.

"You wait for me, Jim," Johnny called after him. "I'll be there, all right. No hard feelings a'tall. I'm still obliged to you for gittin' me out of that Injun camp."

It was less than half a day's ride to the foot of the tallest in the line of hills Jim had pointed out to Johnny Malotte. He thought about pushing on, but he had said he would leave food for him. He had given his word, and even when dealing with a thief like Johnny Malotte, his word was his bond. *The poor bastard's gonna need something to eat by the time he makes it to this hill.* Jim knew the Crows had wasted no food on him.

He began a careful scout around the hills, holding to the trees near the base. While he hunted, he gave a lot of thought to the subject of Johnny Malotte. A young man, Johnny looked to be about the same age as Jim. He seemed genuinely contrite about bamboozling Jim out of his horse, but Jim was not softheaded to the point where he would trust the glib-talking young horse thief. He was convinced that, when it came down to two men and one horse, a man would be a fool to turn his back on Johnny Malotte. Still, Jim wasn't prone to leaving a man stranded with no means of survival. After worrying his mind with it for some time, he decided to leave him food and his pistol, loaded. It was a difficult decision to leave the pistol, even though he used it only on rare occasions—to kill a snake or scare off a bear. If Johnny was as smart as Jim figured him to be, he could walk at night and rest during the day. The pistol would provide him with some defense against hostile Indians. *That's the best I can do for him, and more than he deserves.*

Finding meat proved to be a little more difficult than he had anticipated. It was the middle of the afternoon before he spotted a couple of antelope out on the prairie that rolled away from the base of the hills. With Toby tied to a clump of sage, Jim worked his way around the antelope on foot, keeping downwind. When close enough to risk a shot, he didn't waste it, bringing one of the animals down with a strike right behind the front legs.

He sat there in the cover of the shallow defile he had settled in for a long time, watching the prairie around him. When there was no sign that his shot had attracted the attention of any roaming Indian hunting parties, he left the defile and recovered his meat. Drawing the animal up on Toby's back, he led the horse back to a tiny stream near the base of the hill.

Butchering done, he packed the meat up the hill on his horse just as the shadows began to pool in the gullies and draws. It would be dark soon, and he intended to be long gone from this hill before then. He wrapped part of the meat in the antelope hide and placed it in a prominent spot on the treeless hilltop, where Johnny would be sure to find it. Then he took out his pistol and placed it on top of the hide bundle. "I expect that's the last I'll see of that," he muttered.

Satisfied that he had done as well for the man as could be expected, he led Toby back down the hill to the stream. After winding his way through the willows that framed the tiny water course, he let Toby drink while he knelt down to wash the last traces of antelope blood from his hands. In the next instant his head exploded and he was knocked senseless, floating in a sea of inky darkness, until the shock of his face in the cool water of the stream partially revived him. Completely disoriented, his ears still ringing from the impact and his brain spinning out of control, he tried to push himself up, but succeeded only in sprawling helplessly into the stream.

Johnny Malotte stood over the fallen man, holding the stump of a stout cottonwood limb that had broken in two under the force of the blow. He reached for Jim's pistol after he struck him down, only to find an empty holster. Undeterred, he turned immediately and pulled the Winchester from the saddle sling. Turning back to Jim, he watched impassively for a few seconds while the injured man tried to regain his feet. Jim had managed to struggle to his knees when Johnny cocked the rifle and pulled the trigger. He went down immediately, the bullet slamming into his chest and knocking him down on his back.

Johnny ejected the spent shell and took a couple of steps forward, watching Jim closely as the shallow water around his body became dark with blood. When, after some long seconds, there was no sign of movement, Johnny eased the hammer down and turned back to calm the startled bay stallion. Toby pulled away at first, but Johnny kept a firm hold on the reins while he quieted the confused animal. Soon Toby calmed enough to accept Johnny in the saddle. Once mounted, Johnny took one long last look at the body lying in the tiny stream. "No hard feelings, friend," he said with a smile. "But I've got to get goin' in case some nosy Injun heard that shot."

Chapter 4

"**E**venin', friend."

Nate Wysong glanced up upon hearing the gruff greeting, and involuntarily sucked in a sharp breath. "Ah . . . ah, evening," he stammered, unable to hide his shock. "Can I help you?" he managed. The man was huge, grizzled, and woolly as a bear, with a long white scar down the side of his face. Nate felt around under the counter for the shotgun usually kept there, but could not locate it.

Slocum grinned, amused by Nate's apparent fright, knowing it was fostered by the mere sight of the giant bounty hunter. "Lookin' for a friend of mine," Slocum said. "Jim Culver—I was told he's hereabouts somewheres."

Nate exhaled, able to breathe again. "Oh, you're a friend of Jim's, then. Well, he was here, all right, all winter, but he's gone now."

Slocum's grin froze on his face for a few seconds in his effort to hide his irritation. "Where'd he go?"

"I ain't sure. I just know he rode out of here a few days back." When the surly brute's face turned into a scowl, Nate suggested that Katie Mashburn might know. "Jim stayed over there while him and his brother built Katie a new cabin."

"How do I get to Katie Mashburn's place?"

After giving Slocum directions to Katie's cabin, Nate stood in the doorway of his tiny store and watched as the huge man climbed aboard an iron-gray horse and rode off toward the river. Nate expelled a long sigh of relief as soon as the stranger rode out of sight beyond the bluffs. *He said he was a friend of Jim's,* he thought. *I hope I ain't sent Katie no trouble.*

"Somebody coming," Luke Kendall said.

Katie paused. Leaning on her hoe handle, she pushed her bonnet back a bit in order to see better. It didn't look like anyone she knew, and even at that distance this one looked like trouble. She unconsciously reached down to feel the handle of the Colt she always wore.

Taking another look at the rider coming up the trail, then glancing back to notice the look on Katie's face, Luke dropped his hoe and walked over to the corner of the garden where he had left his bow. With the weapon in hand, he went back to stand beside Katie.

"Mornin', ma'am," Slocum said, reining the gray up at the corner of the garden. He took a moment to look Luke up and down, a natural habit, before he turned his gaze back to the slender young woman. *A damn odd pair,* he thought, *a woman packing a .45 and a half-breed boy carrying a bow.* Doing his best to affect a pleasant facade on a face that had seldom experienced one, he tipped his hat and spoke. "Feller over at the store told me you might know where Jim Culver was headed when he left here."

"Oh?" was Katie's only reply.

Overhearing the conversation outside, Lettie Henderson appeared in the doorway of the cabin, an apron tied around her waist. Slocum nodded politely in her direction before gazing back at Katie. "Yes'm. I'm a friend of Jim's from back in Virginia. I promised him I'd look him up if I was ever out this way."

Katie cut her eyes at Luke in a brief warning, but the boy's face was expressionless. According to what she had learned from his brother Clay, Jim had left Virginia rather suddenly—in the middle of the night, if she remembered correctly. It didn't seem likely that he would have had the time to tell friends where he was going. She didn't like the look of this dark and grizzled stranger, and she had doubts that he was any friend of Jim's. "Well, mister, I'm afraid we can't help you. He didn't say where he was heading. Most likely he headed toward Oregon territory.

Sorry you missed him." That said, she immediately started weeding with her hoe again, dismissing the stranger.

Ignoring her obvious signal that the conversation was ended, Slocum sat there for a long moment, eyeballing the woman and boy in the field. Glancing at the cabin, he noticed that the young lady was no longer standing in the doorway. He considered the possibility that Culver was inside the cabin, but a look around him seemed to indicate otherwise. For one thing, there was no sign of the big Morgan stallion Jim rode.

His ruse as a friend of Culver's obviously a failure, he decided to take a different tack. "Might be you folks could improve your memory a touch if I told you the U.S. Army sent me out here to look for Jim Culver. He murdered an army officer. If you don't help me, I reckon it'll just take me a little longer to find him. But I'll find him. I always do."

Katie looked up again. "Then you'd best get started," she curtly advised. "Oregon's that way."

A slow smile curled the corners of the sinister brute's mouth. "You're a sassy little bitch, ain'tcha?"

Luke tensed at the comment, and started to reach for his quiver of arrows, but Katie stopped him with a raised hand. She did not reply to Slocum's remark, standing defiantly with her hand resting on the butt of her pistol.

Glancing in Luke's direction, Slocum grinned openly. "You pretty handy with that bow, sonny?" Luke's expression didn't change as he continued to stare stone-faced at the unwelcome visitor. Laughing at the lack of response from the half-breed boy, Slocum jerked on the reins, turning the big gray's head back toward the trail. "Much obliged," he said to Katie, his voice heavy with sarcasm. Not one to miss many things in the pursuit of his business, he did not fail to notice the tip of the rifle barrel in the corner of the cabin window.

Heading back down the wagon track at a leisurely pace, he was confident that what the storekeeper and the woman at the cabin had told him was true. Culver had, in fact, left the valley. He was confident the rifle he spotted in the window was being held by the woman he had seen standing in the door. There were still possibilities, however. He was not convinced that they had no idea where Culver was heading. So the thing to do now was to find a good spot to hide out where he could watch the cabin for a while. *One thing for sure: Culver ain't headin' for Oregon territory.*

When Slocum had ridden out of sight, Lettie emerged from the cabin, still carrying the rifle. She walked into the garden to join Katie and Luke. "What did that awful-looking man want? He scared me so bad just looking at him that I thought we might be in trouble."

Katie couldn't help but smile. "So you were going to shoot him," she chided, impressed by the young girl's show of bravado.

"I don't know. I guess I was, if he made one move toward you. That was the meanest-looking man I've ever seen."

"Bounty hunter," Katie said. Then she related Slocum's story to Lettie.

"Jim didn't murder anybody," Lettie exclaimed. "You know what happened in Virginia. That lieutenant shot at Jim first, and Jim shot in self-defense."

"I know," Katie calmly replied. She was thinking hard on what she could do to warn Jim. "We need to let Jim know that animal is after him." She turned to Luke. "You and Clay talked to Jim about seeing the mountains and all that horseshit you men think is so important. Do you have any notion where he was going?"

Luke shook his head. "Nope. He was just going. Him and Clay talked a lot about the Wind River country. I expect he might have rode up that way."

Seeing the sudden distress in Lettie's eyes, Katie laid a comforting hand on the young girl's arm. "Jim strikes me as a man who is pretty good at taking care of himself, honey. I wouldn't worry." Then she looked back at Luke. "All the same, Luke, you'd best go find him. You know that country as well as anyone. If he's up there somewhere, maybe you can strike his trail."

"Yes'm," was all Luke replied. Wasting no

more time, he immediately went about getting some possibles together for a long scout in the mountains. In a matter of no more than half an hour, he was in the saddle and on his way.

"Well, that didn't take long," Slocum muttered. "I didn't have a chance to even make myself comfortable." He stood at the head of a shallow ravine, hidden by thick pines, watching the young half-breed boy as his horse loped by. Motionless until Luke had passed out of sight, he then stepped up in the saddle and rode after him. "All right, sonny, lead me to him."

Chapter 5

Iron Bow pulled his pony up abruptly when he heard the single shot. With a quick motion of his hand, he signaled his warriors to stop and listen. He waited for more shots, but none followed. Earlier that morning they had heard one shot. It had come from the direction Jim Culver had taken with his prisoner. Iron Bow had puzzled over it. Had the young brother of Ghost Wind decided to kill his prisoner? Or had Johnny Malotte managed to overpower him? It aroused Iron Bow's curiosity enough to cause him to want to follow the sound.

Some of the warriors voiced their concern over the wisdom in riding deeper into Shoshoni territory. Already they had ventured deep into the land of their enemies to take back the ponies Malotte had stolen. They had recovered their ponies, they reasoned. Why risk running into a Shoshoni war party? Iron Bow listened to their words and agreed that it would be the wiser thing to break off and return to their own country. But he had taken an instant liking to Jim Culver, so he still had a desire to see if anything had happened to him. "I can only speak for myself, but I'm going to ride as far as the line of hills we see on the horizon." After a brief discussion, the others reluctantly decided to follow, since he intended to go no farther than the hills they could see.

The shot just heard was much closer than the one heard that morning. The hills were no more than three or four miles away now. Iron Bow cautioned his warriors to be alert and keep a watchful eye for Shoshoni hunting parties. Leaving one of the younger men to watch the extra ponies, he led the others toward the sound of the shot.

As they approached the tallest in the line of hills, they came upon the tracks of a shod horse. "Culver's horse," Iron Bow said, and directed his scouts to follow the tracks. The Crow war party was about to follow Toby's tracks up the hill when one of the forward scouts discovered a body lying in the narrow stream at the foot of the hill.

"It's the white man Culver," Wounded Leg reported as Iron Bow brought his pony to a stop before the stream.

"I was afraid so," Iron Bow replied. "Is he dead?"

Wounded Leg bent low over Jim to examine him more closely. Putting his ear to Jim's chest, he listened for a few moments. "He walks the path between life and the spirit world," he decided. "I think his path is closer to the spirit world."

Iron Bow dismounted, and he and Wounded Leg pulled Jim out of the water and laid him on the grassy bank. The others crowded around to watch while the two decided whether it was worthwhile to try to help him. Whether he was aware of the importance of the discussion over him was not certain. But at that moment, Jim opened his eyes.

Iron Bow smiled. "We thought you had already started on the long journey to the spirit world."

Jim managed a grimace that hardly passed for a smile. "I still got things to do here," he uttered, his voice halting and labored.

"You have lost a lot of blood. The rifle ball went all the way through your body. The wound looks very bad. I think you should already be dead," Iron Bow said. "I can take you back to my village. It is a long ride. We will have to travel fast because we are in the land of our enemies, and we are few in number. The ride may kill you. Maybe you would rather stay here and die where you would be more comfortable. It is your choice."

The Crow war chief's candor brought the hint of a smile to Jim's face in spite of his pain. "You don't have much faith in my will to live, do

you? I'm not ready to lay down for old man
Death just yet."

Iron Bow smiled. "Good. We'll make a travois
and take you back to our village. Old Red Wing
will make you well again. He is very wise and
makes strong medicine."

Before they reached the Crow village, Jim
began to wonder if maybe he should have remained back by the stream to die a peaceful
death. Iron Bow's warriors fashioned a travois
using two lodgepole pines lashed to a bearskin
platform, and mounted it on one of the ponies
recovered from Johnny Malotte. After making
Jim as comfortable as possible, the band of
Crows headed northeast. The mountains he had
crossed the day before were now to the west,
but Jim took little note of the direction.

For three days he bounced along over the
rough terrain, his wound weeping almost constantly, relief from the searing pain coming only
with occasional escapes into unconsciousness. It
seemed that every time he awoke from one of
these blackouts, he would open his eyes to discover Iron Bow riding beside the travois, gazing
down intently at him. Jim soon realized that the
somber Crow war chief was curious to see if he
was going to come back to life again. Jim would
do his best to smile at Iron Bow, and Iron Bow
would simply shake his head as if amazed.

On the morning of the fourth day, the party

of Crows entered a wide valley that descended the low hills to a river that flowed serpentine among the willows and cottonwoods. Jim was aware of a general chorus of greetings from the camp as the people welcomed the war party home. But the sounds came to him as if through a dense fog, echoing around his head with bits of speech and laughter, mixed with the neighing and nickering of horses. He didn't know what was happening around him, and he was too weak to care.

It was the following morning before consciousness returned. He awoke from a deep sleep, groggy and confused, staring up into an open flap in the peak of a Crow lodge. The patch of sky visible through the flap was the milky gray of early dawn. He attempted to rise from the bed of animal fur he lay upon, but immediately sank back when a searing pain shot through his chest.

"Well, damned if you ain't alive after all." The voice came from behind him. "I've been waitin' to see if I was gonna have to waste any food on you." The man moved around to Jim's side and knelt down beside him.

Puzzled by the man's speech, Jim stared hard at his benefactor. He was an old man, dressed in animal skins like an Indian, but he was obviously not an Indian. Grinning widely at Jim through a beard almost completely gray, he held a small bowl filled with water up to Jim's lips.

"Here, drink some. It's water." Jim accepted

eagerly. "My name's Newt Plummer. The Injuns call me Red Wing. Iron Bow brung you in here half-dead last night, said you'd been having a battle with death for four days and wouldn't give in." Newt laughed when recalling it. "Told me to patch you up, 'cause you was a warrior. Ol' Iron Bow don't git too folksy with many white men, but he sure took a likin' to you, for some reason." He paused to take the bowl from Jim. "He said you come ridin' right into their camp and told him you was taking your horse and gun. Did you do that?" Jim nodded. Newt laughed again, shaking his head in amusement. "Well, it sure impressed ol' Iron Bow."

Newt got up and went outside to fill a bowl with some boiled antelope from a pot sitting in the coals of a cookfire. When he returned, he helped Jim sit up on his fur bed. "I believe you're gonna make it. You better put some of this in your gullet, though. You lost a helluva lot of blood—need to build your strength back up."

Jim took some of the meat and started to chew it. Reluctant at first because he didn't feel like eating, he soon gained an appetite after a few bites. Newt watched him intently, as if expecting to see the food running out of the holes in his body. After a few long moments of silence while Jim cleaned out the bowl, Newt spoke again. "Yep, I believe you're gonna be all right—just need to rest up awhile till your body mends. Somebody upstairs must think a lot of you. You were mighty lucky. You've got two neat little holes in you where the bullet went clear through. But they were high enough to miss your heart and lungs, else you'd be dead for sure. You'd bled pretty good outta both holes, so I put a hot iron on 'em to seal 'em off last night while you was asleep. You didn't even wake up."

Jim pulled aside the cloth that bound his chest, and stared at the cauterized wound. He could only hope Newt Plummer knew what he was doing. "How do you happen to be here?" he asked.

"I've been with 'em since sixty-one," Newt replied. "I took a Crow woman to wife and come to live with 'em when Iron Bow's daddy was chief. Old Two Bears, he died a year after that when a bunch of Blackfoot raided our village on the Tongue River. Two years after that, my woman took sick and died."

"But you stayed with the Indians," Jim commented.

"Well, sure. They're my people." He grinned. "They think I'm some big medicine. That's why Iron Bow brung you to my lodge. I wouldn't go back to what white folks call civilization now if you held a gun on me."

Jim, feeling tired from sitting up so long, lay back on his bed, reliving the events of the past several days in his mind. It seemed like a month since he had decided to leave the mountain lake and ride to Fort Laramie. "Where the hell am I, anyway?"

"We're camped on the Bighorn, about a day and a half's ride below the Yellowstone." Newt rose to his feet again, preparing to leave his patient to rest awhile. "I expect Iron Bow's right about you being tough enough to whip old man Death this time. But it's gonna take a while before you'll be ready to do any high kickin'."

Almost one hundred miles from the Crow camp on the Bighorn River, as the hawk flies, young Luke Kendall knelt by a narrow stream. Some small stones that had been dislodged near the edge of the water caught his eye as he followed a single set of shod hoofprints. It was not the stones themselves that caught his attention; it was what appeared to be dried bloodstains on some of the stones. On closer inspection, he found traces of blood that had spattered the sand and blades of grass near the water.

Not sure what it meant, but with a sudden feeling of dread, he stood up and looked around him. Someone or something had gotten shot here, but that was as much as the sign told him. It only added to his confusion. At the top of the hill he had found a perfectly good Colt .45 pistol lying beside an antelope hide. From the sign around the hide, it appeared that wolves had been there before him.

He had been confident that the tracks he had followed from the lake down through the hills belonged to Jim's horse, Toby. Toby was a big horse, easy to trail. Besides that, the camp he had found by the lake looked like one a white man might make. If he read the sign correctly, Jim had evidently met up with a band of Indians somewhere on an old game trail that led down the mountain. From the base of the mountain they had started toward the southwest and camped close by a creek. In the confusion of tracks, it had been difficult at times to pick out Toby's shod prints among the many others, but he found enough of them to be sure Jim had still been riding with the Indians.

From the camp, it had become more difficult to follow the trail because of the short grass that covered the prairie, but he had picked out enough tracks to tell him that Jim had left the others and headed out alone. This was what now worried him. The Indians had left the camp, headed in a different direction from that taken by Jim. But before reaching the point where he now stood, they had converged on Jim's trail. When Luke added all this up with the bloodstains by the stream, it painted a picture that he dreaded to take back to Katie and Lettie. It became very clear to him that Jim had been jumped by the Indians he had befriended and camped with. The fact that there was no sign of a body told him that the Indians probably took him with them, no doubt to kill him slowly. There was a possibility that Jim might still be alive, but Luke knew that to be unlikely.

The one thing he had no explanation for was the pistol and antelope hide on top of the hill.

He pulled the .45 from his belt and examined it closely. He remembered that Jim owned one like this. He looked around him again, wondering if he should return to Canyon Creek and tell Katie what he had found. What should he tell Lettie— that Jim was probably dead? He considered the possibility of following the war party's tracks, but they would only lead him deeper into Crow and Sioux country—not a healthy situation for a Shoshoni boy alone. He had no fear of entering enemy territory, it was just that he felt strongly that Jim Culver was beyond any help he could give, and it would be wasted effort.

Watching the hesitant young boy from a clump of sage on the side of the hill, Slocum turned his head to spit. *Hell,* he thought, *he don't know where Culver is. He's just following sign, same as me. He's wasted enough of my time.* Slocum had trailed Luke for almost four and a half days, thinking the boy knew where to find Jim Culver. He might have been irritated enough with Luke to take it out on him, but the army was paying him by the day. So he was a bit more patient than usual. He was willing to bet at this stage that Culver was going to Fort Laramie, judging by the direction the trail was now headed. "Where else would he be going?" he asked aloud as he turned to retrieve his horse.

By the time Slocum returned to the clump of sage, leading his horse, Luke had made his decision. The fearsome bounty hunter watched as the young half-Shoshoni boy jumped upon his pony's back and set off toward Canyon Creek. "Huh," Slocum grunted. "Where the hell's he going? That's the way we just come." He climbed into the saddle and rode down to the shallow stream where Luke had been studying sign.

First he searched the bank of the stream and found the bloodstained rocks and grass that had prompted young Luke to assume Jim Culver was most likely dead. Slocum was not as ready to assume as much. There weren't many stains—he allowed for the possibility that more blood could have been washed away in the water. Culver might just be wounded—or it might not be Culver's blood. A careful search around the stream and the trees that framed it turned up no evidence of a body. He reasoned that the Indians would have left the body where it lay if they had killed Culver. And if animals had eaten him, there would be bones scattered about. So he had to conclude that Culver was still alive.

Next, he looked carefully at the tracks just left by Luke. Try as he might, he could not find any trail older than the one the boy left. *He ain't following no trail*, he concluded. *He's hightailing it back to Canyon Creek.* Slocum didn't spend much time contemplating it. The boy had decided to quit looking for Culver. That was all there was to it. It did not serve to influence the bounty hunter's resolve. He would assume Jim was dead when he found a body.

Still firm in his original assumption, he figured Culver was on his way to Fort Laramie. So he searched in that direction, looking to find tracks that would prove him right. It was easy enough to see that the band of Indians had cut back and headed northeast. Still betting on his instincts as a manhunter, Slocum ignored the multitude of tracks and continued searching on an arc south of the stream. Less than twenty yards from the stream, he found what he was looking for; prints of a single shod horse. And they were heading in the general direction of Fort Laramie. That was enough for Slocum. He didn't waste time tracking, but spurred the dingy gray and took off for Laramie straightaway. "If the boy had took a closer look at all them tracks heading thataway, he'da seed there wasn't no shod horse with 'em." He laughed at the thought.

Chapter 6

Katie Mashburn paused at the doorstep to put her bucket down. Then she turned toward the wagon trace, shielding her eyes with her hand while she sought to identify the lone rider approaching the cabin. "Lettie," she called out when she recognized the familiar figure of Luke Kendall, still a quarter of a mile away. "It's Luke," she said when Lettie came from the cabin.

"Is Jim with him?" was Lettie's first spoken thought as she turned her gaze to follow Katie's pointing finger. "He's alone," she answered her own question when she sighted the young half-breed. The disappointment in her voice prompted Katie to respond.

"That doesn't mean Luke didn't find him and warn him. Jim can take care of himself."

The word that Luke brought back was not good. He explained why he had decided to return home with news of what he had found. He

told them of the scene he had discovered after
tracking Jim's horse to the tiny stream at the
base of the hill, and showed them Jim's pistol.
He could offer no explanation as to why the
weapon was left on the hilltop, but he had to
figure Jim had to be killed or captured for someone to have taken his pistol from him. When
all the tracks had headed north toward Crow
country, he decided it best to bring the news
back to Katie and Lettie.

Katie glanced at Lettie's face before questioning Luke more closely. It was obvious that
Luke's report had hit the young girl with devas-
tating impact. Lettie had not been very successful in hiding her deep feelings for the tall young
brother of Clay Culver. With each passing day
since he had ridden off toward the Wind River
country, Lettie's concern for his safety became
more and more intense until, finally, she confessed her love for him. It was not news to Katie.
The signs had been quite obvious. Katie sympa-
thized with her young friend's plight. It was not
an easy thing to love a man who would always
hear the call of the mountains, and that seemed
to be an inborn trait of the Culver men. Katie
knew this from experience, though she did not
express it.

"You didn't see Jim's body, or any sign of
clothes or anything, though?"

"No, ma'am."

"Then there's a chance Jim's still alive." She
looked at Lettie again. "I think there's a good

chance he's still with the band of Indians Luke said he was riding with. I wouldn't count Jim Culver out just yet." She was trying to be positive for Lettie's sake, but she truly did have confidence in Jim's ability to survive. She did not discount the fact that there was also a pretty good chance that what Luke had surmised might be the truth of the matter. Also, knowing the Shoshoni blood that filled the boy's veins, she understood his reluctance to follow a war party into Crow territory. She wished that Clay were there.

Turning back to Luke once again, Katie said, "Well, I suppose you haven't had much to eat since you've been gone. Put your horse away, and I'll fix you something." She placed a comforting hand on Lettie's arm. "You might want to walk down to the creek and fill the water bucket," she said, thinking the young girl might need to be alone at this time.

Lettie understood and smiled sadly at her friend, glancing at the bucket Katie had just filled. "No, I'm all right." They walked inside arm in arm.

At almost the same time Luke arrived in Canyon Creek, a huge mountain of a man riding a dirty gray horse approached the outermost buildings of Fort Laramie. Looking around him from left to right as he rode, he proceeded past the cavalry barracks and the sutler's house directly to the sutler's store.

Alton Broom had seen his share of grizzled old trappers and half-wild mountain men pass through the store since he started clerking for the post trader. But he had never seen the match of the brooding giant riding the gray horse up to the hitching rail on this morning. Some he didn't remember. This one would be hard to forget, with an oversize body that resembled a mounted grizzly. This was the second time in the past few weeks the big man with the jagged scar down his face had shown up in the sutler's store, claiming he was a friend of Jim Culver's. Alton had told him that Jim left Laramie and headed for Canyon Creek.

Alton paused in a halfhearted attempt to sweep some of the dust from the front steps and watched Slocum dismount. Propping his broom against the wall, he said, "Last time you were in here, you were looking for Jim Culver, as I recollect. Did you find him?"

Slocum didn't respond until he looped the reins over the rail and stepped up onto the porch. He liked to tower over people when he talked to them. "No, I didn't," he said. "Over at Canyon Creek, they said I just missed him. Figured I'd find him here. Ain't you seen him?"

"No, can't say as I have. Leastways, if he's back at Laramie, he ain't been in the store."

Alton's reply genuinely surprised Slocum. He had been so confident that Jim had set out for Fort Laramie that he hadn't made allowances for other possibilities. He was not ready to concede

the fact that his instincts had sent him on a wild-
goose chase. He still felt certain that Culver had
been heading to Laramie. "Are you sure he ain't
been in? Maybe when you wasn't working?"
Slocum's irritation was beginning to show
through in his tone.

"I'm sure he ain't," Alton replied, somewhat
mystified when the sinister-looking brute
seemed to blame him for Jim Culver's absence.
"I tend the store every day it's open. I remember
him well enough—came in here with a young
lady. But I'm telling you, he ain't been in since
early winter, just like I told you last time."

"Well, this time he don't have the girl with
him, just him. Hell, he coulda changed some
since winter. Maybe you just didn't recognize
him this time." Slocum locked his dark eyes on
Alton's, his thick eyebrows knotted in a deep
frown as he appeared determined to force the
clerk to remember.

Alton began to become uncomfortable with
Slocum's unjustified anger, and he felt a mea-
sure of relief when two cavalry troopers walked
into the store. Slocum turned at once to stare at
the two soldiers. Alton, eager to divert Slocum's
intensity, was quick to enlist their help. "Either
of you boys see anything of a young feller name
of Jim Culver around the post lately? He's Clay
Culver's brother—might be looking for Clay."
When his only response was a blank stare and
a shake of their heads, he added, "Feller here's
looking for him."

The soldiers looked at each other, questioning. Then the taller of the two said, "Don't know his name, but a young fellow I ain't seen around here before has been hanging around Cora's for a couple of days now."

Slocum's eyes immediately lit up. He turned back to Alton. "What's Cora's?"

"Cora's a whore," Alton replied. "She's set herself up in a tent on the other side of the bridge. She used to work as a laundress, but she found out she could make a sight more money selling satisfaction to the soldiers."

"How do I find her?"

"Hell, you can't miss her. Go across the bridge, then go to your right and follow the river about a quarter of a mile. She's got a wagon with a tent beside it, right on the river-bank. You can see it from the bridge."

Without another word to Alton, or a thank you to the two soldiers, Slocum turned and walked out the door.

"Damn," Alton swore quietly. "That is one dangerous-lookin' man. I'd hate to have him lookin' for me."

Slocum was more than a little interested in the stranger hanging around Cora's tent. He would take a thorough look around the post, searching for his man, but not until after paying a little visit across the river.

The bridge was new, made of iron, and just completed that very year. As he walked the gray across, he kept his eyes trained on the bank on the other side. From the bridge he could see Cora's wagon and tent, just as Alton had said, and there was a horse tied out front. Slocum gave the gray a little nudge with his heels.

When he was within about fifty yards of the tent, Slocum slowed the gray to a walk to prevent the occupants of the tent from hearing him approach. He guided his horse, plodding slowly through the soft sand of the riverbank, to a stop beside a bay Morgan with a white star on its face. Looking at the horse, Slocum felt his lips part in a thin smile. He dismounted and walked around the horse to find a Winchester .73 riding in the sling. He rubbed his fingers over the other side of the smooth stock until he felt a rough spot. His grin wider now, he drew the rifle out and turned it over to discover the initials J.R.C. carved in the stock. He chuckled. It was almost too easy.

"I've told you, Johnny, you got your money's worth. You know my rules. You have to pay to play, so if you want another turn, it'll cost you the same as the first."

"Hell, after all the money I've paid you this week, I ought to get a free one."

"You know the rules," Cora insisted. It would be another two weeks before the soldiers got paid, and she needed the money. If she let this one have a free one, the word might get out, and she would be arguing with customers over free ones from then on. She wasn't getting any younger. She might not have many good years left. Already a fresh-faced youngster from the infantry barracks was unable to perform because he complained that he felt like he was trying to make love to his mother. It was discouraging to hear, but she *was* old enough to be his mother.

Johnny Malotte stood there with nothing on but his shirt and his boots, trying to make up his mind if another tussle on Cora's straw-tick mattress was worth spending any more of his cash. In her long robe now, she looked considerably more fetching than a short while ago, when they had completed the first transaction. Long overdue when he arrived at Fort Laramie several days before, he had tried to catch up as fast as his constitution would permit. Unfortunately, his meager fortune was literally draining from his lower body parts to the extent that he was soon going to be unable to buy supplies. It occurred to him that he could rectify the situation by knocking the voluptuous Miss Cora in the head and recovering his investment. He was ready to leave Fort Laramie and head to Montana territory, anyway. Pleased with the plan, he cheerfully pulled some currency from his shirt pocket and said, "You win, darlin'. Let's get to it."

After carefully tucking the money away in a little black-and-gold Oriental jewelry box, Cora untied her robe and let it fall to the plank flooring of her tent. Aroused by the anticipation of another bumpy ride along this well-worn trail to sexual fulfillment, Johnny stepped forward, eager to embark. Cora managed a tired smile for him as she settled herself on the straw mattress and once again opened the pale, flabby gates to paradise, the aging hinges sufficiently oiled now by U.S. currency.

If the sagging curves and mushy thighs were of major concern to Cora, they were no bother to Johnny. His needs were more of a primitive and animalistic nature, and he set to his task with a vengeance. Working away with the single focus of a rutting elk, he soon began to tire the lady out. And she realized what Johnny already knew—that so soon after the first trip, it was going to take a good deal longer for him to reach his destination.

"I think you're about finished, honey," she gently suggested.

"Hell if I am. I ain't nowhere near," he replied between rapid grunts for breath.

She endured for several more minutes before announcing, "That's it; you're done."

"The hell you say. I ain't fell outta the saddle yet, have I?"

"You don't get to rent me all day for two dollars. I can't help it if your pump's dry. You got your money's worth."

"You heard the little lady. You got your money's worth." The gruff voice came from behind him. Startled for an instant, Johnny recovered immediately and spun around to defend himself. He was fast, but not quick enough to avoid the rifle barrel that smashed the bridge of his nose and laid him out cold on the rough plank floor.

After briefly checking to make sure Johnny was unconscious, Slocum turned to the terrified woman on the mattress. Taking a few moments to assess the field Johnny Malotte had been in the process of plowing, he suddenly cocked his lip to form a crooked smile. "No reason for you to be afraid. I ain't gonna hurtcha. This here man is wanted by the army back at Fort Lincoln for killin' a soldier in Virginia." Cora was still too terrified to speak, able only to stare wide-eyed at the frightening giant standing over her. Slocum continued to stare back at her until a long-dormant urge began to worm its way into his brain. It was a need that didn't surface but once in a great while, but when it did, it couldn't be ignored.

Having seen that look on the faces of hundreds of men, Cora realized what might be coming next, and the dread of it made her shiver.

Breaking off the eye contact, Slocum turned his attention back to the man lying at his feet. Taking a coil of rope he carried in his other hand, he tied Johnny's hands together. "Reckon I'll have to put his pants on before I tie his feet together." He dragged Johnny away from the mattress far enough to give Cora room to help. "How 'bout pulling his boots off so's I can pull his britches on." It was not a question. Slocum paused when he thought more about it. "What the hell's his boots on for, when his pants is off?"

Cora shrugged, not answering, but immediately did as she was told, hoping she had misread the intent she had seen in the awesome brute's eyes moments before. This was not her day, however.

Pants on and securely hog-tied, Johnny began to groan, his eyelids fluttering, as Slocum dragged him over by the tent flap and dumped him there. Satisfied that his prisoner would await his pleasure, he turned his attention to other matters. "Reckon it's been quite a spell for me, but as long as you're open for business," he said, and began unbuckling his belt.

Oh, God, no, she thought, reaching for her robe in an effort to cover herself. She imagined it might be the same as mating with a buffalo, which held no fascination for her whatsoever. But the man looked so violent, she feared for her life if she refused. Still, she made an effort to avoid the gruesome encounter. "Well, I usually don't receive gentlemen after my lunch hour."

"It ain't no problem then," Slocum responded, " 'cause I sure as hell ain't no gentleman." He could see the lack of interest in Cora's eyes. It didn't bother him. The few times he had done it before were with whores, and they all seemed reluctant. His lust was unusual at this particular time, but there was something about Cora's

wearied body that suggested this was the time
to take care of his biological needs. He untied
his trousers, letting them drop to rest on his
boot tops.

Cora could see that she had no choice. Still,
she was reluctant. "You're too damn big. I'd
have to charge you more," she said, trying to
gain as much as she could from a bad situation.
"It'll cost you double."

"Don't surprise me none," he calmly replied,
and reached in his shirt pocket for the money.

"All right." She sighed loudly, resigned to the
task ahead. With his money in hand, she no
longer feared for her life, and she prepared to
receive him. "Come on, then. Let's get it over
with." He dropped to his knees, hovering over
her like a black storm cloud. "When's the last
time you took a bath?" Cora complained.

He grinned. "I don't know. When's the last
time it rained?"

"Don't it bother you? Him laying tied up
over there?"

"Don't bother me. He ain't goin' nowhere."

It was as she had anticipated: coarse, brutal,
even animal-like, but also short. The comparison
to a bull buffalo came to mind again during the
passionless assault, as she bit her lip to endure
the rough encounter. But soon it was over and
he abruptly withdrew. Without so much as another glance in her direction, he pulled his
britches up, grabbed Johnny by the ankles, and
was gone, leaving her slightly dazed and won-

dering if it had really happened. In only a few minutes' time, she heard the horses moving away from her tent. Unable to move for a brief time, she wondered if it was time to find another way to survive in this world. She was certain of one thing, however: If the situation ever presented itself again, and she were given a choice, she would opt for the buffalo.

Content with himself, Slocum left Cora's tent behind, leading Jim Culver's horse with Johnny Malotte reeling drunkenly in the saddle. They had almost reached the bridge over the North Platte when Johnny's head began to clear and he realized where he was. Aware of a painful throbbing in his face, he remembered the blow that had crushed his nose. He tried to lift his hands to his injured nose, but discovered they were tied to the saddle horn. Lifting his head, he saw the broad back of a huge man riding before him. *Who the hell is he?*

His head clearing rapidly now, he called to Slocum. "Hey! What the hell's going on? Who the hell are you?"

Slocum turned in the saddle to look back at him. "Have a nice little nap, didja? I thought for a minute there I'd cracked you a little too hard. I promised the captain back at Fort Lincoln that I'd do my best to bring you back alive. Course, I might'n be able to do that if you don't behave yourself."

"Fort Lincoln?" Johnny gasped, confused. "I

ain't never been to Fort Lincoln. You got the wrong man, mister. I ain't had no trouble with the army anywhere."

Slocum laughed. "You've been to Virginia, though, ain'tcha? I reckon the army sees things a little different than you do. They don't cotton much to having folks murder their officers. But, what the hell, I reckon some folks is just picky about things like that."

"What the hell are you talking about?" Johnny railed. "I ain't murdered no army officer."

Slocum was enjoying his prisoner's protests. The few men he had brought in alive all protested that he had the wrong man. "Mighta slipped your mind," he said with a chuckle, "about that lieutenant in Virginia."

"Virginia? Virginia?" Johnny repeated in stark amazement. "I ain't ever been in Virginia in my entire life. I'm telling you, you damn fool, you got the wrong man." The absurdity of his situation began to further stoke the fires of his anger. "You big dumb son of a bitch, you busted up my nose so I can't even breathe through it. And I ain't even the man you're looking for." When Slocum merely kept on riding without commenting further, Johnny asked, "What's his name? The man you're looking for?"

"Jim Culver, same as yourn," Slocum replied. "And I ain't lookin' for him no more."

"Well, there, now, you see? That's where you made your mistake," Johnny quickly retorted.

"My name's Johnny Malotte. Now why don't you just cut me loose, and I'll even forget about you bustin' up my face."

"Oh, all right, Mr. Malotte," he said facetiously. "Sorry for the inconvenience. I'll just pull up under yonder shade tree on the other side of the bridge and cut you loose. How's that?"

"That'll do fine." Johnny felt a sense of relief. Things were looking pretty grim for him up to that point. But he promised himself one thing: When this wild-looking giant cut him loose, he would put a bullet in him for busting his nose.

In silence now, Slocum led the horses across the bridge and guided them up under the shade of a tall cottonwood tree, just as he had said. He dismounted and untied Jim Culver's Winchester from a strap on his saddle. Walking back to stand by Johnny's stirrup, he said, "Now, Mr. Malotte, was it?"

"That's right. Johnny Malotte."

"Right. Well, you see, what throwed me off was you being about the right age, and carrying this here rifle with J.R.C. carved in the stock, and riding that big dun with the star face that I tracked in here from back north a piece. Why, I thought to myself that you must be Jim Culver. Looks like I made a mistake." He reached up and untied Johnny's hands, freeing him from the saddle horn.

Satisfied that he had convinced the seemingly

guileless brute, Johnny relaxed in the saddle. "Now, I'll just take my rifle, and I'll be on my way," he said.

"Shore," Slocum said. "Here it is."

Johnny was not expecting the events that took place in the next few seconds. He sat there unsuspecting for a moment while Slocum took a step forward to transfer all his weight to his lead foot, insuring plenty of leverage when he swung the rifle. Holding it by the barrel, he caught Johnny just below his ear, knocking him out of the saddle. Stunned, Johnny nevertheless tried to scramble to his feet, only to feel the force of the rifle stock against the back of his skull. It would be the last thing he remembered for a while.

Turning to cast his gaze upon a soldier who had stopped on the bridge to gawk, Slocum glowered at the young trooper until the startled spectator decided that what happened under the shade of the cottonwood was not his affair and quickly went about his business. Slocum shifted his gaze from the bridge back to the buildings of the fort. There were many soldiers, as well as civilians, coming and going, but none close enough to meddle. Satisfied, he reached down and picked Johnny up, grabbing him by his collar and the seat of his pants, and threw him over the saddle. Taking his time, he tied Johnny's hands under Toby's belly, then looped the rope over the saddle horn to keep him from sliding upside down. That done, he climbed aboard the

gray and started the long ride to Fort Lincoln
with his prisoner. "I can't abide a lying, whining
bastard," he muttered as he passed by the outer
buildings of Fort Laramie.

Chapter 7

"Ah, I see Dead Man is back from the land of the spirits," Iron Bow called out cheerfully as he approached Newt Plummer's lodge, referring to Jim by the Crow name he had given him.

Newt glanced toward his patient, who was sitting outside the lodge, dozing in the morning sun. "Yes, he's getting stronger every day. His wound is healing very well, although I wasn't sure he was going to make it for a while."

Jim opened his eyes upon hearing the two men talking. He could not understand what was being said, since they spoke in the Crow tongue, but he turned to greet Iron Bow as the Crow war chief walked over to him. "Good morning," Jim said.

"Good morning to you," Iron Bow returned, now speaking in English. "Red Wing tells me you are getting stronger." He smiled warmly at Jim. "Soon we will hunt buffalo together."

Jim returned Iron Bow's smile. "You better give me a few more days. I might fall off my horse right now."

Jim's recovery took a good deal longer than a few days, but once it started, he began to regain strength rapidly. Having lost everything he owned except the clothes he was found in, he owed a great deal to the charity of Newt Plummer and the people of Iron Bow's village. Iron Bow made him a gift of the horse that had transported him back on the travois, and Wounded Leg's wife sewed a fine deerskin shirt for him to replace his that had been torn away to treat his wounds. In the days that followed his initial recovery, Newt showed him how to make an Indian saddle. Before long Jim was taking short rides up and down the river. The people of the camp would smile and nod as he passed them in their daily routine—the women working with animal hides or harvesting roots and berries, the men on their way to or from their hunting. It seemed a peaceful way of life, and one that Jim could easily have adopted. But he had some unfinished business to take care of, so he knew his stay in the Crow camp would not be extensive. The biggest problem facing him was the fact that he had no weapons. And a man without weapons was no man at all in this country.

Since there was no way to acquire a rifle, Jim determined that he was going to learn to use a bow. Newt offered to help him make one, but he suggested that Jim should ask Wounded Leg to help him. "I reckon I could show you how the Crows make one, but I ain't never tried to make one myself. Now, Wounded Leg would most likely be glad to help you, and ain't nobody in the village can make a better bow than Wounded Leg."

When Jim approached Wounded Leg with his request for help, the Crow warrior enthusiastically agreed, humbly flattered that his help had been sought. So, for the next few days, the making of the bow became Jim's obsession. He climbed on his Indian pony, and he and Wounded Leg rode up into the hills to find a suitable piece of wood. Wounded Leg was not easily satisfied, so they scoured the trees until a young mountain ash was deemed the perfect candidate.

Jim watched closely as Wounded Leg showed him how to shape his bow from a three-foot section of the wood, strengthening it with sinew on the back and fashioning a grip made of strips of hide wrapped around the center. More buffalo sinew was employed as the bowstring. Arrows were formed from shoots of the same ash, the shafts shaped by continuous passing of the wood through a hole drilled in a piece of horn, then rubbed smooth between two grooved stones. Through the use of sign language and a few fundamental words repeated often, Wounded Leg explained each step of the process.

It was a simple weapon when finished, almost harmless-looking, like a child's toy. But Jim was amazed by the power of the bow when he took it out to practice with it. Wild at first, he soon became fairly proficient with his primitive weapon. Having been blessed with a sharp eye and a steady hand, he progressed each day until his percentage of hits versus misses became quite respectable. His first kill with his new bow was a sage hen, with a shot of approximately twenty yards' distance. He was as pleased as when he killed his first deer at age thirteen near the banks of the Rapidan River. Sitting around the fire with his Crow friends that night he was subjected to a great deal of good-natured teasing about his kill. He didn't care, and laughed with them. He felt, in time, he could become quite accurate with the weapon.

There were other things he needed before he could consider leaving his Crow friends and going in search of the man who stole his horse and rifle and left him for dead. Basic supplies for staying alive had been lost along with his horse—little things like flint and steel, extra clothes, salt, coffee—things that contributed to the simple pleasures and necessities, a razor and a whetstone. He needed money to acquire many of these things. Since money was impossible in his situation, his only opportunity was trade, and the most lucrative item to barter with were buffalo hides. Consequently, when scouts came back to camp with news that a large herd of buffalo had been sighted moving through the upper part of the valley near the Yellowstone, he was anxious to join the hunt.

Jim was not so naïve as to imagine he was skilled enough with his new bow to go into the hunt with that weapon. He needed a rifle, and one became available to him when Newt decided to stay in the village. Newt offered to let Jim use the rifle in exchange for a share of the meat. Jim quickly agreed. He was interested mainly in the hides. So early the next morning, Jim set out with most of the men of the village toward the Yellowstone, Newt's early-model Henry rifle resting across his thighs.

Iron Bow told Jim that this would not be like the grand-scale hunts that would take place later on, when provisions were made for the winter. Later in the summer the whole village would follow the herds—women, children, everyone. On those hunts, there would be much planning in order to trap as many of the huge animals as possible, usually by stampeding them over a cliff, or into a box canyon, where they could be slaughtered. This time the hunters would descend upon the herd, killing individual animals on the run. It was a time when the young men competed to exhibit their skill and daring, darting in and out of the mass of thundering beasts on their nimble ponies, most with bows only. The hunt would not last long, Iron Bow explained, because they were very close to the land of their enemies the Blackfeet. This suited Jim just fine. He was in a hurry himself.

Just as the scouts predicted, the herd was sighted, moving slowly through a wide, grassy draw. It was· an awesome sight to young Jim Culver. The dark current of moving bodies flowed along the length of the draw for as far as he could see. Iron Bow shook his head sadly as he told Jim that a herd this size was as nothing when compared to the herds of several years ago. "The buffalo used to cover the land, but the white man has come and slaughtered them for the hides, leaving the meat to rot on the prairie."

Hearing Iron Bow's lament, Jim felt a tinge of conscience, because he knew he had come on the hunt for exactly that reason. The difference, he convinced himself, was that the meat would not be wasted, as well as the horns, hooves, and other useful parts of the animals. They would all be packed back to the Crow village, along with the hides he planned to take.

The band of Crow hunters rode along the ridge above the draw after deciding to cut into the moving mass as it turned into the narrow end. Jim pulled a cartridge into the chamber of the Henry. He had brought no extra cartridges, satisfied that the fully loaded magazine would be sufficient for his purposes. Cartridges were precious to Newt, so Jim took no more than he thought he needed. He was confident enough in his expertise with a rifle—any rifle—to know he wasn't going to miss a target as big as a buffalo. Having never fired the Henry before, he might be a little off with the first shot, but he would adjust on the second. Newt said it had a tendency to shoot low, but Jim would have to see for himself. Sometimes a jerky trigger finger caused a rifle to pull down slightly. Maybe Newt wasn't as smooth on the trigger as he should be.

When Iron Bow gave the signal, the hunt was on, and the riders plunged down the side of the ridge, straight into the sea of bobbing humps. The first buffalo cow dropped within seconds. Jim held his pony back while the others charged after the leaders. He had no intention of wasting even one cartridge, so he watched the first animals to fall, especially those felled by an arrow to see where the shots were placed. Behind the last rib—a lung shot. Jim knew Newt's rifle was not a real buffalo gun. Like the Indians with their bows, he would have to place his shots strategically in order to fell each buffalo with just one cartridge. Ready now, he released his restraint on the reins, and the buckskin bolted into action.

Racing along at full speed, the buckskin provided an almost steady shooting platform. Jim put his first shot right behind the last rib of a large bull. It was a couple of inches lower than he had aimed. *Newt was right*, he thought as the bull dropped to its knees and then tumbled head over heels. Jim adjusted his aim on the next target, then methodically squeezed off fifteen more rounds, dropping fifteen more buffalo. His rifle empty, he pulled off to the side while the hunt continued up the draw, the hunters shouting and whooping at the beleaguered animals, a long cloud of dust lying over the herd like a brown shroud.

He looked behind him as the tail end of the stampeding herd passed through the grassy draw, grunting with the effort of their flight, swerving in their path to avoid the fallen carcasses. Among the random humps he could determine his kill, strung out in a neat, almost straight line. Sixteen carcasses—that should be enough to barter for the supplies he needed.

As the last few stragglers passed the point where he sat on the buckskin, he was struck with a question. Could he take a buffalo down with his bow? *There's an easy way to find out,* he thought, and slung the rifle on a loop of rope on his saddle. Taking his bow from the hide case on his back, he notched an arrow and urged his pony to give chase once more. The buckskin reacted immediately to his command and was soon racing down beside a large buffalo cow. *Right behind the last rib,* Jim reminded himself as he drew the bowstring fully. He released the arrow, oblivious to the sting of the sinew bowstring as it slapped his bare arm. His arrow sailed under the belly of the cow, only to ricochet harmlessly off the grass and land under the hoof of an old bull some twenty yards distant. Jim watched, disgusted, as the huge beast broke the arrow shaft in pieces. Then he looked around to see if any of the other hunters had witnessed his lack of proficiency with his bow. They were too far away to have seen him, all except one. Even at a distance, he could see the broad smile on Iron Bow's face as the war chief gazed in his direction. "Damn," Jim uttered.

The work of skinning and dressing would take the rest of the afternoon, even with the men working as rapidly as possible. Since the Crows were well into enemy territory, Iron Bow sent scouts out to make sure the hunting party was not surprised by a Blackfoot war party. After the hunters had butchered and packed their kills, they set to work helping Jim.

Iron Bow was truly impressed with Jim's marksmanship, using a rifle he had never fired before. "You are very good with a rifle," he said, astounded by shooting so rapid that it was no more than a quarter of a mile from the first kill to number sixteen. He nodded his head in admiration, then gave Jim a little wink. "I think you must practice a little more with your bow." The other men seemed puzzled by the remark, but Iron Bow did not offer an explanation. Instead he said, "The packhorses cannot carry all the meat. We will have to make travois."

* * *

Jim's problems were only partially solved when the hunters returned to camp. The hides he had taken would buy him most of the basic things he needed, but he was going to need a packhorse to carry the hides. And while they might do well to outfit him with new possibles, like blankets, a frying pan, coffee and sugar and such, they were not enough to replace his precious Winchester .73 and Colt .45. The only way to do that, in his mind, was to find Johnny Malotte, and that was what he was determined to do, if it took the rest of his life. *Iron Bow was right. I'd better go back to practicing with my bow.*

He kept only a small portion of the meat he had brought back, all that he could really handle. After giving Newt his share, there was still plenty to be divided among the people. His gesture was well received. A large feast was held on the first night the hunting party was back in the village, and great quantities of buffalo hump were roasted over the cook fires. It was a jubilant banquet that lasted until the early-morning hours, with many tellings of Jim's expertise with a rifle.

Jim's quest soon became common knowledge among the people of the Crow village, and there was genuine approval of his desire to find the man who had left him for dead and then stolen his possessions. Many of the men offered encouragement; among them Iron Bow's son, Wolf Paw, seemed to take the most interest in the young white man. Jim's grasp of the Crow language was expanding daily, until he became able to converse with the people of the village without interpretation from Newt or Iron Bow. Had his determination to have his revenge not been so powerful, Jim might have considered lingering in the Crow village for a time. Newt had a warm, roomy lodge he was happy to share. The women of the village took great delight in helping him scrape and dry his buffalo hides. And when it became obvious to everyone that his one pair of trousers was wearing thin, Wounded Leg's wife sewed him a new pair from softened deerskin. He began to develop an appreciation for his brother Clay's embrace of the Shoshoni way of life. It was going to be hard to leave his Crow friends.

In the days that followed the buffalo hunt, Jim practiced with his ash bow until he became competent enough to hunt game larger than rabbits and prairie chickens. Before long he advanced beyond mere competency to become deadly in his ability to place a powerfully launched arrow where he aimed. And all the time he worked at honing his skill with the primitive weapon, he thought about Johnny Malotte sitting on Toby's back, cradling his Winchester.

Sometimes at night, when lying awake listening to the steady drone of Newt Plummer's snoring, Jim thought of someone other than Johnny Malotte. It was during the deep hours, after Newt turned on his side and the snoring subsided—when the camp was still, with nothing to break the silence but occasional nickers and whinnies from the pony herd, when she came to his mind. As he lay there in the darkness of the tipi, he would try to see her face, but it appeared in his mind's eye as if seeing her reflection in the rippling waters of a stream, her features vague and constantly changing.

There had been a long period of time when he had not consciously thought of Lettie—when he was recovering from his wounds, suspended between the living world and the land of dreams. He even thought at one time that he was already forgetting the troubled feelings he had had for the slight young girl. He was not unaware of the shy glances he received from some of the young Crow maidens as he rode in from the hunt with an antelope carcass across his saddle. And he had to admit that he gave some serious thought in that direction. But as he regained his strength, she came to him more and more. Soon he was forced to tuck thoughts of her away in order to concentrate on his preparations to search for Johnny Malotte, bringing them out again at night in the darkness. He knew he was going to have to make a decision about his feelings for Lettie, but he told himself it would have to wait. Johnny Malotte came first.

"Well, I see you got your moccasins," Newt said as Jim approached, carrying his boots in his hand. "What did they cost ya?"

Jim smiled. "Two antelope hides. They're right handsome, aren't they?" He turned a heel up and looked down to admire White Feather's handiwork. "They're right comfortable, too. I ain't gonna throw my boots away, though. There's still some wear left in 'em."

"Yep, they shine smart enough," Newt said, looking the moccasins over with a critical eye. "You're lookin' more and more like a Crow warrior ever' day. You're gittin' mighty handy with that bow of yourn, too. You might not need your rifle back."

Jim's face turned sober at the mention of his rifle. This was what he had come to talk about. "Newt, I reckon I'm ready to trade my hides and get on with my business." It was time. His wounds had long since healed, but he had become much too content living with Iron Bow's people. He and Iron Bow's son, Wolf Paw, had developed a strong friendship, hunting together almost daily. And there were times when Jim went several days without remembering his vow to find Johnny Malotte.

Newt nodded solemnly. "I figured you was about ready to cut loose. I ain't tryin' to tell you what to do. But if it was me, I wouldn't waste my time taking them skins to the Crow agency. I know they do a little tradin' over there, but they ain't never give the Injuns a fair deal. Back in the spring, some fellers opened up a trading post on the Yellowstone—built a stockade close to where the Bighorn ties in. They call it Fort

Pease, although it ain't really no fort. Anyway, you'll most likely get a better trade up there than you will from an Injun agent."

That sounded like good advice to Jim, so the next morning he loaded his hides on one of Newt's horses, and he and Newt prepared to set out, planning to follow the river to the Yellowstone. Jim didn't particularly need any help. Newt just had a craving for a drink of whiskey. Jim was glad to have the company. They were joined by Wolf Paw and another young warrior, Leads His Horses. Together the four of them rode out of camp, heading north up the Bighorn valley.

Chapter 8

Johnny Malotte turned his head painfully to the side in an effort to squint through the eye that wasn't swollen shut. Mercifully, he had fallen asleep from sheer exhaustion two hours before, in spite of being trussed up, hands behind his back, lying with his face in the dirt. The sleep provided some escape from the stabbing pain in his head. But awake now, he found no relief from the aching in his arms and shoulders, and his wrists were bound to his ankles by a length of rope too short to allow him to straighten his legs.

Unable to see his captor from this position, Johnny bit off a groan as he forced his body to roll over on its side. Hearing the faint cry of pain, Slocum turned to look at the tormented man. "Well, now, did you enjoy your little nap?" Slocum asked sarcastically. Sitting on the end of a log by the fire, the huge man ripped off a mouthful of salt pork while he gazed at

Malotte. He scooped up a spoonful of boiled beans and loaded them in with the pork, chewing noisily while he studied his prisoner. "You know, you ain't been a helluva lot of company on this trip. I almost wish I hadn't cracked your head so hard." He paused in his chewing for a moment. "Almost," he added, grinning at his humor. "While you was layin' around sleepin', I've been fixin' us some supper. I bet you could eat a little, couldn't you?" When there was no response from Malotte, Slocum got up from the log, lifted the iron pot from the coals, and walked over to stand before the prone figure on the ground. "I'm gonna be honest with you," he said. "I wouldn't waste the beans on you, but if I don't keep you alive, that prissy-ass captain won't give me my money."

"I ain't Jim Culver," Johnny forced through swollen lips.

"Course you ain't," Slocum said, grinning broadly. "Here, here's you some beans." He spooned out a little pile of beans on the ground in front of Malotte. "I hope you'll excuse me, but I musta misplaced my tablecloth."

Johnny stared at the beans piled on the bare ground. He wanted to tell Slocum where he could shove them, but he had not eaten in two days and he was hungry. "Untie my hands," he said.

Smiling, Slocum slowly shook his head back and forth several times. "Now, Jim, you don't really expect me to do a damn-fool thing like that, do you? Git down there and eat 'em like a dog."

"You son of a bitch," Johnny growled.

Still grinning, Slocum went back to his seat by the fire. "Eat 'em or leave 'em, all the same to me."

Johnny tried to restrain himself out of sheer defiance, but his hunger was overpowering, and he knew he must take nourishment or he would grow steadily weaker. After only a few minutes, he rolled over on his belly again and stuck his face in the beans, gulping them down as fast as he could. Slocum chuckled softly in the background.

Johnny had tried repeatedly during the first couple of days on the trail to convince the obstinate giant that he had captured the wrong man, but it was to no avail. Slocum had put two and two together and it had come up four in his mind, and he was not one to be swayed. To a man who made his living tracking down fugitives, Johnny's claims were not in the least unusual. Slocum would have been surprised if Johnny *had* admitted he was Jim Culver. Johnny had even confessed that he had killed Jim Culver and taken his horse and rifle. This was after trying to convince Slocum that he had bought them from an Indian. Slocum just displayed that contemptuous grin until he was tired of hearing Malotte complain. Then he had silenced him again with the butt of Jim's rifle, which had caused the swollen eye. Johnny had given up after that, convinced that there was no chance to alter the single-minded bounty hunter's convictions. He would hold his tongue and hope for the best when they reached Fort Lincoln. It had been bad luck that led him across Slocum's trail. But luck just might swing over to his side before this was over and done with. He promised himself that if he got the chance, he wouldn't waste it. He'd open the big son of a bitch's throat from ear to ear. That would give him a nice scar to match the one down the side of his face.

Capt. Thomas Boyd looked up from his desk when Master Sergeant Cochran appeared in the doorway. The bugle had just sounded Recall minutes before at eleven-thirty, signaling the end of morning drill. "Captain Boyd, sir," Cochran said with his customary absence of emotion, "Major Rothmeyer wants to see you."

"Now?" Boyd asked. "He wants to see me now—or sometime today?" Boyd was preparing to go to the officers' mess. He would prefer to see the adjutant after he had eaten.

Cochran shrugged. "He didn't say, sir. I reckon he meant now."

"All right," Boyd replied with a heavy sigh. Cochran paused for a second, then turned and left the room. The captain slid his chair back and got to his feet. He didn't care much for Major Rothmeyer, and he was satisfied that the feeling was mutual. "What's the old son of a bitch complaining about this time?" Boyd muttered to himself. Boyd had been led to believe that he would be given the position of post adjutant when he was assigned to Fort Lincoln. Instead the post was held by Philip Rothmeyer, a blocky, gray-haired officer who had been a schoolteacher before the recent War Between the States. He claimed to be a distant cousin to Phil Sheridan, the general in command of the Division of the Missouri. Boyd suspected that was the man's chief qualification for the position he held. It chafed the captain to have to report to Rothmeyer, but he had no choice in the matter.

Rothmeyer was busy shuffling through some papers when Boyd entered. "Ah, Captain Boyd," the major greeted him. "Take a seat," he said, waving his arm toward a chair in front of his desk.

"Sergeant Cochran said you wanted to see me," Boyd said.

"Yes. I've just been looking through these papers you filed on this civilian in Fredericksburg. This case has been open for quite some time with no progress toward conviction that I can see. I'm trying to clean up all the old dead files, and I think this is one we can close out. If I read this correctly, it appears we are paying this man, Slocum, to track the fugitive on a per-diem basis. I'm not sure how you got that approved, or even if the army is legally bound to honor the arrangement. There is no contract that I can find."

Incensed by the implication, Boyd replied. "It was a spoken agreement," he insisted. "You approved it yourself."

Rothmeyer seemed unimpressed. "I did, did I? You must have caught me in a weak moment. Anyway, since I approved it, as you say, then I'm officially disapproving it now." When Boyd started to rise to his feet in protest, the major stopped him. "You don't stand a chance of convicting this man Culver, even if your bounty hunter finds him. The only witnesses to the shooting, four enlisted men and a civilian sheriff, have all testified that your Lieutenant Ebersole fired at Culver first."

"Begging your pardon, sir—" Boyd started, now on his feet, but Rothmeyer interrupted.

"I think you may have a personal interest in this, but there'll be no more discussion on the matter. The army can't afford to pay some lazy bounty hunter who's probably lying around with some squaw somewhere. General Custer has ordered that we stop wasting time on matters that are unrelated to this post. I'm sorry, Captain, but this matter is closed. I'm authorizing one month's pay for Slocum, no more."

Boyd made one more attempt to protest, but Rothmeyer cut him off again and told him he was dismissed. Feeling the anger all the way down in his boots, Boyd snapped a sharp salute, did an about-face, and left the room. Outside the major's office, he grumbled to himself about the incompetent ex-schoolteacher. He was one of Lieutenant Colonel Custer's boys—still addressing the post commander by his brevet rank, currying favor at every opportunity.

Captain Boyd was no longer passionate about trying Jim Culver for Ebersole's murder. That emotion had waned over the months. He was livid, however, over the treatment he had received from his immediate superior. Who the hell was Philip Rothmeyer to make judgment on the case? As far as the tracker Slocum, Boyd had not heard anything from him since he left Lincoln. He had planned to cut off his per diem in a week or two anyway.

At approximately four-thirty on a cloudy afternoon, Slocum rode into Fort Lincoln, leading his prisoner. The bugle's last notes of Stable Call were drifting over the parade ground as the two riders approached the adjutant's office. The hulking bounty hunter riding the iron-gray horse scowled as he met the inquisitive stares of the troopers on their way to the stables. Slocum didn't have a lot of use for soldiers—too many rules. Snorting his contempt, he turned away and guided the horses to the building where he had first talked to Captain Boyd. He dismounted and tied the horses to the corner post of the porch. After untying the rope under Toby's belly that had held Malotte's feet in the stirrups, he grabbed his prisoner by the shirt and pulled him unceremoniously to the ground. Johnny grunted when he landed hard on his side, then cursed Slocum. Slocum paid him no mind. His thoughts were now on the anticipated payday for bringing the prisoner in.

A young private stood gaping at the grizzled bounty hunter as he stepped up on the porch. "Go fetch Captain Boyd, sonny," Slocum said. "Tell him I brung him something."

When Boyd was told that a man who looked like a grizzly bear wanted to see him, he knew immediately who it was. It could be no other than the vile manhunter Slocum. The private said he had a prisoner with him. This was enough to cause Boyd to rise quickly from his desk, anxious to see Jim Culver in irons. In spite of the recent order from Major Rothmeyer, Boyd at once revived thoughts of pleading his case again. With the prisoner in custody, Rothmeyer might change his mind about trying Culver.

Boyd stepped out on the porch to confront the intimidating figure of his hired bounty hunter. Having once been exposed to the fearsome countenance of Slocum, he thought it inconceivable that the man's image could fade from memory. Yet Boyd was still taken aback somewhat to confront the tracker face-to-face again. "Slocum," he said, nodding acknowledgment; then, looking past the huge bulk of the man, he stared at his captive. Johnny Malotte stared back at him in angry defiance. "Who's this?" Boyd asked, puzzled.

Confused by the captain's question, Slocum let the malevolent grin slowly fade from his face, and he turned to look at Malotte. The defiant prisoner, standing on the bottom step with a rope around his neck, much like a dog on a leash, stared back at Slocum with a smirk on his face. Slocum looked back at the captain. "Jim Culver," he replied, "the son of a bitch you're paying me for."

Boyd stepped down off the porch to take a closer look. Even with Malotte's battered face, there was no uncertainty in Boyd's mind. Still, he studied Johnny's swollen features for a few long seconds. Then he turned back to Slocum. "I don't know who the hell this is, but he's damn sure not Jim Culver."

Slocum was stunned and, for the moment, speechless. He jerked his head around to gape at his prisoner. Johnny found his voice. "I told you my name's Johnny Malotte, you dumb son of a bitch." He looked at Boyd then. "I tried to tell him all the way between here and Fort Laramie, but he's crazy. You need to lock him up for trying to kill me."

Boyd was now faced with a dilemma. He hadn't the faintest notion of the identity of the man whom Slocum had mistakenly captured, nor did he particularly care. His orders were to terminate Slocum's services, and that was what he was about to do. The battered man at the end of Slocum's rope was probably justified in demanding Slocum's arrest, but Boyd knew the army had no interest in pursuing that. At this point he just wanted to be through with both of them. Before he could speak, Slocum recovered his thoughts.

"What the hell you mean, he ain't Culver?" he demanded. Stalking down the steps, he stood beside Toby. "This is Culver's horse. There ain't no doubt about that. And this here's sure as hell that fancy new Winchester he carries—got his initials carved right in the stock." He held Jim's rifle up to show Boyd.

Boyd paused to think about it again, peering at Johnny Malotte, reassuring himself. "They might be Culver's," he quietly agreed. "But this man's not Jim Culver. I'd know Jim Culver if I saw him. A bullet from that rifle passed right under my arm before it took the life of Lieutenant Thomas Ebersole. No, this isn't Jim Culver." The matter finished as far as he was concerned, he turned to go back inside. "I suggest you turn that man loose, and the two of you go on about your business."

"Wait a minute, here," Slocum protested, catching the captain's sleeve to detain him. "You owe me pay for tracking Culver."

Boyd glanced down at the hand on his sleeve for a moment, waiting for Slocum to retract it. When he did not, Boyd jerked his arm away. "I don't owe you anything," he pronounced curtly. "You weren't being paid to go chasing after this saddle tramp." Then the thought struck him. "What are you doing with that horse and rifle, anyway?" he demanded of Johnny.

Malotte hesitated for a moment, sensing he

might yet be in trouble with the army. "I bought the outfit from a fellow at Fort Laramie. I didn't ask him his name."

"You lying bastard," Slocum exclaimed, getting madder by the minute. "You told me you killed Jim Culver."

"Well, I didn't. I just said that. I never killed nobody."

Slocum jerked his head back to confront Boyd. "He's still hiding out there. I'll find him for you," he insisted.

"The army no longer needs your services," Boyd coldly replied. "We have no further interest in Culver." Once again he turned to go inside.

"So that's how it is," Slocum growled. "I track all over Injun territory for you, and you ain't gonna pay me for it."

Boyd paused. He was authorized to pay Slocum for one month's wages—Rothmeyer had told him that—but he had decided against it. He felt the army shouldn't finance a wild-goose chase that resulted in the capture of the wrong man. "It was your decision to waste the army's time chasing after the wrong man. You're dismissed." He turned to the private standing on the porch who had witnessed the entire confrontation. "Private, untie that man." Looking back at Malotte, he said, "Both of you clear out."

"Yes, sir," Johnny Malotte replied cheerfully as the private loosened the knot around his neck. Luck had clearly shifted over to his side, so he was quick to take advantage. "That there's my rifle he's got."

"Give him the rifle," Boyd instructed the private.

Slocum was seething, his huge body trembling with a rage that was steadily building, but he did not protest when the trooper pulled the Winchester from the strap on his saddle. He had been cheated, and he didn't take being cheated well. The mocking smile on Johnny Malotte's face, as his former prisoner took the rifle and climbed aboard Toby, was almost enough to set the angry giant off in spite of the appearance of several additional soldiers attracted by the loud discussion. But Slocum said nothing as he watched Johnny ride across the parade ground. There would be a reckoning. Johnny was a dead man.

With a brief glance at the soldiers gathered around the captain, Slocum then turned back to lodge one final protest. "You hired me to go after Jim Culver. All I had to go on was that damn horse and his rifle. I didn't have no damn picture of the man. I done my job." Then, in slow, deliberate motions, he untied the iron-gray horse from the corner post and stepped up into the saddle. With a hard glint, he favored Boyd with one last glare, an unspoken promise, before turning the gray to follow after Malotte. Feeling the anger like a hard knot in his belly, he fervently wished the day would come when he caught the arrogant captain away from the fort and his soldiers. *Dismissed, am I? We'll see who is dismissed, all right.* Slocum was due for payment, and he meant to have it, if not in U.S. currency, then in blood. And the memory of Johnny Malotte's snide smile was burning in his brain like a white-hot coal.

For the sake of his immediate health, Johnny Malotte deemed it of utmost importance to first put some distance between himself and Slocum. He had no intention of simply running from the loathsome brute, for he had promised himself restitution for the cruel beatings he had absorbed from the not-so-gentle hands of Slocum. But before he reversed the roles to become the stalker instead of the prey, he needed a good head start on the big man. Battered, broke, and hungry, he turned Toby toward Bismarck, six miles to the north, confident that Slocum would follow him. He checked the Winchester and determined that it was fully loaded. It would have been more satisfying to simply kill Slocum right then, but they were in the midst of several hundred soldiers. And he was smart enough to know that he would most likely come off second-best in a showdown with Slocum at this point. Bushwhacking was more Johnny's style. *I'll have my chance*, he promised himself as he kicked his heels into Toby's flanks, leaving the post at a gallop.

Slocum watched as Johnny galloped away. "Run, you bastard; it won't do you no good," he muttered under his breath. Settling for a more leisurely gait, he started out after Malotte. Slocum had no intention of coming up empty-handed after hauling Johnny Malotte all the way from Fort Laramie. He considered the horse and the Winchester his property and just payment for the trouble he had been put to. He would not stop until he regained them. In addition to his desire for these material possessions, he had developed a burning hatred for Johnny Malotte, primarily for not being Jim Culver. He had cost Slocum a lot of time and ultimately his rightfully earned money.

After pushing Toby hard for almost a mile, Johnny let up on the big Morgan. Looking back over his shoulder toward the buildings of Fort Lincoln, he couldn't see any sign of Slocum on the trail behind him. *He'll be coming,* he told himself, and began looking around him for a suitable ambush site. The flat, endless prairie offered little in the way of concealment for a man and a horse; the many gullies and washes by the river were the most promising. He rode on for another mile before sighting a treeless ravine a short distance off the wagon road, and deep enough to conceal the horse. The grass along the rim of the ravine grew high and thick, enough cover to hide him as he lay in wait for the big bounty hunter.

After another look over the wide expanse of prairie behind him to make sure Slocum was not close, he guided Toby down into the bottom of the ravine. Stepping down from the saddle, he staggered slightly, his knee almost buckling, and he realized he was even weaker than he had thought. He was suddenly feeling the results of the days on the trip from Laramie, when Slocum denied him food beyond a few beans strewn on the ground, and those only occasionally. Adding to his extreme hunger was the fact that he had been unable to sleep at night, due to having been trussed up like a hog to market.

He steadied himself with his hand on the saddle horn for a few minutes until he felt he had his feet under him again. Then he drew the Winchester and started back up the side of the ravine, grunting with the effort. Reaching the rim, he dropped down in the grass and waited. It would not be a long wait.

Slocum was good at his craft, in part because he prided himself on being able to think like the cutthroats he stalked. He figured Malotte knew he would be coming after him. And knowing the kind of man Johnny was, Slocum could pretty much bet on an ambush. With that in mind, Slocum had no intention of following Johnny along the wagon track to Bismarck. Instead he guided his horse off the road and worked his way north along the riverbank. It was slower, but he was confident Johnny would wait for him.

Come on, you big bastard, Johnny pleaded. It was getting late in the afternoon, although this time of year there was plenty of daylight left. Lying in the tall grass, the rifle resting on the ground before him, he was almost of a mind to give it up. The constant gnawing in his empty stomach pleaded with him to forget his revenge for the time being. If it were not for the vivid memory of the brutal beatings administered by Slocum, he might have given in to his hunger and gone immediately into the town of Bismarck. *He'll come.*

Slocum might have passed right by the ravine where Johnny lay in ambush, had he not been warned by his horse. The iron gray and Toby had traveled together from Fort Laramie, and when Toby recognized the familiar smell of the gray, he nickered a greeting. The gray returned the greeting, causing both men to react immediately. Realizing Slocum had gotten behind him, Johnny rolled over on his back, blindly firing his rifle as rapidly as he could. His shots ricocheted off the rocks on the side of the ravine, whining and whistling as they spent themselves harmlessly. By far the cooler head, Slocum backed his horse around a protruding rock formation and quickly dismounted. Pulling his pistol, he scrambled up the bank to the rim of the ravine and circled around to approach from the direction Johnny had been watching until the horses nickered. As he suspected, Johnny was crouching halfway down the side, his back to him as he watched the mouth of the gulch.

A slow grin began to creep across the grizzled

features of the bounty hunter as he stepped up to the rim of the ravine. He paused to enjoy his advantage while Johnny nervously craned his neck, watching for some movement from the direction of the river. "You're wasting a helluva lot of ammunition," Slocum said.

Johnny tried to whirl around, but he made it only halfway before two .45 slugs from Slocum's pistol ripped into his side. He yelped like a dog hit with a stone, as much in surprise as in pain. Dropping to his knees, Johnny tried to maintain his balance, but could not, the impact of the two slugs causing him to fall over on his side. Slocum followed his victim down the side of the ravine as Johnny rolled over and over until coming to rest facedown at the bottom. Slocum stooped to pick up the rifle Johnny had dropped on his way down. When he reached the mortally wounded man, he rolled him over with his toe and stood over him for a few moments, silently watching him for signs of life.

Johnny's eyes fluttered open, and he grimaced in pain. His hands, clutched tightly over his wounds, could not stop the flow of blood that oozed through his fingers and covered his wrists. "You killed me, you son of a bitch," he forced out between clenched lips.

Slocum smiled. "Looks that way, don't it?"

"God damn you." Johnny groaned, clutching his side even tighter in an effort to stop the pain. "I'm gut-shot," he moaned. He could feel the blood filling his stomach, and the pain was becoming unbearable. Looking up at the hulking brute standing over him, he pleaded for mercy. "You've killed me. Go ahead and finish it."

Slocum slowly shook his head as if sympathizing with the suffering man. "Like you said, you're dying. Don't make no sense to waste ammunition when you're dying anyway." He reached down and unbuckled Johnny's gun belt, then unceremoniously pulled it from under him, causing Johnny to yell out in pain. "It ain't gonna help you none to cry like a baby," Slocum chided. "You can't last much longer, so you might as well be quiet about it." He threw Johnny's gun belt over his shoulder and straightened up while he looked his victim over carefully. "I've been admiring those fancy boots of yourn ever since we left Laramie. Too bad they ain't a bigger size. Might be worth somethin', though." He grabbed Johnny by his heel and started tugging on his boot. Johnny was helpless to stop him, and when he strained to pull his foot away, the effort caused his throat to fill with blood from his stomach. He was forced to lie writhing with the pain while Slocum methodically robbed him of everything that might be of value. Indifferent to Johnny's suffering, Slocum loaded his plunder on Toby and prepared to take his leave.

"Don't leave me like this," Johnny pleaded. "I can't stand this pain—just one bullet—please!"

About to step up into the saddle, Slocum paused to consider the dying man's request. Without another word, he withdrew his foot from the stirrup and walked back to stand over Johnny once more. Then very deliberately he pulled his skinning knife from his belt, grabbed a handful of Johnny's hair, pulled his head back, and cut his throat. Amused by the look of shock in Johnny's eyes, he stepped back and watched his final convulsions. Stepping up in the saddle then, he took one last look at the now-still corpse and muttered, "I can't abide a whimpering man."

Riding up from the ravine, leading Toby, Slocum continued on toward Bismarck. He could cross the river there and head back to Indian territory. The anger that had consumed him at Fort Lincoln had been only partially satisfied. And at the root of that anger was Jim Culver. As Slocum saw it, all the time he had wasted, the money he had been promised and then denied, was all the fault of Jim Culver. Malotte had claimed at one time that he had killed Culver, then denied it when questioned by Captain Boyd. The more Slocum thought about it, the more he was convinced that Culver was still alive. More than likely Malotte had stolen the horse and rifle. He thought back over the trail he had followed from Canyon Creek. He had no idea where Johnny Malotte had come into the picture; maybe he had been riding with the Indian war party. But since it was Malotte who had left that little stream at the foot of the hill, headed for Fort Laramie, instead of Culver, then it was likely that Culver was with the party of

Indians that had headed north toward the Crow agency. Stroking his chin whiskers thoughtfully, he thought, *Seems to me I recall hearing about a new trading post some fellows built on the Yellowstone.* It was supposed to be near the place where the Bighorn forked off, and that wasn't too far from the Crow agency. That was as good a place as any to start looking for Jim Culver, he decided. *If he's alive, I'll find him.* Slocum had been cheated, and he would not rest easy until he found Culver and watched him die.

Chapter 9

Jim crawled up beside Wolf Paw and lay flat on his belly. The rock outcropping they lay upon was still warm from the sun, even though it was late in the afternoon. It went unnoticed by Jim. His mind was on the line of Indian warriors filing by silently near the river below them. "Sioux," Wolf Paw said softly, "Lakota Sioux."

Jim counted seventeen riders, all warriors, wearing paint. "They're a little out of their usual territory, aren't they?" He knew the Sioux and Crows were natural enemies.

Newt Plummer crawled up behind them in time to hear Jim's question. "Here lately they've been sending out scouting parties damn near ever'where," he said. They watched in silence for a while, until the war party moved on down the valley. "I wonder where the hell they're goin'," Newt muttered. "They're mighty damn close to Iron Bow's camp. Might be they're thinkin' about stealin' some Crow ponies. Maybe we oughta warn Iron Bow.''

While they watched, Newt explained the volatile situation to Jim. "The army's been threatening to go to war agin' the Sioux for over a year now. They told all the Sioux to go back to the reservation and stay there. Some of 'em *are* staying. But a helluva lot of 'em ain't about to give up their way of life to go rot on a reservation. Sittin' Bull and his bunch, and Crazy Horse and his crowd, they ain't signed no treaties with anybody, and they're staying out. Our scouts say that Sittin' Bull is calling for the reservation Injuns to come join him—not only the Sioux, but the Cheyenne and Arapahos too. I'd be surprised if the army really knows just how many warriors they're gonna have to fight." He scratched his head, considering his own words. "Trouble is, the Crows is been friends with the army for as long as I can remember, and they might catch some hell from the damn Sioux, too."

"You think we should go back to warn Iron Bow?" Jim asked, concerned now for his new friends in the Crow camp.

Newt scratched his head again, thinking. "Well, seventeen ain't enough to worry about if they've got fightin' on their mind. But they might be planning to go after the horses. Maybe I oughta go on back. I'm just going with you because I've got a cravin' for a drink of whiskey. But there ain't no need for you to come back with me. Go on and trade your hides."

"I'll go," Leads His Horses volunteered. "I can follow them until they make camp. Then I'll go around them and alert the village."

"I'll go with you," Wolf Paw said.

The issue decided, Jim and Newt continued on toward the Yellowstone while their two Crow friends followed the Sioux war party.

"Well, lookee here what the cat drug in," the man sitting by the short step of the storeroom called out in a halfhearted attempt to sound cordial. "I was wondering when you'd pay us another visit." He got up from his seat on a three-legged stool and took a few steps forward to greet the visitors. A man known only by the name Chambers, he was one of the original company of men who had built the trading post.

"I see you fellers ain't been run off yet by the Injuns," Newt replied, grinning.

"Why, hell, no," Chambers responded. "We're doing business with all of 'em—Crow, Sioux, Blackfoot." He craned his neck to look around Newt. "I see you brought somebody with you. You fellers step down, and let's have a look at them hides you got there." He nodded briefly at the tall young man, dressed in buckskins with a bow strapped on his back, and walked past him to examine the buffalo hides on the packhorse.

"This here's Jim Culver," Newt said. "Them hides is his. I've just got a few plews I'm lookin' to trade for some of your rotgut firewater."

Chambers stopped short and took a closer look at the stranger still seated in the Indian saddle. "Damn," he exclaimed apologetically. "I'm sorry, young feller. I took you for one of Newt's Crow friends. Jim Culver, is it?" He extended his hand, which Jim reached down to accept. "My name's Chambers. Always glad to see a new face, especially with a load of hides like these. Looks like you come to do a heap of trading. If the ones on the bottom look as prime as those on top, you could buy a helluva lot of whiskey."

"I need a new outfit," Jim said. "I don't need any whiskey."

Chambers looked surprised. "Well, come on in the store. I expect we've got most anything you need. Like I said, those hides look in fair shape." He glanced at the two bundles of fox and beaver pelts slung over Newt's saddle. "Them plews you got, Newt, ain't worth much more than a couple of jugs of whiskey, but I reckon it'll be enough to scald your gizzard."

Jim looked around him in the small stockade. There were perhaps a dozen white men engaged in various activities. Two of them were stacking wood against the side of the store. Beyond them, toward the open end of the fort, a blacksmith was busy shoeing a horse while his partner brought up another from the corral. One of the others was involved in an animated discussion with several wildly gesturing Indians as they argued over the value of a couple of buffalo robes. The rest seemed to be busy with nothing more than taking their ease in the morning sun. All paused to take an inquisitive glance at the two new customers.

After Chambers inspected Jim's hides, he set a price on the lot, then led Jim and Newt into the store, where Jim went about selecting items to replace those lost to Johnny Malotte. After his basic supplies, he had plenty left to buy a good skinning knife, as well as a .45 single-action pistol and ammunition. But the only rifles Chambers had to offer were some late-model flintlocks and one single-shot Springfield. Jim decided to save his money, still determined to recover his own Winchester from Johnny Malotte. Satisfied that he had done the best he could for himself, he figured he was ready to start back down the Bighorn. He hadn't figured on Newt's thirst for firewater.

Before Jim got into serious trading with Chambers, Newt cashed his plews in for two jugs of whiskey. He watched the dickering between Chambers and Jim for only a few minutes before retiring to take a seat on a large sack of coffee beans, and began the long-awaited reacquaintance with what he lovingly referred to as Fort Pease panther piss. What Jim was to learn, and Chambers already knew, was that Newt was good-natured and entertaining after a few drinks of the prairie poison Chambers sold. Unfortunately, Newt was never content to limit himself to those few mellowing drinks. Larger doses of whiskey would tend to gradually transform the easygoing old trapper until, by degrees, he would become every tavern owner's nightmare.

With each additional drink, Newt's view of his world narrowed to focus upon nothing but the bitter reflections of every rotten deal life had dealt him—from the final days of the rendezvous when beaver had lost its shine and once-hospitable Indian tribes came to look upon the white man as competition for the very land they hunted upon, to the evil sickness that had taken his Crow wife from him. Lost from his mind's eye were the simple joys of his life with Iron Bow's people and the honored position he enjoyed as a medicine man. There reached a point, usually after more than half a jug had been consumed, where the bitterness became a galling serpent in the pit of his belly. And each additional drink taken to drown it only intensified the misery it caused. It was a battle over which Newt had no control. To Chambers and his men at Fort Pease, he was simply a mean drunk.

Knowing what to expect, Chambers gently suggested to Jim that it might be best for him and his friend to take their trade goods and ride on down the river. "If you ain't of a mind to start back home before morning," he suggested, "there's a good place to camp about four miles south on the east side of the river."

At first Jim didn't understand. Chambers seemed like a friendly enough fellow. Why, he wondered, was the trader inclined to withdraw the welcome mat he had so cordially spread earlier? He glanced over at Newt, still perched on the sack of coffee beans. The old trapper's face was strangely devoid of expression. His eyes narrowed and he stared unblinking at the jug, now empty, at his feet. Jim glanced back at Chambers, who smiled and slowly nodded. It was Newt, then, that Chambers would have depart. But why? Surely Chambers could not expect to sell a man whiskey and not expect him to drink it? In the next instant, Newt himself answered the question.

Jim had already turned back to face Chambers when he heard the thud of the empty whiskey jug as it collided with the log wall of the store and bounced unbroken to the floor. He quickly turned back to discover the old man standing now, although none too steadily. His face a twisted mask of rage, apparently because the jug had failed to shatter, he pulled his pistol from his belt and started shooting at the offending vessel. In the close confinement of the store, the shots sounded like cannon fire. Chambers dived for cover behind the rough plank counter as Newt's slugs slammed into the log walls, each one wildly missing the jug. Chambers's men came running from all directions, and as soon as Newt's firing pin clicked on an empty cylinder, they descended upon him, pinning him to the floor. Cursing and flailing like a captured mountain lion, Newt struggled against his captors until he ran out of steam. Subdued at last, he settled unresisting on the floor.

Jim, completely stunned by the wild display that had caught him by surprise, watched in fascination as his friend was restrained. He looked at Chambers, astonished. "Happens every time," Chambers replied to Jim's unspoken question. "The man just can't handle his liquor." He nodded toward a heavyset man with a bushy black beard who was presently sitting astraddle Newt's chest. "Broke Blackie's nose when he was in here a couple of months ago, caught him square in the face with his rifle barrel. Blackie was ready to kill him right then and there, and I reckon he would have if I hadn't stopped him."

Jim looked at the man called Blackie. He was a good bit younger than Newt and looked to be three times as big. Then he looked again at Newt. The old man's eyes were glazed as he stared up helplessly, his arms and legs pinned to the floor with Blackie on top of him. He was spent.

"Are you all right, Newt?" Jim asked. Newt didn't reply, but blinked a couple of times, then continued to stare at the ceiling. Jim couldn't help but be reminded of the dazed look of an animal caught in a trap. "Looks to me like it's all over," he said to Chambers.

"Not yet it ain't," Blackie remarked. His heavy beard was parted now by a wide, surly grin. "I reckon it's time to teach the old bastard how to behave—time to pay for breakin' my nose." He drew his fist back.

"I reckon not," Jim softly stated. In a flash like a striking rattler, his hand clamped onto Blackie's wrist, stopping the punch in midair. "Let him up," he ordered.

Blackie, unaccustomed to being challenged by any man, was startled at first. Then, angry, he strained against Jim's grip, but found the lean young man's arm unyielding. Enraged and shamed to find he was unable to overpower this unexpected adversary, he started to reach for a large skinning knife in his belt. With reactions a step faster, Jim drew his newly purchased pistol with his free hand and had the muzzle against Blackie's ear before the big man cleared his knife from his belt.

Slow to react before, the men holding Newt's arms and legs suddenly came alive at the sight of the drawn pistol. Quickly now, they scrambled up and stepped back. One of them gave brief consideration to pulling his own pistol, but a warning glance and a slow shake of Jim's head convinced him it would be folly to try.

Blackie, frozen with his hand still on the handle of his knife, the hard, cool barrel of the pistol bumping his ear, burned inside with anger and humiliation. But he was in no position to resist. Chambers, an astonished spectator up to that point, finally spoke. "Let him up, Blackie." He then turned to Jim. "No harm done, I reckon, if you'll just get him the hell outta here before he goes crazy again."

Jim nodded, still keeping his eye on Blackie. "We're already on our way." He took a couple of steps back, the pistol still trained on the big man.

"You're lucky Chambers is here," Blackie mumbled in a feeble attempt to save face at having been bested in the standoff. "He's the boss, so I reckon he saved your ass this time." He slowly removed his bulky frame from Newt's chest and got to his feet, his eyes now glowing black coals of hatred.

"Just a little misunderstanding," Chambers said, directing his words toward his own men. "We don't want any bloodshed here. When all's said and done, nobody got killed." Chambers was a fair man, and he could understand that Jim was doing what he had to. He moved over to stand beside Jim while the young man helped Newt to his feet. "You'll be all right, young fellow. Nobody's gonna take a shot at you." He looked again at Newt, standing reeling and exhausted. "Some people just can't handle whiskey," he said. "Mostly it's the Injuns that go crazy with it. Maybe old Newt's been living with them Crows too long. You're welcome back here anytime." He smiled. "But I don't reckon I'll sell Newt any more firewater."

"Much obliged," Jim replied, but continued to hold the pistol in his hand. "Come on, Newt," he said, leading a subdued and confused old man toward the door.

Chambers instructed his men to stay put until Jim and Newt were out of the stockade and on their way. Blackie paced back and forth across the floor, his face twisted and scowling with anger. Finally he stopped and confronted his employer. "We could have jumped that son of a bitch and settled his hash before he got to the door."

"I told you, that ain't the way I do things. It was just a little misunderstanding that almost got out of hand—wasn't worth somebody getting shot over. I don't want the word spreading that we're a bunch of outlaws and murderers. We'll have folks afraid to come trade with us."

Blackie's pride was not satisfied by the explanation. "I was just gonna fix the old coot's nose the way he done mine," he grumbled. "But I'da kilt that young feller for pulling a gun on me. He was just lucky he sneaked it out on me."

Chambers laughed. He couldn't resist chiding his angry employee. "If you'd have been in here when he packed up his plunder, you mighta noticed he hadn't opened up that box of forty-five cartridges yet. His pistol wasn't even loaded."

It was the same as if Chambers had hit him in the head with a limb. Blackie's face flushed scarlet behind his whiskers, and for a long moment he was speechless. Glaring at the men standing around, he silently dared anyone to make a comment. Knowing his temper, none were foolish enough to remark. Finally words came to him. "You knew that?" he demanded of Chambers.

"I knew," Chambers calmly replied. "Now let's everybody get back to their own business." He stood there watching his men disperse, a sharp eye on the brooding monster who gave him a long, hard stare before turning to do as he was told. The simpleminded brute was going to give him trouble one day. Chambers could feel it in the insolent stare. *That may have been a big mistake*, he thought. *That and that gun-happy Larson—I should have never hired those two.* Out of a total complement of just under fifty men, when everybody was in camp, two bad apples were probably nothing to complain about.

Jim held to a steady pace after leaving Fort Pease behind them. Chambers seemed to be a sensible and coolheaded man, and Jim was convinced that he was sincere in his efforts to preserve peace. Still, there was no sense in taking any chances. Some of his crew didn't look to be as forgiving as their boss, especially the one called Blackie. For that reason, Jim had planned to keep riding until almost dark before making camp, and he would have, had it not been for Newt.

Still in a daze when Jim helped him climb onto his horse, Newt was fairly wobbling in the saddle, not really fit to ride. Jim had never seen a man so drunk. He was unable to hold the reins, so Jim led his horse and trailed the pack-horse behind Newt's. Before passing through the gates of the stockade, Newt had keeled over forward, lying on his horse's neck. He seemed secure there, so Jim let him be. Newt rode that way for almost seven miles before sliding over sideways and landing in a heap on the hard, rocky ground. Jim dismounted and walked back to pick him up. A disgusting sight, the old man lay crumpled, sick as a dog. His gray whiskers were streaked with vomit, mixed with red flecks of blood. Glancing up at his horse, Jim saw a long reddish-green trail down the side of the animal's neck where Newt had vomited before falling off. The poor old man was literally poisoning himself with rotgut whiskey. Jim shook his head sadly at the sight. Too many years of drinking bad whiskey, he supposed.

"Newt," Jim asked, "can you stand up?" There was no answer from the old trapper. He just lay there as though he were dead. For a moment Jim feared that he was. But then Newt uttered a low moan, and his eyes flickered briefly. "Can you stand up?" Jim asked again. When there was still no response, Jim shrugged and sighed. "All right, then; this is as good a place to camp as any, I reckon." He reached down and rolled Newt over onto his back. Taking his wrists, he pulled him up on his feet. Then, crouching, he let Newt fall across his shoulder. When he straightened up with the drunken man on his shoulder, the pressure against Newt's belly caused the poor man to lose the rest of the whiskey down the middle of Jim's back.

"Damn!" Jim yelped, and came very close to dumping the old man back on the ground. Realizing the damage was already done, however, he told himself that Newt couldn't help it. So he grabbed his horse's reins and started walking toward the edge of the river, cursing Newt, and Chambers and his rotgut whiskey.

Selecting a spot among some willows, Jim dropped the reins and started to lower Newt to the ground. He hesitated for a few moments, looking now at the shallow water a few feet away. The foul stench of Newt's stomach contents served to help him make up his mind. Moving down to the water, he stepped in up to his knees before rolling Newt off his shoulder and dropping him in the current. Newt's limp body flopped with a loud splash and immediately sank to the bottom. Jim waited for a few seconds, but Newt failed to bob up to the surface. Afraid now that he had drowned the old man, Jim scrambled to pull him up again.

At last showing signs of life, Newt started sputtering and spitting as Jim dragged him up on the bank. "What happened?" Newt asked, his mind in a state of complete confusion.

"You fell in the river," Jim immediately answered.

"Oh," Newt replied, bewildered by it all. He rolled over on his side and coughed up some of the river water he had consumed, still fighting a need to vomit again. "Well, much obliged for pulling me out," he mumbled, and sank back against the cool sand of the bank.

"Anytime," Jim said with a smile, amazed that the old man had no idea how he happened to land in the river, and seemed not to care one way or the other.

While Newt lay there on the side of the river, apparently having passed out again, Jim peeled off the deerskin shirt that White Feather had made for him and scrubbed the remnants of Newt's stomach contents from it. When it was as clean as he could get it, he hung it on a willow, spreading the arms to help it dry faster. That done, he glanced again at Newt to make sure the old-timer was still breathing before going about the business of building a fire and scaring up something to eat.

"They didn't git far." Blackie chuckled to himself when he caught sight of a flame in the fading light, flickering through a stand of willows along the riverbank. He drew up on the reins and listened. There was no sound that would indicate that the horses in the camp had discovered his presence. He decided it best to leave his horse there and make his way on foot from that point. Sliding his rifle out of the sling, he stepped down from the saddle and carefully moved through a sparse line of cottonwoods that bordered the willows.

Making his way through the brush as quietly as a man his size could, he stopped suddenly when he spotted something in the trees beside the campfire. It took a few moments before he realized what he was seeing. When it hit him, he grinned, for he recognized the buckskins that Jim Culver was wearing, still new and bright. It was too good a target to pass up. Culver seemed to be standing in front of the fire, his arms spread to each side as if telling some wild story to the man on the ground. Blackie couldn't have asked for better. He could take care of Culver before the old man could even start to get out of his blankets. Then it would be a pleasure to settle Newt's hash.

Jim studied the new tin coffee cup in his hand without really turning his mind to it. Sitting with his back to a V-shaped willow trunk, he slowly chewed the last bite of salt pork and let his mind wander to the cabin on the banks of Canyon Creek and a certain young lady who dwelled there. It was the first time in a while that he had allowed his mind to linger in that recess. He had been gone now for much longer than he had planned. He wondered if Lettie might have decided he had left for good. The thought worried his mind, for he realized that he would very much like to see her again. What would stop him from heading out for Canyon Creek the very next day? He glanced over at Newt, still sleeping soundly—only now there was no question that he was alive, unless dead men snored like a bull elk in rutting season. He could see that Newt got back to the village safely, then start out for Canyon Creek. But then thoughts of Johnny Malotte crept into his mind, and he knew he couldn't go back without Toby and his Winchester. Just the name *Johnny Malotte* was enough to make his muscles tense, and he knew there was no question where his priorities lay. Further thought on the subject was interrupted by the sudden report of a rifle and the distinct snap of a bullet passing close overhead.

Like a startled mountain cat, Jim was on his belly, his eyes searching the trees behind him, looking for the source of the attack. At first he could see no one, his vision obstructed by the willows between him and the cottonwoods. He glanced up to notice the neat hole through his buckskin shirt. "Damn," he swore, then immediately returned his gaze to the trees behind him, his pistol ready. Within seconds another shot was fired, and he looked up to discover another hole in his shirt, this one close to the shoulder. "Dammit, that's enough," he muttered, his ire totally aroused now. He reached up and pulled the shirt down before their unknown assailant made a sieve out of it. Concerned now for Newt, he looked back to find his friend sleeping through the attack. With what happened in the next few seconds, Jim didn't have time to alert Newt.

When Blackie saw the shirt disappear from the willows, he naturally assumed he had hit his target. He scrambled up from his position behind a tree and charged through the brush like a runaway moose, intent upon rushing the old man. A man of his immense proportions created a sizable racket as he crashed through the scrub before the river; even so, Jim determined that there was only one assailant, in spite of the noise. So he simply rolled out of his path and waited. His main concern at that point was that Newt might finally awaken and get in the way.

A triumphant grin stretching his thick black beard, Blackie burst into the small clearing, his rifle searching for a target. Seeing Newt still rolled up in his blanket, he brought his rifle to bear on the sleeping man. Before he could take aim to shoot, he heard his name called.

"Blackie!" Jim commanded.

Startled, Blackie jerked his head around to discover Jim lying almost at his feet. His expression of astonishment was forever frozen on his face when Jim pumped three slugs into his chest. Already dead, the huge man stood for a few long moments, his eyes staring but unseeing, before collapsing heavily to the ground. Jim had to roll out of the way to keep from being crushed by the falling body.

After the noisy confusion of the assault, everything was suddenly still, accented by the quiet gurgle of the river's current. "Son of a bitch," Jim uttered softly, amazed by the events of the prior few seconds. Hearing grunting sounds from Newt, he glanced over as the old trapper raised himself up on one elbow.

"What's all the fuss?" Newt inquired, scratching his tangled gray hair. "I swear, whiskey gives a man a terrible thirst." Paying no attention to the corpse sprawled on the ground no more than fifteen feet from his blanket, the old man crawled down to the edge of the river and dunked his head in the cool water. Jim was too astonished to speak.

"Who the hell's that?" Newt wanted to know when he staggered back to the campfire.

"That's what all the fuss was about," Jim answered, amused that Newt seemingly had no idea what had taken place. "This is your friend Blackie, come to call."

"Blackie," Newt replied, showing some concern for the first time. "He's a mean one. Is he dead?"

"I reckon. He ain't moved in a while."

A little steadier on his feet now, Newt walked over to examine the body. He placed a toe in Blackie's side and attempted to roll him over, but the huge man was too heavy, so he reached down and grabbed him with both hands. After the corpse was faceup, Newt stood over it, staring thoughtfully at the remains of the man he had so thoroughly disliked. "Yessir, he was a mean one. What's he doin' here, anyway? Why'd you shoot him?"

" 'Cause he was fixing to shoot you," Jim replied. "He'd already put a couple of airholes in my new buckskin shirt." He held it up for Newt to see.

"Well, I'll be go to hell," Newt marveled. He shrugged his shoulders. "Like I said, he was a mean one. Some folks is just born with the devil in 'em—don't know why he would have it in for me, though."

Jim couldn't suppress a smile. "Maybe 'cause you broke his nose."

Newt paused and gave that some thought. "Yeah, maybe, but that was a while back. Just no accountin' for some folks, I reckon." He studied the three holes in Blackie's chest. "Three holes pretty close together—looks like that pistol you bought shoots pretty straight."

"Hell, he was almost standing on me. It would have been pretty hard to miss."

Newt nodded, thinking about the confrontation that took place practically on top of him. "No wonder I woke up," he muttered to himself.

"We were trying to be as quiet as we could, Blackie and me. We didn't wanna disturb you if we could help it." He couldn't resist teasing the old man.

Jim's humor was lost on Newt. It was the second time in as many encounters with demon whiskey that he had no recollection of what had occurred during his drunken state. Could be that whiskey was turning on him in his later years. Maybe, he thought, it was time he went back to his Crow village and stayed away from men like Chambers and his rotgut. But he had drunk a riverful of whiskey in his life. It was probably just a bad batch.

The following morning saw a fully recovered Newt Plummer, one without so much as a grain of remorse for the trouble his drinking had triggered. As far as he could see, the world was a better place without the likes of Blackie, and he was more than a little puzzled with Jim's concern over the disposal of the huge body. "Hell, the buzzards and the wolves will take care of it," he said, unable to understand Jim's need to justify his actions. "A man ain't held to account for it when he kills·a rattlesnake."

Jim could understand that his concern was highly unusual in a land where every man was his own judge and jury. But he had never killed a man unless that man had tried to kill him, and he felt it his responsibility to inform the company of traders at Fort Pease of the circumstances of Blackie's demise. Against Newt's argument that it didn't make a fart's worth of difference in a tornado, Jim held that he wanted it clearly understood that Blackie had jumped them, and not the other way around. For that reason he deemed it necessary to deliver Blackie's body back to Fort Pease and let Chambers know how the man had met his death—and why Jim now claimed Blackie's horse and rifle. Jim reasoned that he needed both, and since the rifle had been used in an attempt to take his life, and the horse delivered his assailant, then the two rightfully belonged to him. Newt still thought it to be a waste of time. But he helped him heft the heavy corpse onto Blackie's horse and dutifully followed him back toward Fort Pease, the arms and legs of the stiffened body protruding on either side like oars from a rowboat.

"Well, I'll be . . ." Chambers murmured as he walked out the door. He didn't have to be told that the stiffened body lying across the pack-horse was that of the missing Blackie. "So that's where he went." Chambers strode out to meet the two riders.

No one had noticed when Blackie rode out the day before shortly after Jim and Newt had departed. And he wasn't missed early this morning. The sullen giant had few friends among the men of the company, Daniel Larson being the only one who had much to do with him. The other men kept their distance from the two bullies as much as possible—Blackie because of his intimidating size and mean streak, Larson because of his lightning-fast gun and his eagerness to have a reason to pull it. Blackie always had a habit of being scarce when the morning chores were being done. It wasn't until breakfast that his absence was discovered, for Blackie seldom missed a meal.

Since most of the men were away, cutting firewood for the coming winter, there were only half a dozen left to greet the two riders. Jim pulled up in the middle of the small courtyard and waited while Chambers and the others gathered around him. Newt held back a respectable distance with the packhorses just in case there might be trouble and he had to cover his partner's back.

"Didn't expect to see you back so soon," Chambers remarked casually while he moved past Jim to take a closer look at Blackie's corpse. "Shot through the chest," he said after a moment. Then he walked back to stand beside Jim's stirrup and waited for the explanation. It did not escape his notice that Jim had exchanged his Indian saddle for Blackie's. Chambers was a sensible man, and he had a fair idea of what had taken place. Blackie had obviously decided to take revenge, and it had cost him his life. It didn't figure that Jim Culver would have brought the body back if it hadn't happened that way, and he and Newt had lain in ambush for Blackie. Chambers couldn't help but think he should thank Jim for taking care of a problem for him down the road.

"He jumped us and there wasn't much choice but to shoot him," Jim said. "I brought him back to let you know what happened, I reckon so you

could bury him if you wanted to." He sat there
while Chambers's men moved in closer to gawk
at the body. "Anyway," he continued, "we'll be
moving on now." He pulled his horse around
until he was beside Blackie's horse. When he
was even with the head, he reached over and
shoved the body off of the horse's back. Rigid
in death, Blackie's corpse landed on its feet and
seemed to pause upright for a long moment, his
evil scowl glaring unseeing, causing the few
men closest to jump back, aghast. It was only
for a second; then the massive body keeled over
to land heavily, like a felled cottonwood. Jim
touched his finger to his forehead in a casual
salute to Chambers and started to leave. There
was one, however, who was not ready to accept
Jim's explanation.

"Hold on!" Larson called out, and grabbed
hold of Jim's bridle. "You've got a heap more
explaining to do, mister. You can't just come riding in here with poor Blackie's body and some
tall tale about him jumping you. Blackie was a
pretty stout man. I'd say you'da had to shoot
him in the back. Might be that you and that old
rumhead there murdered him for his horse and
rifle." He glanced around him to see if his argument was garnering support from the others.
There was no evidence of commitment to his
cause. Most of the men felt it good riddance to
be done with the sullen bully.

Jim took a moment to take stock of this new
threat. He noted the pistol carried in a holster

that rode just about even with the man's right hand. The leather was oiled and polished. He addressed Larson's accusations then in a calm and even tone. "Any fool can see he was shot in the chest. It happened like I said, and now I'm done with it." He attempted to pull his pony's muzzle away from Larson's grasp, but Larson held on, obviously working himself up for a confrontation.

"Let it go, Larson," Chambers commanded. "Blackie made a mistake and paid for it. It was gonna happen sooner or later, anyway."

Larson was reluctant. "Dammit, Chambers," he whined, "you're lettin' a man get away with murder here." Turning his hostile glare to Jim again, he challenged, "I'll just take that there rifle you stole, and that horse, too."

Jim was already tired of Larson's complaints, but he maintained his calm. "I'm claiming the horse and the rifle as payment for these two holes in my shirt." For emphasis, he cocked the rifle. "I'll ask you to let go of that bridle unless you wanna lose that hand."

Larson flared angrily and briefly considered reaching for his pistol. The sound of Newt cocking his rifle behind him was enough to give him pause, however, and he realized the foolishness of trying to make a move. Reluctantly he released Jim's bridle and stepped back, but he wasn't finished. Just as Jim had looked him over, Larson had pretty much sized Jim up as well. The tall man in buckskins might be handy with a rifle, and even with the bow he wore across his back. But Larson figured Jim, like most mountain men, had little use for his pistol. Added to that, the pistol was new, and Jim had not even had enough sense to load it right away, pulling an empty gun on Blackie the day before. Larson almost smiled at the thought. Men the likes of Jim Culver were just what he was looking for. A man could build a reputation on men like Jim Culver. After all, he had killed Blackie, as mean a son of a bitch as ever lived.

"Mister," Larson said, "you're mighty damn brave when you've got a rifle on a man, and another'n behind him." He took a couple more steps back to give himself room, pulling his coat back from his holster. "Now I'm callin' you out, you back-shootin' son of a bitch. You've got a pistol. Step down off'n that horse, and let's see if you're man enough to use it." He glanced back at Newt. "And keep that old fart out of it. This ain't none of his affair."

Being the sensible man that he was, Chambers was quick to step in. "Now hold on, Larson; there ain't no call for this. You know Blackie better than most of us. You know he was spoiling for a fight."

"Stay out of it, Chambers," Larson ordered. "This is between me and this murdering son of a bitch. I'm callin' him out fair and square, man to man." He turned back to Jim. "How 'bout it, back-shooter? You either throw that rifle down and hightail it outta here on that Injun pony, or stand up to me like a man.''

Chambers wasn't willing to see what he knew would amount to murder. He pleaded with Jim. "Turn around and ride out of here, son. It ain't a fair fight. Larson's as fast as greased lightning with that pistol. He practices with it all the time. There won't be any shame in riding out."

Jim, silent to Larson's challenge up to that point, smiled at Chambers and said, "I appreciate your concern, but I'll be happy to accommodate this jackass." Taking his time to dismount, he glanced over at Newt. "It'll be all right, Newt. No need to take part in this. You just hold my horse over there. I don't wanna take a chance on this jackass hitting him with a stray bullet." His remark was met with a snide smile from Larson as he squared himself and got ready to draw.

Talking to Chambers, Jim said, "First, we've gotta set some rules."

"Rules?" Larson exclaimed. "We don't need no rules except you go for your gun and I'll go for mine."

"When you call a man out, I figure you mean to have a face-off, fair and square. I believe that's what you said, ain't it?"

"Yeah, yeah," Larson replied, anxious to get on with it, "fair and square."

"All right then," Jim went on. "I see you don't carry a bow. I'm pretty damn handy with a bow, so it wouldn't be a fair fight if I insisted on bows and arrows. Same thing with pistols. I don't practice shooting a pistol, and according to what Chambers just told me, you practice all the time."

"What is this shit?" Larson interrupted, thinking Jim was trying to talk his way out of fighting him. "You ain't gittin' outta this now. You've done run your mouth off about standin' up to me."

"Oh, we're gonna fight," Jim assured him. "We're just gonna have a fair fight, that's all." He looked at Chambers. "You can be the judge. "We're both right-handed. So the only fair way to do it is to take some rope and tie our right arms behind us. Then we'll both draw left-handed."

Chambers almost laughed out loud. "By God, that's fair enough, all right." He turned to the men gathered around watching the drama. "Boys, somebody get me some rope." There was an immediate scramble as several started to run toward the corral at the same time, anxious to comply. There was no one among them who had any use for Larson, and this fight had the makings for a promising outcome.

Standing dumbfounded for a moment, Larson finally found his voice. "What the hell . . . Wait a damn minute! I ain't drawing left-handed."

Newt chimed in. "What's the matter, Larson? Seems fair to me. You've got just as good a chance as Jim has. Be a good time to find out what kinda guts you've got."

Larson had no immediate reply. His brain was in a total state of confusion, and he began to fidget, nervously shifting his weight from one foot to the other and back again. In no time at all, one of the men was back with a couple of coils of rope. Jim's confident smile, as he stepped forward and placed his arm behind him, didn't serve to bolster Larson's confidence. Jim's arm was already in the process of being tied by the time one of the other men approached Larson and reached for his right arm.

"I'll be damned," Larson muttered, and jerked away from him. Shoving the man aside, he went for his gun. He *was* fast, but his pistol had not cleared the holster when Newt's rifle ball smashed into his breastbone, knocking him backward. Flat on his back, Larson strained to raise his pistol. A second shot from Newt's rifle split his forehead, and the belligerent bully lay still.

In the confusion that followed, Jim quickly freed his right arm and drew his pistol, ready to meet any counterattack toward Newt. There was none, the men gathered there having been shocked into stunned paralysis by the sudden gunfire. After a few moments, it became apparent that there was no thought of retribution. Such was the level of contempt the men of the company held for the late Daniel Larson.

"I reckon we've overstayed our welcome," Newt remarked softly as Jim stepped up in the saddle.

Jim immediately turned his pony and slowly backed it toward the gate, keeping a wary eye on the handful of men watching him. While Jim led Blackie's horse toward the entrance, Newt moved over to the gate and stood covering him.

"I've got no quarrel with you, Chambers," Jim said in parting. "But if another one of your men comes after us, I ain't gonna take the time to bring him back—just so you know."

"I know," Chambers answered. "We've got no quarrel." He looked around him at the rest of his men. "I don't think anybody here can say that Larson didn't bring it on himself."

When they had cleared the stockade, Newt reined his horse back and waited for Jim to come alongside. "I reckon you must be pretty good with your left hand to come up with a slick stunt like that."

"Hell, no," Jim replied. "I'd have probably shot myself in the foot."

Chapter 10

Jake Pascal had seen enough to convince him that the little trading post at Fort Pease would not long be a safe place for a white man. There had been too much talk about trouble with the Sioux lately. The word that had reached Chambers from Fort Ellis was that Crazy Horse and Sitting Bull continued to defy the army's demands to report to the reservation. Chambers assured his men that they shouldn't expect trouble from the Sioux, but Jake decided that Chambers refused to see the writing on the wall. Once the Sioux started raiding, no little outpost like Fort Pease would be spared. And after the episode a few days ago, there were two less men to defend the fort. Blackie had been a bully, and Jake had little doubt that the world was a better place without him. But if the Sioux decided to raid the trading post, Blackie and Larson would have provided added firepower.

So Jake had decided to *git while the gittin' was*

good. Chambers had tried his best to talk him out of leaving, but Jake had seen enough. He considered himself to be as adventurous as the next man, but he didn't agree with Chambers's confidence that the raiding Sioux would spare the little trading post. So he decided it was safer to get himself to a military post. After telling Chambers he was quitting, he had ridden out, heading for Fort Laramie two days after Larson was killed by Newt Plummer.

Crossing the mountains that separated the river valleys, he had made his way from the Bighorn, to the Tongue, then the Powder before finally cutting over to the Belle Fourche. He had been lucky in that there had been no sighting of Indians, although he had found plenty of sign that told him several bands were on the move. There was also evidence of movement of small bands moving west from the great Sioux reservation in the White River country. It served to strengthen his conviction that the Sioux were gathering somewhere, probably in Sitting Bull's camp. And the last he had heard before deciding to leave Fort Pease was that Sitting Bull had moved his people halfway up the Powder River valley. Jake felt a good deal safer after leaving the Powder far behind, safe enough to make an early camp by the Belle Fourche and rest his horses for a spell. Fort Laramie was still about three days' ride now, but Jake felt that most of the threat from hostiles was behind him.

*   *   *

Slocum stroked his beard thoughtfully as he studied the camp below him in the bluffs. *White man*, he thought, *two horses. Looks like he's fixin' to rest up a spell. Wonder where his friends are?* He looked in all directions around him, paying close attention to the banks up and down the river. After several minutes of watching, Slocum decided the man was alone. Feeling confident that there was no one else lurking about, he climbed into the saddle again and made his way down into the bluffs.

Evening shadows were already lengthening when Jake was suddenly jolted alert by a booming voice no more than seventy-five yards away. "Hallo, the camp," Slocum yelled. "I'm comin' in."

Jake quickly rolled over on his belly, grabbing his rifle as he did. He searched frantically left and right, but could not spot his caller. Keeping low to the ground, he called back, "Who be you?"

"A white man," Slocum answered. "Just a traveler headed for Fort Laramie. No need to git spooked. I mean you no harm."

Jake was not ready to accept just any stranger's word on that. What was a man doing alone in Indian territory, anyway? After thinking about it for a second, he had to wonder if maybe the stranger might be thinking the same thing. "Well, come on in, then," he called out. It might not be a bad idea to have some company on the way to Laramie. He rose up on one knee, his rifle still handy, and awaited his guest. When Slocum suddenly walked his horse out of a patch of willows, Jake almost dropped his rifle in fright.

"Blackie!" Jake gasped, his voice almost choking. Thinking he was being visited by an apparition, he was too stunned to move a muscle. He believed in ghosts, but before this moment he had been blessed never to have seen one. "Oh, sweet Jesus," he moaned, undecided whether to take flight or beg for mercy.

Puzzled by the man's strange behavior, Slocum continued to ride slowly up to Jake's camp, wondering if he had come across a victim of prairie fever. He had heard of men—prospectors or trappers—who had roamed alone for too long, until they became tetched in the head. This might explain why the man traveled alone in Indian territory.

Keeping an eye on the seemingly terrified man, Slocum dismounted and walked up before Jake's campfire. Jake began to shake all over. Slocum stared at him for a long minute before demanding, "What the hell's wrong with you?"

"Whaddaya want with me, Blackie? I never done you no harm," Jake blubbered, cowering from the fearsome bully standing before him.

"Blackie?" Slocum replied. "So that's what you called me when I started in. Hell, I ain't Blackie. Blackie's my brother."

Still almost in a state of shock, Jake realized the form standing there was, in fact, flesh and blood. And though macabre in appearance, it was not a vision at all. "Brother?" Jake croaked. "You're Blackie's brother?"

"That's a fact," Slocum replied, eyeing Jake suspiciously. He hadn't seen Blackie in several years, but he could understand why someone might mistake him for his twin brother. The thing that triggered his suspicions was Jake's frightened reaction when he thought he was Blackie. Frowning now, he said, "Maybe you got some reason to be skeered of Blackie. You looked like you was about to piss your britches a minute ago."

Jake was immediately alarmed by the sudden change in the stranger's expression, and he rushed to reassure him. "Nossir. I never got crossways with your brother, not me. I was just skeered because I thought you was a ghost, seein' as how Blackie's dead and buried."

Stunned, Slocum took a step backward. "Dead! Blackie's dead? What the hell are you talkin' about?" The instant storm that developed behind those dark brows was enough to terrify Jake. He yelped like a frightened pup when Slocum suddenly stepped right across the fire and grabbed him by his shirt. Pulling the petrified man up by his collar, he demanded, "How did he die? Who killed my brother?"

Jake did wet his britches then. His face no more than inches from the fuming giant's, he felt his legs go limp as the warm urine spread in his pants. "Wait, wait," he pleaded, afraid the infuriated beast was about to extract his vengeance from him. "I didn't have nothin' to do with it. Please, put me down, and I'll tell you the feller what done it."

Still fuming with a rage that only he was capable of, Slocum slowly released his hold on Jake's collar, permitting the frightened man to sink back to the ground. "Who?" Slocum demanded impatiently.

"A young feller back at Fort Pease," Jake blurted. "He shot him three times in the chest." He was trying hard to recall the name. "Just give me a minute. I'll remember his name."

Slocum's eyes narrowed again as the storm intensified in his face. "I'll give you about thirty seconds. You come up with his name or I'll crack your skull for you." He grabbed Jake's collar again.

"Wait! Wait!" Jake squealed. "I got it! I remember!" Slocum eased his grip a little. "Young feller's name was Jim something." Then it came to him. "Culver, Jim Culver, that was his name."

The roar that followed caused Jake to shrink back, once more in fear for his life. The menacing giant bellowed like a wounded grizzly. His dark eyes flashed with an anger that sprang from his very soul. *Jim Culver!* The name caused the angry bile to boil deep inside him, temporarily blurring his vision and impairing his capacity for rational thought. In his need to strike out at one who had brought him frustration, and now pain and insult, Slocum launched his massive body toward the closest living thing in his path. And that was Jake Pascal.

Horrified, Jake tried to scramble out of the crazed beast's path, certain that his judgment day was at hand. Slocum grabbed the cowering man—one massive hand clamped around the back of his neck, the other taking a handful of the seat of Jake's britches—and lifted him up over his head. Poor Jake was held there, squirming and begging for mercy for a moment, before Slocum slammed him to the ground.

The pain that shot through his chest caused Jake to fear that something inside him had broken when he crashed to the ground. He was helpless to defend himself and unable to run. Just as he would have had he been attacked by an angry bear, Jake lay still, pretending to be dead. Slocum stood over him, glaring down at the seemingly lifeless form at his feet for what felt like an eternity to Jake. Gradually Slocum started to recover from the explosion of rage that had touched him off, and after a few minutes he took control of his anger. As if noticing Jake lying before him for the first time, he stepped back and said, "Git up from there. I ain't gonna hurtcha." The storm over, he moved back and sat down by the fire. The need for vengeance against Jim Culver that already burned deep in the pit of his stomach was now magnified tenfold. He knew that he would stop at nothing until Jim Culver was dead.

Now that the baleful monster was no longer

standing over him, Jake began to slowly move one leg and then the other, like a possum emerging from a death pose. When there was no violent reaction from Slocum, Jake proceeded to sit up, groaning quietly as the pain in his ribs caused him to catch his breath. Convinced that he had almost had an introduction to the great beyond only moments earlier, he was still leery of the menace that now sat silently beside his campfire.

"Where is he?" Slocum asked, his voice deadly soft and even, his eyes locked on Jake's.

"I don't know," Jake answered, his voice shaking, afraid the violent man might explode upon him again. He hastened to offer any information he possessed about Jim Culver. "I swear, I never saw him before he come into the trading post that day with Newt Plummer. I don't know what his trouble with your brother was. All I know is, he shot him. When he left Fort Pease, he didn't say where he was headin', but I expect he went back to that Crow camp with Newt."

"What Crow camp?"

Jake quickly explained that Newt Plummer lived with a band of Crow Indians, and Jim had evidently spent some time there recently.

"Where is that Crow camp?"

"I think they said they was camped on the Bighorn, but I couldn't say fer sure."

"That's a good piece west of here," Slocum said. "You sure about that?"

Jake was quick to reply. "No. Like I said, I

couldn't say fer sure, but that's what I recollect. Iron Bow's village, I think. At least that's the one Newt was livin' with. I reckon Culver was goin' back there with him."

Slocum considered the matter for a few moments. He decided Jake was probably telling him everything he knew about Jim Culver. The man was too frightened not to. "All right, friend," he said, his voice reflecting a friendlier tone. "I reckon I'll be on my way west at first light. What kinda grub have you got? We best have ourselves some supper before we turn in."

Although his fearsome guest appeared to have taken control of his explosive emotions, Jake didn't sleep much that night. Fearing the worst if he closed his eyes, he fought to keep his lids from dropping. The surly giant slept fitfully and loudly. Once, when Slocum suddenly issued a loud threat to some antagonist in his dreams, Jake sat upright in his blanket, thinking an attack was coming. Early in the predawn hours, Jake decided his life was losing value with every minute he remained in the violent man's presence. *He will surely rob me and kill me,* his exhausted brain told him.

Deeming it prudent on his part to be gone when the belligerent bounty hunter awoke, Jake rolled out of his blanket as quietly as he could manage. Carefully placing each foot, so as not to make a sound, he eased his saddle up on one shoulder and tiptoed toward the willows where his horses were tied. *If I can get a couple hours' start toward Laramie,* he told himself, *I'll be in the clear. As set as he is on going after Jim Culver, he ain't gonna waste time coming after me.* It seemed a reasonable assumption that Slocum would set out due west.

Although Jake was as careful as he could possibly be, the horses spooked a bit when he suddenly approached them in the darkness. Jake's own horses, used to his scent, merely stamped their hooves in nervous tension. Slocum's horses, Toby in particular, snorted loudly to challenge this sudden intruder. In a moment of panic, Jake tried to quiet the big horse. He grabbed Toby's bridle and tried to soothe the nervous Morgan, but Toby pulled away. *Damn you!* Jake thought, and frantically jerked at the reins. He never heard the loud report of the rifle as the impact of the bullet slammed him in the back, ripping through his heart.

"I can't abide a horse thief," Slocum stated quietly as he walked over to confirm his kill. With the toe of his boot, he rolled Jake over and watched him for any sign of life. When it was obvious that Jake was dead, Slocum returned to his bed. He placed a couple of limbs on the fire, then, oblivious to the body near the horses, rolled up in his blanket again. It would be over an hour before daylight.

Approaching the outer buildings of Fort Laramie, Jim couldn't help but recall the first time he had entered this army post. It would soon be a year since he and Lettie had arrived here. It seemed more like three years to him now, so much had happened. One thing was certain: He was a different man from the Jim Culver who had ridden in that day. Events of the past year had dulled the sharp edge of youth that had followed him from Virginia, and he could no longer be thought of as a greenhorn. Like many others before him, he had experienced the magnetic charm of the Rocky Mountains. And the scars on his chest and back attested to the fact that he had met their violent element as well. Dressed in animal skins, rifle in hand, and bow strapped on his back, he rode with the confidence of a man firm in the knowledge that he could deal with whatever God or nature decided to send his way.

As he guided the buckskin Indian pony toward the sutler's store, he thought about the friends he had recently left behind. The people of Iron Bow's camp had been uncommonly friendly toward him, and he had to admit to a certain bit of reluctance at having to say goodbye. After all, he owed his life to Iron Bow and Newt Plummer. The Crow war party could just as easily have left him to die from Johnny Malotte's bullet when they found him lying half dead in that stream. Thinking about his visit in the Crow village brought a smile to his face when he pictured Newt. The salty old trapper had proven to be a competent medicine man, as well as a patient teacher of Crow customs. Jim had given Blackie's horse to Newt as a token of his appreciation and promised that he would get back for a visit soon after he had finished a little piece of business with Johnny Malotte—and maybe a ride over to Canyon Creek to see Lettie Henderson.

Alton Broom glanced up briefly from the sack of meal he was tying off when the broad-shouldered young man in buckskins walked through the doorway. He quickly took another look when it occurred to him who it was. "Why, hello there, stranger," he greeted Jim. "I swear, I didn't know who you was for a minute there." He extended his hand as he looked Jim over thoroughly. "I know you're Clay Culver's brother, but I can't call your name right off."

"Jim," Jim answered. "I reckon it has been almost a year, at that."

Eyeing the transformation in the young man who had passed through the previous October, traveling with a young woman, Alton couldn't help but remark, "Looks like you've took to life on the frontier quick enough." He finished tying off the sack of meal. "Did that friend of yourn ever catch up with you?"

Puzzled, Jim replied, "Who would that be?"

"Why, I reckon it's been quite a while now. Big fellow, said he was a friend of yourn from back east." Seeing the puzzled look on Jim's face, Alton continued. "He said you and him was friends from back in Virginia."

Jim stroked his chin thoughtfully. He could recall no such friend who fit the description that Alton proceeded to give him, of a huge bear of a man with a jagged scar down the side of his face. "Must be some mistake. Did he ask about me by name?"

"Sure did," Alton assured him. "There was a couple of soldiers in the store, and they told him there was a stranger visiting Cora's wagon. I told him that the feller they was talkin' about had been in the store. He said his name was something I can't recall right now. But I told that friend of yourn it weren't you; if you'd been in Laramie, you hadn't come by the store. He mighta gone lookin' for you over at Cora's anyway. Then I guess he just moved on. At least he didn't come back here."

Jim felt the muscles in his arms tense. "The young stranger over at Cora's, was his name Johnny Malotte?"

Alton grimaced, trying to recall. "I don't know. Coulda been. I ain't sure."

Jim's mind was racing as he considered what Alton had told him. There was a strong possibility the stranger who had passed through was Johnny Malotte. As far as the other man, Jim could only shake his head, at a loss for even a guess as to who might be looking for him from back east. He was inclined to be suspicious about anyone from Virginia who came looking for him, although his only trouble might be from the army. And according to Alton, this man was not a soldier. "Doesn't sound like anyone I know," Jim finally declared. Satisfied that he had found out all he could from Alton, he inquired, "Do you know if my brother is in camp?"

"He is," Alton replied. "He was in the store yesterday. Said he was fixin' to ride out with a patrol in the morning. So I guess you just caught him this time."

"Much obliged," Jim said, and took his leave.

"Damn, I hardly recognized you, little brother," Clay Culver exclaimed when he spied his younger brother approaching his campfire. "You look like you've gone plum Injun." He got to his feet and stepped around a small campfire to greet Jim.

With a wide grin, Jim reached out to grasp his brother's arm, and the two pounded each other on the back affectionately. "They told me over at the cavalry barracks that you'd be camped over here by the creek. How come you're way out here by yourself? Won't the soldiers let you camp with them?"

Clay laughed. "I like peace and quiet, and there's a racket of some kind or another going on all the time with those troopers. Half of 'em's foreigners, anyway. You can't even tell what the hell they're talking about." Grinning from ear to ear, he stepped back and took a long look at his brother. "You're looking pretty spry for a dead man." When Jim was obviously puzzled by his remark, Clay explained. "I got word from Canyon Creek that Luke had tried to find you after some fellow came to the cabin lookin' for ya. Luke couldn't find you, but he found enough sign to make him think you'd been bushwhacked. Anyway, that's the word I got. I didn't put much stock in it, and I wouldn't believe it till I had a chance to talk to Luke about what he'd seen. I was fixin' to ride out toward Wind River to see if I could pick up any sign as soon as I got back off this patrol."

There it was again. Someone had gone to Canyon Creek looking for him. Then he showed up here at Fort Laramie. Jim was going to have to deal with it pretty soon. Thinking about the report Luke had taken back, he explained. "Luke wasn't far wrong. I was left for dead, all right, but it wasn't by anybody trailin' me."

"Come on and sit down while you tell me about it." He motioned Jim toward the fire. "Hungry? I've got a little bacon here and some beans."

"I could eat," Jim stated thoughtfully, and followed Clay to the fire.

"You make some coffee while I slice some of this bacon," Clay said. "The coffee beans are in that sack yonder by my saddle. I ain't got a grinder, but there's a couple of smooth rocks laying by the sack that do a pretty good job." Never one to miss many details, he glanced up at Jim again. "I was wondering why you took off after we finished Katie's cabin. Kinda figured you might stay close to that little Henderson gal. From the looks of you, you musta been visiting with the Injuns. Crow, I'd say."

Jim smiled. "Yeah, Iron Bow's village, but how'd you know that?"

"That bow," Clay replied. "Those are Crow markings." He paused while he casually picked a worm from the bacon. "Iron Bow, huh? Is old Newt Plummer still above ground?"

"Alive and kickin'," Jim replied. "He's the main reason I'm still here, I guess, and how I happen to be riding that buckskin pony."

"I was gonna ask you about that. I didn't think you'd ever part with Toby. I notice you ain't carrying that fancy Winchester of yours either."

With the quiet patience of a man who had lived much of his life in the high mountains, and consequently accepted most events with little emotion, Clay listened to Jim's recounting of the circumstances that brought him to Laramie on this day. His only display of concern was a grave nod of his head when Jim told of the incident with Johnny Malotte that had left him near death until Iron Bow had found him.

When Jim finished his story, Clay sat back on his heels to digest everything he had heard. "Damned if you ain't had one helluva summer," he finally exclaimed. Thinking of the lieutenant in Virginia, the man called Blackie, and Larson at Fort Pease, he commented, "You're leaving a string of dead men behind you."

"Not by choice," Jim quickly insisted.

"I know," Clay responded, knowing from his own experience that a man didn't always have a choice. "So now I reckon you're looking for this Malotte fellow."

"I reckon," Jim replied.

"Then I reckon I'll help you," Clay decided. "I've promised to lead a patrol back toward Horse Creek in the morning. I'll have to do that first. We'll only be gone for ten days at the most. Then we'll see about this Malotte fellow. Whaddaya say?"

"Fair enough," Jim replied, welcoming his brother's help. "I need to go have a little visit with a whore named Cora. I reckon I could do that in the morning." He laughed when he saw the grin on Clay's face. "It ain't what you think." Then he told him he suspected Johnny Malotte had visited Cora. He also told him about the *friend* who had come to Laramie looking for him. "I think I'll go over and talk to the lady. Maybe I can figure out who the hell he might have been."

Clay nodded. "Sorry I wasn't here when he came lookin' for you. He sounds pretty damn persistent."

Jim and Clay sat watching the formation of the cavalry patrol that Clay was to lead. There was very little conversation between the two brothers as they waited patiently for the troopers to go through the formalities of getting

started. It was an awful lot of useless commands
and wasted time, as far as Jim was concerned.
Clay, having served in the army during the recent war, agreed with his brother, but understood the necessity for the routine.

"Like I said," Clay advised, "I shouldn't be
out more'n ten days or so. Some settler down
past Horse Creek says some Injuns ran off some
of his stock. When I get back, it might take some
time for us to find this Malotte fellow, and I've
been thinkin'. Maybe you might better ride over
to Canyon Creek and let Katie and Lettie know
you ain't dead." When Jim didn't respond right
away, he said, "It would be the right thing to
do. That little girl thinks a helluva lot of you."
He grinned and added, "God knows why."

Jim couldn't hide a blush. "Shit," was all he
replied.

"Ride over there," Clay insisted. "We're likely
gonna be gone a helluva long time."

"I might as well," Jim conceded, "as long as
I've gotta wait around here for you."

"Good. You might as well stay there, and I'll
meet you there." Clay didn't express it, but he
had a hankering to look in on Katie Mashburn
as well.

The decision made, they sat in silence for a
few minutes more before a young lieutenant signaled Clay that he was ready. "See you in Canyon Creek," Clay said as he prodded his horse
into action.

Jim remained there to watch the patrol file out

in a column of twos. Then, following the simple directions given him by Alton Broom, he crossed the bridge and rode along the riverbank until he reached the tent described to him. It was attached to the bed of a wagon by a canvas flap that was tied to the rear wheel spokes. Dismounting, he called out to see if anyone was about. After a moment or two, a pale woman with tired eyes and lips painted ruby red pushed the entrance flap aside and stuck her head out. Seeing the tall, broad-shouldered young man, she immediately affected a smile and came outside to greet him.

"Well, sir, what can I do for you?" she asked, her enthusiasm fostered by the prospect of a customer she might actually enjoy servicing. "In need of a little female companionship?"

"No, ma'am," Jim replied. "It's a little early in the day for me. It's a tempting thought, though," he lied, not wishing to insult her. "Is your name Cora?"

"It might be," she replied, suspicious of any man who called on her for other than business reasons.

"I'm looking for a man that came to see you maybe a couple of months ago."

Before he could say more, she laughed and replied, "Ha! I don't remember who was here last night, let alone a couple of months ago."

"His name is Johnny Malotte," Jim continued.

Cora replied at once, "Oh, him. I remember Johnny, all right. He spent the best part of a week around here." She paused to recall. "I swear, I believe he'da stayed longer if that big scary bastard with the scar down his face hadn't knocked him in the head and dragged him outta here." She shook her head in wonder and shuddered involuntarily as she remembered Slocum's surprise visit to her tent.

Jim was puzzled. "Somebody knocked him in the head? Who? Was it a lawman?"

"No," she answered, then hesitated. "Well, maybe. I don't know. He didn't say he was the law, just said Johnny was wanted by the army in Fort Lincoln."

"Fort Lincoln?" That didn't make sense to Jim. "If he was wanted by the army, why not turn him over to the army right here at Fort Laramie?"

"You got me, mister. All I know is he said he was wanted at Fort Lincoln." She paused, trying to recall. "For something he did in Virginia, I think he said."

Virginia? That definitely struck a chord, and Jim immediately became impatient for answers. "Did this man say he was taking Johnny Malotte to Fort Lincoln or Virginia?"

Now Cora's patience was beginning to thin. "He didn't say where he was going." She threw her hands up helplessly. "If you coulda seen that man . . . I wasn't about to ask him where he was going. I was just glad to see him go."

Seeing that he was going to get no more information from Cora, Jim thanked her, started to leave, then as an afterthought, gave her a couple of dollars for her time. She curtsied sweetly and graciously accepted the money, then invited him back when he desired something more than answers. "I could get real generous with a man like you."

"Much obliged," he said as he stepped up in the saddle. "Maybe another time." Then he wheeled the buckskin pony around and rode off down the riverbank. There were a lot of facts that didn't add up swimming around in his mind. *I'm looking for Johnny Malotte. Some stranger is looking for me. But he finds Malotte and hauls him off to Fort Lincoln.* It didn't take a genius to figure out this fearsome stranger Cora had talked about had mistaken Johnny Malotte for Jim Culver. He knew now that he had been dead wrong when he assumed the army would not pursue his arrest. From Cora's description of the incident, the huge man didn't waste much time making sure he had the right man. *The fact that Malotte was riding my horse and carried a rifle with my initials on it didn't help Johnny a drop.* By now this bounty hunter—and Jim was sure that was what he was—had to know that he had captured the wrong man. He would be back. The question in Jim's mind was, after all this, where was Johnny Malotte? Maybe he was in Fort Lincoln, or anywhere west of the Missouri . . . or dead. Knowing it might be impossible to track Malotte down, he was still determined to settle that score. But first, his common sense told him a more urgent concern might be the bounty hunter. *I'd better go back and see if I can find out more from Alton Broom about my so-called friend from Virginia.*

Chapter 11

"Well, if the bastard's in the camp, he ain't showed his face all day long," Slocum complained aloud, his impatience about to get the best of him. Never good at the waiting game, he was getting more and more antsy as the sun sank lower in the afternoon sky. He had spent the entire day watching the Crow camp, looking for some sign of the young white man he hunted. He had spotted an old white man who he assumed was Newt Plummer, the man Jake had described. So he was pretty confident that the village he was watching was that of the Crow chief Iron Bow.

He squinted as he strained to watch a group of Indian women as they made their way, laughing and talking, along the riverbank after emerging from a thick stand of willows. Slocum guessed there must be some berry bushes beyond the willows, because the women were carrying baskets. He followed them with his eyes as they returned to the circle of tipis. From his position on a high bluff, he could now see hunters, some individuals, some in groups, returning to the camp—but no sign of a young white man among them.

"Dammit!" he exclaimed aloud, reluctantly coming to the conclusion that he had wasted an entire day watching the Crow village. He could feel the hot blood of frustration heating his veins as he thought of the man he hunted. Jim Culver . . . in the beginning he was just another rabbit, to be tracked down and skinned for the reward money. But Jim Culver had caused Slocum a great deal of humiliation—as well as a sizable reward payment—when he mistook Johnny Malotte for the wanted man. Slocum hated the fact that he had brought in the wrong man, more than the loss of the money. After the berating by the contemptuous army officer, Slocum tended to heap the entire blame upon Jim Culver, and he developed an intense hatred for the man. Discovering that Culver had killed Blackie added so much fuel to Slocum's rage that he could not rest until Jim was dead. He did not hold that much affection for his brother. Slocum hadn't seen him in years. It was more the fact that Culver had the audacity to kill *his* brother. It ate away at his insides that the young fugitive had escaped him so far.

Maybe Jake Pascal had lied to him about Jim Culver being in Iron Bow's village. Slocum frowned at the thought. "I ain't gonna wait much longer," he mumbled. "I'll find me one of them Injuns alone and beat it out of him." It was an idle threat, Slocum's natural reaction to resort to violence as a solution to every problem. But the angry comment caused him to consider approaching a member of the village to find out if Jim Culver was, in fact, among them. He had to know for sure. Spurred by his growing impatience, he decided it was the best thing to do. *What I gotta do is catch one of 'em alone*, he concluded.

This thought brought his attention back to the willows where he had seen the women. "Maybe there's still some of 'em picking berries or whatever they was doin'," he mumbled as he got to his feet and made his way back down the bluff to where his horses were tied.

It was close to sundown by the time he circled around to approach the riverbank below the stand of willows. Leaving his horses tied again, he moved through the trees to the water's edge until he discovered the patch of serviceberry bushes where the women had evidently been. There was no one there now. Disappointed almost to the state of fuming, he angrily turned on his heel and stomped back through the trees to his horses. He was just shy of emerging from the cover of the willows when he caught a glimpse of a buckskin-clad figure through the foliage.

Quick as a wink, Slocum dropped to one knee and drew the pistol from his belt. Moving very slowly, he reached up and pulled a willow branch aside and peered through the leaves to discover the slightly bent figure of Newt Plummer standing by his horse. Slocum waited and watched for a few minutes before deciding what to do about his surprise visitor. It was the old white man he had seen in the village earlier, and here he was snooping around his horses. After watching Newt for a short while, Slocum decided the old man was simply curious about finding a couple of horses tied among the gullies, especially one with a white man's saddle. He decided to try a friendly approach, counting himself lucky that it was the old white man snooping around instead of an Indian. He knew some sign language, but none of the Crow dialect.

Newt was surprised, but not startled, when a man called out from behind him, "Howdy. I reckon you might be Newt Plummer."

Newt turned to face the stranger who suddenly appeared from the willows. At once taken aback to find himself confronting Blackie, or Blackie's ghost—he wasn't sure which—he nevertheless kept his emotions in check. His common sense told him that Blackie was dead. He had witnessed his death. But this man looked enough like Blackie to be his twin—except for the scar on the side of his face. It was this feature alone that convinced Newt he was looking at Blackie's twin brother. "I'm Newt Plummer, all right," he replied, "but how'd you know that?"

"Oh, I heard you was livin' with a bunch of Injuns," Slocum said, smiling. "I'm lookin' for a friend of mine, and I was told he was runnin' with you."

"Is that so?" Newt replied, looking Slocum over thoroughly. "And who might that be?"

"Jim Culver," Slocum said. "I've got some news for him from Virginia."

"Is that a fact?" Newt responded. He had a pretty fair idea why Blackie's brother would be looking for Jim, and it wouldn't be to bring him any news from Virginia. "You're kinda takin' a chance, sneakin' around Iron Bow's camp, ain'tcha?"

Slocum grinned. "Well, maybe. But I wasn't exactly sneakin' around. I was just fixin' to ride in. I'm a peaceable man."

Newt had lived in the high mountains long enough to know a skunk when he met one, and he was certain he was facing one now. For sure, this oversize polecat was no friend of Jim Culver's, and he must have found out that Jim had killed his brother. "Well, I can save you the trouble of ridin' into Iron Bow's camp. Jim Culver left over a week ago."

"That so? Heading where?" Slocum asked.

"He didn't say," Newt replied.

"Maybe he headed back to that little valley they call Canyon Creek. You reckon?"

"Like I said, he didn't say," Newt replied dryly.

Slocum's eyes narrowed behind heavy black

brows, and a lascivious grin slowly spread across his woolly face. "You'd tell me if you knew, though. Right?"

Newt shrugged in response, feeling no need to reply. He turned to fetch his pony, which was pulling up some grass near the water's edge. "I best get back to camp. I reckon you'll be anxious to get on your way before some of Iron Bow's warriors catch your scent. They ain't exactly fond of white men right now."

Slocum raised an eyebrow at this. "Why, hell, you're a white man, ain'tcha?"

"They don't look at me as one. I've been livin' with 'em long enough so's they look at me same as a Crow." He prepared to mount his pony.

"Well, that's just dandy, ain't it?" Slocum's grin returned to part the hairy mass of beard that obscured the lower half of his face. "Much obliged for your help," he said as he stepped closer and extended his hand. Newt reluctantly took it.

Slocum continued to grin, staring directly into Newt's eyes, as he gradually increased the pressure of his hand. Newt tried to squeeze back at first, but the old man was no match for the powerful grasp that was slowly intensifying with bone-crushing power. Newt tried to pull away, but he could not free his hand. Slocum laughed at the old man's attempts and continued to apply pressure until suddenly there came the sharp crack of bone breaking, and Newt cried out in pain. Desperate now, he tried to lash Slocum's face with the reins he held in his other hand. Annoyed by Newt's feeble efforts, Slocum emitted an angry grunt and responded by drawing his knife from his belt. Newt drew his breath in a sharp gasp of surprise as the blade sank deep under his ribs. His whole body tensed helplessly, and he grimaced with the fiery pain that seared his innards.

"Damn you," was all Newt could manage to mutter through clenched teeth. He knew he was done for. His efforts to free himself became more and more feeble.

The grin still in place, Slocum continued to hold Newt up with the knife embedded deep in the old man's organs, watching him die. "You're done for," he crowed. "You might as well tell me where Culver is."

"You can go to hell," Newt gasped with his final breath. The light of life in the mortally wounded man quickly faded away until it went out, and Newt slumped limply. In one sudden move, Slocum snatched the knife from Newt's belly and let his body drop to the ground.

"I can't abide a renegade Injun lover," Slocum stated dispassionately as he cleaned his knife blade on Newt's shirt. Killing the old man provided a certain amount of satisfaction for Slocum, because he knew Newt was a friend of Jim's. So it was almost like killing a little piece of the man for whom he had built such a strong hatred. If he had his way, Slocum would kill everybody in Jim Culver's family. There was a practical reason for killing Newt beyond pure satisfaction, however. Slocum didn't doubt for a minute that Newt would have sicced his Indian friends on him as soon as he got back to camp. With Iron Bow's Crow warriors in mind, he decided he'd better remove Newt's body from the vicinity in case someone from the camp chanced upon it. That decision made, he picked Newt up and flopped him across his pony's back.

He led the horses along the riverbank, remaining in the cover of the cottonwoods and willows until he deemed it safe to mount up and head south down the valley. He was satisfied that Jim Culver was no longer in the Crow camp, and he had made a decision to head for Canyon Creek. He had a notion that maybe Jim wouldn't stay away from those two women in the new cabin there for very long. After putting some distance between himself and the Crow camp, he released Newt's pony. He would have ordinarily kept the horse, but at this time he didn't want the extra burden. So after watching the Indian pony wander off toward a berry thicket with the old man's body teetering to and fro across the saddle, Slocum led Toby off toward the end of the valley.

Chapter 12

Jim looked up into a heavy gray sky as a light shower of snowflakes began to settle softly upon the trees along the narrow trail he followed. The snowfall was unexpected. The sky had been almost cloudless the day before, and it was still early for cold weather. It was not unusual, however. According to Newt, more times than not the weather turned cold overnight in this part of the Rockies this time of year. High up near the peaks, it could be a sunny fall day on one side of a ridge and a spine-freezing winter squall on the other. It was just one more thing about the high mountains that fascinated him. Less than a week before, he had been riding in warm sunshine as he made his way through the Bighorn valley country, his senses almost overwhelmed by the pungent aroma of the sage that grew there in such abundance. Now he could possibly be faced with plowing through snowdrifts before he made it through the narrow pass to Canyon Creek.

He found himself thinking more and more about Lettie Henderson as he urged the buckskin pony along a trail barely wide enough to permit a wagon to pass. On either side of him, the wind whispered softly through lodgepole pines that stood so tall it strained a man's neck to look up to their tops. This was such a peaceful place that Jim found it difficult to concentrate on the likes of Johnny Malotte and the mysterious stranger who seemed to be dogging his trail. Instead his thoughts kept straying ahead to the cabin in Canyon Creek and the slight young girl there. Many weeks had passed since he rode out of Canyon Creek, not only to follow an inborn call to see the other side of the mountains, but also to give his mind a chance to rid itself of thoughts of Lettie Henderson. It hadn't worked. Even after all this time, and all that had happened, she still crept into his thoughts.

"What in hell could I offer her?" he suddenly blurted, wondering how he could even think about supporting a wife. Surprised by the sudden outburst, the buckskin turned its head to eyeball the troubled young man. "Hell, I ain't nowhere near ready to settle down," he offered in answer to the horse's apparent question. "I've got a helluva lot of unfinished business to tend to before I'm ready to think about the plow." He unconsciously fingered one of the bullet holes in his deerskin shirt as if to recall his attention to the business ahead. Silently he reprimanded himself for entertaining such thoughts about the young lady.

"Hell, she might not even be in Canyon Creek," he voiced his thoughts again. "I've been gone a long time. She could have decided I wasn't coming back, and decided to go back to St. Louis." This time the buckskin didn't bother to even acknowledge its master's foolish prattle, but continued its steady pace along the narrow pass. The pony's previous Crow owner never wasted breath talking to himself. Jim rebuked himself again for thinking foolish thoughts. "She ain't gone back. They would have told me back at Fort Laramie if she had passed through there."

Exasperated with himself, he shook his head vigorously in an effort to sweep troubling cobwebs out of his brain. He still had almost half a day's ride before reaching Katie's log cabin by the river and a cup of hot coffee. He wondered how long it would be before Clay arrived, and tried to convince himself that the reason he wondered had nothing to do with how much time he might have to spend with Lettie.

"Reckon a fellow could get a cup of coffee around here?"

Lettie whirled around so suddenly she almost dropped the armload of firewood she carried. "Jim!" she exclaimed, unable to contain her excitement upon seeing him. Fearing he was dead, she had prayed every night for his return. Now she was shocked almost speechless by his sudden appearance before her. Her composure lost for only a moment, however, she quickly reined her emotions in. "I declare," she said, "you're as bad as your brother—sneaking up behind folks."

"I didn't mean to startle you," he said, even though he was aware that he was, in effect, returning from the dead. He figured she would have heard the soft padding of the Indian pony had she not been engrossed in chopping wood. There was one who had heard him approach, however. Jim nodded to Luke at the corner of the corral. "Howdy, Luke," he said.

Luke acknowledged the greeting with a nod, stunned to see Jim alive. He had been convinced that the Crows had killed Jim at that little stream near the base of the Wind River foothills. Happy that he had been wrong, he immediately strode forward to shake Jim's hand, at the same time feeling a heavy shroud of guilt for reporting him dead. "I thought you was dead," he confessed apologetically. "I followed your trail to that stream and . . ." His words trailed off.

"Well, I almost was, I guess," Jim replied. "You weren't far from right. If I hadn't been found by a band of Crows, I reckon I would be dead." He quickly returned his attention to Lettie. "Looks like you folks are doin' all right," he offered as he reached out and took the load of firewood from her arms. Suddenly he was speechless. He wanted to say more to her, but he lacked the courage to tell her that she was really the only reason he came back to Canyon Creek before searching for Johnny Malotte. He was saved for the moment when Katie appeared in the doorway.

"Well, for goodness' sake," Katie said, a wide smile on her face. "We'd almost given you up for dead." She took a step toward him, then stopped to look him up and down. "It's a wonder anybody recognized you. You look like an Injun."

Jim grinned. "I didn't think I was gone that long," he said. "You folks oughta know I'm harder to kill than that."

Katie stood there a few moments longer, beaming with her delight to see Clay Culver's younger brother again. She had constantly bolstered Lettie's faith in Jim's return, while not completely convinced that Luke's original opinion had been an incorrect one. It was with a sigh of relief that she now glanced at Lettie and winked. The young girl immediately flushed red. Katie shook her head in mock exasperation and turned back to Jim. "Well, don't just stand there with that armload of wood. Bring it on in the house, and we'll get some coffee on the stove."

Luke took Jim's horse, and Jim dutifully followed Katie into the cabin. "Keep your eye on him when you unsaddle him," he called back to

Luke. "He has a fondness for taking a nip outta you if you ain't watchin' him—been that way ever since I swapped saddles on him. He don't like that big saddle too much." He stole a quick glance in Lettie's direction, then looked away when he discovered her doing the same.

"What happened to Toby?" Luke asked.

"Long story," Jim replied. "I'll tell you after you put my horse up."

"Did that big, ugly-looking grizzly ever find you?" Katie wanted to know when they got inside.

"No," Jim replied. "I heard he showed up here." He didn't particularly like the notion that this man who was looking for him knew about Canyon Creek. He told them he had not encountered the man, but was aware that the man was trying to trail him. Even after hearing Katie's description of the stranger, it didn't occur to him that the man she described sounded a helluva lot like Blackie.

While Katie busied herself with the coffeepot, Lettie stirred up the fire in the iron cookstove in preparation for starting supper. Jim sat down at the table. In a few minutes they were joined by Luke, and Jim recounted the events that had taken place since he last saw them—from his encounter with Johnny Malotte to his stay among Iron Bow's Crows. "If it hadn't been for Iron Bow and Newt Plummer, I guess I might still be floating in that stream." He looked over at Luke and grinned. "I guess they more or less took me into their tribe, so I reckon that sorta makes me and you natural enemies."

Luke returned the grin. "I reckon," he answered. "But then, I guess you're Clay's natural enemy, too."

"Dang, I guess I am at that," Jim replied, laughing. He had forgotten Clay's close ties with the Shoshonis. "Well, friend or foe, Clay's supposed to meet me here in a few days."

His remark captured Katie's attention at once, and she hoped the sudden flush in her face had not been noticed. She quickly turned back to the gray coffeepot on the stove in an effort to hide her emotions. She was not quick enough to avoid Lettie's glance, however, and her young friend's quizzical gaze. "This hot stove is making me flush," Katie mumbled lamely.

Lettie didn't comment, but for the first time she began to suspect that Clay Culver might be more than a friend to Katie. It occurred to her then that Katie always seemed to become extremely quiet whenever the subject of Clay Culver came up. The thought caused a little smile to form on her face as she continued to gaze at the other woman.

Alarmed that Lettie might have read her innermost thoughts, Katie attempted to bluster. "Another mouth to feed," she said to Jim. "But I reckon he's welcome, since you and him built this cabin." She could tell by Lettie's expression that her young friend was on to her ruse.

Jim smiled, knowing Katie's comments were

no more than bluster. There was not a more compassionate and giving person in the whole territory than Katie Mashburn, although few of her neighbors realized it. "That's right," he said, "another mouth to feed." He reached over and poked Luke on the shoulder. "I don't know how you're fixed for food, so I reckon Luke and I better go huntin' in the morning—see if we can bring some meat in." Luke smiled his approval of the suggestion.

"Maybe you could kill a couple of those deer that have been feeding in my garden," Katie replied. "What with the damned deer and the cool weather, there ain't much left of the garden."

Lettie, having returned her gaze to settle on Jim once more, could not help but comment. "Haven't been in the house for an hour, and already you're talking about heading to the woods." As soon as she said it, she blushed and looked away, only to catch Katie's smug grin, as the previous situation was now reversed.

Jim and Luke, blissfully unaware of the silent conversation between the two women, the communication having been conducted solely with their eyes, were already talking about the best place to jump a deer. As the afternoon wore on and evening approached, the mood was light-hearted, with Jim and Lettie renewing their acquaintance after many months apart. Katie watched the two young people, amused by the stolen glances each would take when the other was not looking. The two would make an excellent couple, she decided, if Jim ever got it through his thick skull that he needed Lettie. *Just like his brother*, she couldn't help but think. And the thought brought a wistful look to her eyes as she formed a picture in her mind of Clay Culver, sitting tall and straight in the saddle. Where was he at this moment? Jim said he was on his way here as soon as he was back from leading a patrol. *What the hell do I care where he is?* she scolded, bringing her thoughts back to the present. Her resolve had slipped for a moment. She tried never to let herself think about Clay Culver as anything more than a friend.

At the precise moment that Katie Mashburn had wondered about his whereabouts, Clay was not sitting tall and straight in the saddle, as she had envisioned. In contrast, he was lying flat on his belly behind a clump of prairie sage that ringed the rim of a deep defile. Below him, beside a trickle of a stream, a half dozen Sioux warriors were engrossed in the butchering of Bailey Palmer's milk cow. A few yards upstream, two more were watering the raiding party's ponies. Among the ponies, Bailey's two mules and one saddle horse crowded their muzzles in to compete for access to the tiny stream.

The raiding party had not been hard to follow, and it had not been hard to figure where they were headed. The trail was leading straight to the Spotted Tail agency. Clay unconsciously shook his head as he thought about it. It was hard to blame the Indians for raiding the settlers' livestock. *Hell, they're starving! I might raid too, if I was hungry.* Clay didn't like this part of the job. If the government insisted that the Sioux stay on the reservation, then they should provide the food and supplies they had promised. After a few moments he pushed away from the sage, keeping his body low behind the rim of the defile. Once he was far enough away so as not to be seen by the Indians, he got to his feet and made his way back to his horse.

After a ride of approximately a mile, he came upon the cavalry patrol resting their mounts while they awaited his return. Clay rode up to the lieutenant and dismounted. "They're about a mile ahead," he said as he stepped down. "They stopped to butcher the cow."

"How many?" Lieutenant Fannin asked.

"I counted eight," Clay replied, "two of 'em just boys."

Fannin nodded, satisfied that the odds favored his fifteen-man patrol. Clay had told him before that the tracks indicated less than ten riders, but it was reassuring to have visual confirmation. He had no intention of getting his ass kicked by attacking a war party bigger than his patrol. There were only four men in the patrol who had actually been blooded in Indian fighting. The rest were green troops, most of them foreigners, just transferred over from Fort Lincoln, and probably enlisted because of difficulties in finding jobs in the civilian population. Fannin knew they hadn't received a great deal of training, so he wasn't willing to rely on their ability to perform unless the odds were heavily in his favor. "All right, then," he said, "we'd best get moving." He turned to his sergeant. "Sergeant, get the men mounted."

"No need to hurry," Clay said. "From the looks of it, they just started to butcher that cow."

At Clay's suggestion, Lieutenant Fannin split his detachment and sent half of his troops to the west of the defile. Led by Sergeant Dubois with orders to advance no closer than fifty yards, they would be able to cut off the Indians' retreat. When Fannin, with the rest of the patrol, was within two hundred yards of the narrow stream, he halted his men and waited for the sergeant to get his troopers into position. While Fannin waited, Clay made his way forward to the clump of sage he had originally hidden behind to watch the Sioux raiding party.

Let's don't mess this up, boys, Clay thought as he rose to one knee and signaled the lieutenant that the raiding party was still there. After seeing Fannin acknowledge with a wave of his arm, Clay turned back to keep an eye on the Indians. All of them were young warriors, two barely old enough to be called warriors. How, he wondered, would Red Cloud be able to keep these young warriors from jumping the reservation and flocking to join Sitting Bull or Crazy Horse? He held no animosity for these young fighting men. They were not his enemies. To the contrary, he could well sympathize with their plight. They were born hunters and fighters, no more able to adapt to reservation life than a grizzly or mountain lion. For a brief moment he wished he had not found them. But, he told himself, they raided a settler and stole his livestock, so it was best to run them to ground. He had done his job—he had tracked them to this spot—now he would let the lieutenant do the police work. "Come on, Fannin," he said under his breath. "I've got things to do." His mind was already jumping ahead to Canyon Creek and his brother waiting there. He shifted his gaze from the two young boys watching the horses back to the butchering of the cow. *I wonder if that cow gave much milk?*

As it turned out, the successful completion of the hostiles' capture was doomed by the greenness of the lieutenant's troops. In his excitement over his first actual combat with Indians, one of the troopers with Sergeant Dubois accidentally fired his carbine before the detail had a chance to get into position. The result of the sudden gunshot was a wild scramble as the Sioux warriors ran to their horses. Since Dubois was not in position to cut them off, the hostiles were able to escape the trap, galloping off to the west.

Fannin quickly ordered his troops to pursue, but it was too late. The Indians already had too

great a head start. Riding low on their swift ponies, the Sioux warriors soon stretched the distance between them and their pursuers. Bailey
Palmer's horse and mules followed behind the
fleeing Sioux for a while before trailing off and
giving up the chase. The soldiers gamely attempted to pursue the hostiles, but Fannin soon
realized it was a losing proposition and gave the
order to halt. He detailed a couple of soldiers to
round up Palmer's livestock, and headed back
to the little stream where Clay stood waiting.

When the shot that startled the Indians into
flight had rung out, Clay just shook his head in
amused exasperation. Since there was no longer
a need for concealment, he stood up and casually watched the hostiles as they jumped on
their ponies and fled. He could have easily
picked off a couple of them with his rifle, but
he was not of a mind to. Instead he stood there
for a few moments, watching the cavalry in useless pursuit. After the dust settled, he took his
horse's reins and led it down the bank to the fire
where the butchering had been done. Lieutenant
Fannin and his patrol returned to find him
squatting by the fire, roasting a piece of beef
over the flame.

"Well, damn," was all Fannin could think of
to say as he dismounted. The sight of the big
scout leisurely sampling the meat caused a bit
of confusion in his mind. For a moment he was
undecided whether or not he should be ordering
Clay to stop. But then the incident struck him as

kind of humorous. Looking around him, he couldn't help but notice the interest generated among the men as they eyed the half-slaughtered carcass. It took Sergeant Dubois to settle it.

"Well, by God, Lieutenant, since them damn Injuns got away, we might as well have us a feast. I mean, since they was kind enough to fix it for us." Without waiting for Fannin's permission, Dubois pulled out his knife and started hacking off a piece of the cow. The rest of the men hung back at first, undecided.

Fannin laughed. "I guess you're right. No sense in wasting the meat." He looked at Clay. "At least we got Palmer's mules and his horse back."

Clay nodded and stepped away from the fire to make room for the troopers now eagerly shouldering one another aside to get at the carcass. "Do you aim to go after them?" he asked Fannin.

"Hell, no," Fannin replied after a moment's consideration. "There ain't much doubt where they're heading—back to the reservation. By the time we got there, they'd be scattered everywhere."

"I expect so," Clay agreed.

The decision made to return to Fort Laramie, Fannin ordered an hour's rest. The order was met with a cheer from his men, and the feast was continued. After four days of salt pork, the tough beef was a banquet indeed. There was very little sympathy for Bailey Palmer's loss.

After every man had a chance to cut off a slab of meat, Clay carved off another and sat down beside one of the troopers. The young soldier was one of the men recently arrived from Fort Lincoln. He studied Clay out of the corner of his eye for a few moments before asking a question. Hesitant, because most of the men regarded the quiet scout as something of a mystery, he nonetheless sought to satisfy his curiosity. "Your name's Culver, ain't it?"

"That's right," Clay acknowledged.

"Have you got a brother?"

Clay turned to look at him. "I've got three."

"Any chance one of 'em's named Jim?"

This piqued Clay's interest. "Matter of fact, one of 'em is. Why? Do you know Jim?"

"No," the trooper replied. "It's probably just a coincidence; probably ain't your brother a'tall. I just heard about a fellow named Jim Culver when I was at Fort Lincoln. I was pulling fatigue duty one day, sweeping the yard around the post adjutant's office, when this bounty hunter brought some fellow in hog-tied to a horse. He was sure his prisoner was Jim Culver, but the captain said he'd brought in the wrong man." The trooper shook his head to emphasize his story. "And I mean that feller didn't like it a bit."

Clay threw the piece of meat he had been eating into the fire, no longer interested in food. "This bounty hunter, what did he look like?"

"Trouble," the trooper replied. "One of the

meanest-looking sons of bitches I've ever seen—
and big as a grizzly, bigger than you, I expect."
He could see from Clay's expression that the
scout was more than a little interested. "And,
boy, he was fit to be tied when he found out he
had the wrong man. I believe if there hadn't
been a bunch of us soldiers standing there listening, he mighta jumped on the captain for not
paying him."

The soldier's description of the bounty hunter
caused a new feeling of urgency in Clay as he
recalled Jim's account of the stranger who
seemed to be tailing him. The description
matched that of the man asking about Jim in
the sutler's store. Suddenly the picture began to
become clear in his head. He strained his mind
to remember the name of the man who shot Jim
and left him for dead. *Johnny something . . . Ma-
lone, Mallard . . . no, that wasn't it.* "You said the
bounty hunter had the wrong man. Did he say
what his name was?"

"I don't recall," the trooper said, stroking his
chin in an effort to remember. "I remember he
said his name; I just can't recall it."

"Malotte?" Clay suddenly remembered. "Was
it Johnny Malotte?"

"You know, it coulda been. It was a name like
that, anyway."

The picture was all too clear now. Jim had a
bounty hunter on his tail for sure. And if the
man was as mean as the trooper described, Jim

was in real danger. Clay didn't need to hear any more. He got up from the bank and strode over to Lieutenant Fannin. "I'm gonna be leaving you now. You don't need me anymore. You know the way back to Fort Laramie." That said, he didn't linger for any explanation, but turned and went immediately to his horse.

"What?" Fannin exclaimed, and jumped to his feet to follow the tall scout. "Where the hell are you going?"

Clay stepped up into the saddle before answering. "I've got some important business to take care of, and a lot of ground to cover before I even get there."

"What about your pay?" Fannin asked. "You're supposed to get paid for guiding the patrol."

"I'd appreciate it if you'd handle it for me. You can just put me in for pay up till today. I can't take the time to ride back to Laramie." At this point, Clay was unconcerned about pay. It had suddenly dawned on him that Jim was in real danger. If he had known before what he had just learned from the trooper, he would have had Colonel Bradley send one of the other scouts to lead this patrol. And he would have gone with Jim to Canyon Creek.

Fannin stepped back when Clay wheeled his horse and gave the stallion his heels. "All right, Clay," a perplexed Fannin called after the departing scout. "I'll take care of it."

"What the hell's eatin' him?" Sergeant Dubois asked as Fannin stood dumbfounded, watching Clay's trail of dust.

"Damned if I know," the lieutenant replied. "Something set him off, that's for certain."

Chapter 13

"Well"—Lettie sighed—"I guess these clothes aren't going to wash themselves." She picked up the two buckets by the door and walked outside.

Katie looked up from her sewing, watching her young friend for a few moments before she put Luke's torn shirt aside and got up to follow Lettie outside. She glanced briefly at Luke sitting by the doorstep braiding a rope out of rawhide before looking toward the barn to where Jim sat cleaning his rifle. "With all these men around, looks like you could get some help filling up that washpot," she called out in a loud voice, loud enough to be heard at the barn. Jim glanced up at her, then turned to look at Lettie, who was walking down the path to the river. Luke put his rope aside and started to get to his feet. Katie placed a hand on his shoulder and said softly, "Let Jim do it."

Jim glanced again at the cabin and, seeing no

movement from Luke, propped his rifle against the barn and got up to intercept Lettie. Smiling, Katie nodded to herself and returned to her sewing.

"Here, let me give you a hand," Jim said as he fell in step with Lettie.

"Why, thank you, kind sir," Lettie responded playfully, "but I'm used to doing this without help." She let him take the buckets from her. "As long as you're going to help, though, I'll go back and get the dirty clothes and you can take the buckets on down." She turned to return to the cabin. "I'll be right back. You can go ahead and start filling the washpot, if you want to."

Now I'm doing the wash, he couldn't help thinking as he followed the path down by the river. He knew it was a foolish thought, one that was strictly defensive. Since he had returned to Canyon Creek, he found himself constantly thinking up negative thoughts about marriage, giving himself as many reasons as he could manufacture to remain a single man. When he was completely honest with himself, he had to admit that there had been no outward sign from Lettie that she entertained the slightest interest in him beyond simple friendship. If he had given it more thought, he might have surmised that this was the reason for his attitude. The slight young girl had been in his mind on so many nights when he was away from her that there was now a definite fear that she held no special fondness for him. Her feelings for him might be of his own imagining. That was why it was better to shun marriage. "Damn!" he exclaimed, shaking his head vigorously to drive thoughts of Lettie from his mind.

The path ended at an open spot by the river where a huge iron pot sat on some stones. The pot had been brought from Fort Laramie by Nate Wysong, along with the iron stove in the cabin. It reminded Jim of one that was used back on his father's farm in Virginia at hog-killing time. This one was used to wash clothes, since Katie had no hogs.

I expect she'll want a fire built, he thought as he set the buckets down beside the iron pot. There was a small stack of firewood a few yards away. Using a stick of wood for a poker, he raked some of the old ashes from underneath the pot and laid a new bed of dry wood. *I reckon she'll bring something to light a fire with,* he thought. The fire ready to light, he picked up the buckets and walked down to the water's edge. He had filled the huge pot halfway by the time Lettie appeared with a bundle of clothes.

"Thanks for your help," she said cheerfully as she dropped her bundle in the huge pot. "I think that's plenty of water."

"No trouble," he replied, suddenly feeling embarrassed. He wasn't sure if he wanted to linger, or if he should leave her to her chore. She made up his mind for him.

"I'm glad you're back, Jim. I was worried about you; we all were. Luke was pretty sure something bad had happened to you, from the signs he found around that creek."

He shrugged his shoulders as if the incident were trivial. "I guess it was understandable he would figure I was done for. It musta looked pretty bad. I wasn't sure myself for a spell, but I was lucky. I had a first-rate medicine man taking care of me." He smiled when he thought of Newt and made a mental promise to go back to visit his friend when the business with Johnny Malotte was finished.

She gazed at him, searching his eyes for a few moments, as if waiting for something more from him. When he said nothing, she knelt before the wood he had laid, and busied herself lighting a fire. Once she had a promising flame, she backed away and turned to face him again. Pointing to a log a few yards away, she said, "We can sit over here while we wait for the water to get hot." That said, she picked up a crudely carved wooden paddle that had been propped against the pot and poked the soaking clothes with it.

He waited for her to join him before sitting down on the log. "Who carved the paddle?" he asked once they were seated.

Lettie smiled when she answered. "That's Katie's work."

"Well, don't tell her I said it, but I almost broke it up for firewood." They both laughed at that.

There was an awkward silence between them

as they sat watching the fire, both aware of deeper thoughts lying just beneath the surface of the idle conversation. The stern lecture Jim had delivered earlier about the burdens of marriage was far from his mind. And he found himself helplessly thinking back to the lonely nights in the Crow village when he would think of her. Sitting next to her now, he could feel her, even though they were not touching, and the sensation left him confused and bewildered.

Finally she broke the silence. "What are you thinking about?" she asked.

"I don't know," he started. "I mean, nothing, I guess." He dared not tell her that he was at that moment wondering what it would be like to feel her in his arms. "What are you thinking about?"

She shifted her position so that their elbows were touching, making herself more comfortable. "I was thinking that this is the first time we've been alone, just you and me, since we rode from Plum Creek together—on our way to Fort Laramie."

"Yeah," he said, his gaze firmly fixed on the fire, "that seems like a long time ago, doesn't it?"

She didn't answer at once, but turned to gaze at him, wondering if he was even capable of having deep emotions. When he continued to stare into the fire, she shook her head and sighed. "I guess there's really nothing holding me out here. I know my aunt wants me to return to St. Louis to live with her." She watched him closely for his reaction. Since he continued to face the fire, there was none that she could see, so she went on. "I know Katie would hate to see me go. She needs my help, and we've become such good friends, like family really." She paused again to allow for his response. There was none. "But she's the only person who really needs me to stay." Again she waited. He remained frozen in a state approaching despair but outwardly resembling indifference. Finally she threw up her hands in disgust. "Dammit, Jim Culver, you're as dense as that iron washpot! Do you want me to stay or go back to St. Louis?"

"What?" he blurted. Completely flabbergasted by her sudden demand, he couldn't think of anything to say at first. "I don't know," he finally managed. "I can't tell you what to do."

"Damn right you can't," she shot back at him, her impatience blossoming into real anger at his seeming inability to respond to her. "I didn't ask you what I should do. I simply asked you if it makes a damn to you whether I go back east or stay here. Because if it doesn't, I might as well go back to civilization." Glaring at the stunned young man beside her, she demanded impatiently, "Well?"

Lettie was very young, but she was sensible and strong-willed. At this moment she was certain that she was in love with Jim Culver. But she also knew that in this wild country nothing was certain. She felt reasonably sure that he had strong feelings for her, if he only had sense enough to know it. Men like Jim were always looking toward the mountains, hearing the cry of a hawk, and in dread of being tied down. It was her misfortune to fall in love with a man of this breed. But she also knew that he was born with a serene strength and a sense of integrity that made him stand out among lesser-endowed men. And she felt that he was capable of loving her with the same intensity with which she loved him. In spite of this, she had her own integrity and pride. She would not wait forever for Jim to get his head out of the clouds. She would not permit a future for her like Katie's—alone, wearing a pistol on her hip, and dreaming of Jim's half-wild brother, Clay. With an unblinking gaze, she repeated her demand. "Well?"

Jim was stunned, shocked by the unexpected attack from one so young and seemingly innocent. He had known that Lettie had spunk, more than the usual amount for a girl of her tender years. But he had never before witnessed the force of her resolve. He had been in a state of confusion over his feelings for her before this. Now he was approaching panic. Of course he wanted her to stay. He wanted her to always be near him. But how could he make a commitment to her now? There were things to be settled first—Johnny Malotte and the mysterious rider who searched for him.

They sat for what seemed to be a long time with nothing but the bubbling of the water boiling in the iron pot to break the silence. After a few minutes Lettie got up and went to tend it. After she raked the hot coals from under the pot, she dropped some chips from a bar of lye soap into the boiling water, and stirred the clothes with the paddle. That done, she turned again to face Jim, her hands on her hips, an uncompromising expression on her face, but she said nothing.

"I guess I want you to stay," he stated humbly, as if confessing a crime.

His answer didn't fully satisfy her. "You guess you want me to stay," she echoed. "Why, Jim? Why do you want me to stay?"

Totally dismayed and weary of this unforeseen interrogation, he threw up his hands in a gesture of frustration. "I don't know." He hesitated. "You know . . . Katie needs you. . . ."

"Katie needs me," she repeated, getting worked up again. "So if Katie didn't need me, then it would be all right for me to go?"

Cornered, he suddenly rose to his feet. Flushed with frustration, he replied, "You always were like a thorn in a man's foot, ever since you insisted I had to take you to Fort Laramie last fall." He appeared to be angry as he confessed, "Yes, dammit, I want you to stay!"

The stern expression on her face immediately relaxed and her eyes softened. It was commitment enough for her at this point. Considerably short of a wedding proposal, it was enough to warrant further investment of her time. Leaving the paddle in the pot, she walked over to stand before him. Gazing up into his eyes—eyes that still sparked with anger—she lifted her face to be kissed. When he stood unbending over her, she reached up, placed her arms around his neck, and gently pulled his head down to her. In contrast to the stern manner with which she had forced his hand, her kiss was as gentle as the caress of a butterfly. He was immediately lost in the embrace. Thoughts of high snow-capped mountains, cold, clear mountain streams, and the excitement of the hunt—as well as thoughts of revenge—were all dissolved in the warmth of her kiss. At that moment he was completely vulnerable.

"Ain't that sweet," Slocum growled under his breath. The front sight of his rifle was centered right between Jim Culver's shoulder blades. "I can git him and the gal with one shot." The thought brought a crooked grin to his grizzled features. It was the kind of thing that brought him pleasure. Feeling absolutely certain that this time he had found the right man, he slowly closed his finger on the trigger. At a distance of one hundred and fifty yards, he wanted to be sure not to jerk the trigger and cause an off-center shot. He had waited a long time to get Jim Culver in his sights. This man had caused him one helluva lot of trouble, and it suddenly occurred to him that he was reluctant to end it so painlessly. The thought made him hesitate and relax his trigger finger. *Maybe I oughta take him alive and make him pay a little more for the trouble he's caused me. I might even drag his half-dead carcass all the way back to Fort Lincoln and dump it on that prissy captain's doorstep. The army would have to pay me then, because that's what he contracted with me to do.* The idea intrigued his devious mind. He rolled the notion over in his head while he drew his rifle down on Jim's back again. It had always been his custom to take the easy shot because a corpse was always less hassle to deliver than a captive. But this was a special case. This was personal. He had developed a special hatred for Jim Culver and he was reluctant to let him off with a quick death. The prospect of administering a slow death was almost too tempting to pass up. On the other hand, if he brought Culver in alive, as had originally been specified, he might still recoup some of his lost wages. Still undecided, he brought his rifle down and rested it on the dead log he lay behind.

Unhurried in making up his mind, because it appeared the lovers weren't going anywhere anytime soon, Slocum took a few moments to look the area over again. He decided he couldn't have planned it better himself. He had Jim Culver isolated from the cabin and his horse, in a spot by the river that offered ample foliage for concealment. *A man could move up to within twenty yards of the two of them without them even knowing he was there.* He liked the prospects.

His mind working on a new plan now, Slocum got up from behind the log and worked his way cautiously around to a point where he could see the back of the cabin. There was no sign of anyone. *They're either inside or out by the barn*, he thought. His concern was not only for the half-breed boy, but for the gun-toting woman with the no-nonsense bearing. He did not doubt that she wouldn't think twice before using her .45. Satisfied that there was no worry for him from that quarter, he retraced his steps to the spot where his horses were tied.

He led the two horses in a wide circle around the small clearing where the two young people were embracing, weaving his way through the tangle of berry bushes and laurel until he reached the riverbank. Leaving the horses there, he worked his way through the trees to a point almost directly behind Jim and Lettie, and no more than fifteen yards from them. It was in his mind that he still might decide against taking Jim back to Fort Lincoln, but he had decided he would take him alive now and make his final decision later.

Her lips were soft and moist, and she pressed her slender body tight up against his as their lips met again, this time with deeper passion than the first kiss, a passion that had grown over the long summer months when they were apart.

Jim's head was swimming, intoxicated with the closeness of her. He had thought of what this moment might be like during long, lonely nights when he couldn't even be sure she would still be in Canyon Creek when he returned. Now in the whirlwind of the moment, it was more than he could ever have imagined.

They parted for a moment, and he held her by her shoulders as he gazed into her smiling face. Radiant, she beamed lovingly, her expression saying all that needed to be said. Then, in a moment, her expression turned quizzical, and just as instantly to one of distress. Puzzled, he started to question her when she uttered a warning. "Jim," was all she had time to say, her voice frightened.

"Well, now, I sure do hate to break up such a sweet time." Slocum smirked as he stepped into the clearing, his rifle leveled at Jim.

Jim whirled about to find himself facing a ghost. Stunned by the sudden appearance of Blackie, a man he had killed back on the Bighorn, he instinctively pushed Lettie behind him and prepared to defend himself. But Slocum did not attack. Instead he stood savoring this long-awaited moment, his heavily bearded face twisted into a wicked grin. "Mr. Jim Culver," Slocum growled, pronouncing each word slowly, as if tasting each one. "You and me got a little unfinished business."

Confused by something that didn't make sense to him, Jim was nevertheless unafraid. "I don't know how the hell you came back to life, Blackie, but you've got no quarrel with this girl." He glanced briefly back at Lettie. "Go on back to the house, Lettie."

"I expect you'd better just stay right where you are, Lettie," Slocum warned. This was the second time someone had taken him for his brother's ghost. The prospect amused him. "That's right, Culver. I'm Blackie, come back from the grave to take my revenge."

Studying the massive figure confronting him, Jim noticed the jagged scar down one side of his face. That was the first clue that he might not be talking to a ghost after all. Blackie had no such scar. The more he looked at him, the more he realized that he was looking at flesh and blood, and not a specter. His biggest regret at the moment was that his rifle was propped up against the side of the barn. "The hell you say," he finally said. "You ain't Blackie, but you're damn sure his twin, and just as ugly. I killed your brother because he came after me. It was his doing. I didn't go after him. He put these two bullet holes in my shirt. It was just his bad luck that I wasn't wearing it at the time. He didn't give me a choice. Now, whaddaya say we let the girl go on back to the house? She didn't have anything to do with it."

"You think you're talkin' to a damn fool?" Slocum demanded. "The little bitch stays here." He scalded her with a look that told her she had better do as she was told.

Lettie took a couple of fearful steps behind Jim. She recognized Slocum as the same menacing stranger who had come looking for Jim before. "You've got no call to bother us," she finally found the courage to say. "Jim shot that lieutenant in self-defense. Why don't you go away and leave us in peace?"

Amused by Lettie's attempt to plead for her man's life, Slocum smiled. "It ain't about that little deal with the army no more. No sir, your sweetheart here has caused me to go to a whole lot of trouble. To top it off, he ups and shoots my own brother." Looking back to focus on Jim then, his smile gone, he said, "That was a big mistake."

"I told you that was self-defense," Jim stated coolly.

"Yeah, that's what you said, just like that army officer you shot." Slocum's eyes narrowed. "You gun down a lot of people in self-defense, don't you? A real stud panther. Well, mister, you've finally met up with the man that tames all the panthers in the territory." He motioned toward the trees with his rifle. "Now, I've had all the conversation I want. It's time for you to make a choice. You can chance a play for this rifle and get shot right here. Or you can go peacefully and hope I git careless somewhere on the trail back to Fort Lincoln."

While he gave Jim his options, Lettie slowly began to move toward the washpot and the wooden paddle propped against the side. Anticipating some form of attack from the spunky woman, Slocum watched her out of the corner of his eye. And when she suddenly made her move, he was ready for her. Grasping the paddle, she lunged toward Slocum. He waited calmly, the rifle trained on Jim, until she raised the paddle and swung it at his head. In one quick move he blocked the paddle with his rifle, and slugged Lettie square on the nose with his fist. The impact of his huge paw crushed Lettie's nose and sent her reeling backward to land on her back. The assault on Lettie threw Jim into an uncontrolled rage. With no thought for his own safety, he charged the sneering brute.

Fully expecting a wild reaction from Jim, Slocum stepped quickly out of the way of his charge and administered a sharp rap on the back of Jim's skull with the barrel of his rifle. Jim struggled to get to his feet, but was laid out cold by another blow from the rifle barrel. Satisfied with himself, Slocum calmly looked from the motionless body at his feet to the sobbing woman a couple of steps away. "I can't abide a sassy woman," he said as he went to fetch a rope.

Her will to fight having been knocked out of her, Lettie cringed on the hard-packed soil of the clearing, sobbing quietly while Slocum lifted Jim up on Toby's back and tied him hand and foot. Leaving Jim slumped over on the horse's neck, Slocum turned his attention to Lettie. Seeing the brute approach, she tried to back away from him. Her face was already swelling as a result of the broken nose. The pain was becoming intense as the shock of the blow began to wear off, and she could feel each beat of her heart pounding in her eyes. Terrified by his appearance, and fearful of his intentions, she tried to defend herself against whatever horrors he planned for her. Shrugging off her efforts as if they were the playful flailings of a child, he grabbed a handful of her dress with one hand and held her while he punched her again with the other. Lettie immediately went limp. Slocum dropped her to the ground, stood over her for a moment to make sure she wasn't moving, then turned back toward his horse.

Feeling as if his skull were cracked, Jim gradually began to regain his senses to the point where he realized that he was on a horse. He didn't remember how he got there. The only thing he knew for sure was that his head was spinning and he felt like he was going to vomit. Struggling to right himself in the saddle, he then realized he was tied to the horse. It didn't register until later that the horse was Toby and the saddle was his. In the next few moments the events of the prior minutes came rushing back to him, and his first thought was, *Lettie!* Dreading what he might see, he looked back, searching for her, but he could no longer see beyond the opening of the clearing. Fearing the worst, he turned to look at the massive figure on the horse leading his. Looking to either side of him, he recognized the narrow path between the cabin and the river. *I couldn't have been unconscious for long,* he thought, *just long enough to get tied to this horse.* At the same time, it occurred to him that Slocum was heading for Katie's cabin. He had to warn them.

"Luke!" he yelled. "Katie! Watch out!"

Unconcerned by Jim's efforts to warn his friends, Slocum didn't even glance back at his prisoner. For he could see the cabin now, and his rifle was cocked and ready. Jim's warning would save him the trouble of calling them out of the building.

Dropping the rope he had been weaving, Luke sprang to his feet just as Katie came out the door. They both sighted the two horses at the same time. "Quick!" Katie cried when she realized what was happening. "The rifle!" As soon as she said it, she pulled the pistol from her holster. Looking in the direction Katie had pointed, Luke spied the rifle Jim had left leaning against the wall of the barn. Without hesitating, he sprinted to retrieve it.

In unhurried motions, Slocum raised his rifle, took careful aim, and cut the young half-breed down before he got halfway to the barn. Before Luke stopped tumbling, Slocum put another slug in his already-dead body just to make sure.

"Luke!" Katie screamed in horror as Luke finally lay still in the dust. Behind Slocum, Jim roared in frustrated anguish and strained against his bonds. But Slocum was very efficient in tying his knots, and Jim was helpless to come to the aid of his friends. Katie, stunned by the sight of the youngster she had practically raised lying dead in the dusty soil, was unable to move for a few moments. When she recovered her senses enough to use her pistol, it was too late. Slocum pulled Jim's horse up beside him in order to use Jim to shield himself from Katie's fire. Then, while Jim watched helplessly, Slocum laid a barrage of rifle fire upon the doorway of the cabin, forcing Katie to retreat inside amid a hailstorm of splintered wood. Keeping Jim between him and the cabin, he headed for the wagon trace that led toward the north end of the valley at a gallop, leading his captive behind him.

Heartsick and feeling as helpless as a newborn calf, Jim grieved over the death of the young boy. He was afraid to let himself dwell upon what Lettie's fate might have been. Doubting that he would ever see her again in this life, he deeply regretted the fact that he had not told her he loved her. For he knew now that he did, and always would. After witnessing the cold, emotionless execution of Luke, Jim couldn't hold out much hope that Slocum planned to take him all the way to Fort Lincoln. He was as good as dead. He could only hope for the sullen beast to make a mistake, and the prospect of that happening didn't seem promising. He could hardly appreciate the irony of his situation. After all that had happened to him since the last time he left Canyon Creek, he ended up riding Toby and getting his head cracked with his own Winchester rifle. There were many confusing thoughts running around in his head. One among these was the question of how Slocum wound up with his horse and rifle. He had to have gotten them from Johnny Malotte, and judging by what had just happened, Jim had to figure Slocum hadn't come by them peacefully. *Well, it ain't over till this son of a bitch puts a bullet in my brain.*

After pushing the horses hard for a few miles, Slocum eased back on the pace. Accustomed to calling the shots in every situation he was involved in, he felt comfortable with the present one. He at last had his man, and the only threat of pursuit had been wiped out, leaving him to entertain himself with Jim Culver at his leisure. He had planned to kill the boy all along, knowing he was a threat to follow him. The two women didn't worry him. They weren't going to try to trail him. He turned in the saddle to take a look at Jim, who stared back defiantly. *Yessir,* he thought, *I've been waiting a long time for this.* Chuckling to himself, he picked up the pace a bit, anxious to leave the valley behind.

Chapter 14

Clay Culver pressed on through the night, stopping only when it was necessary to rest his horse. Sleeping for short periods while his horse rested, he had pushed across the open prairie, through South Pass and the mountains beyond. Morning would find him near the pass that led to the small valley called Canyon Creek.

During the past several days he had sighted three Sioux hunting parties ranging far beyond the boundaries of the Red Cloud and Spotted Tail agencies. And there had been a great deal more sign that told of many Sioux parties moving about the territory. It was unusual for this time of year, when most bands were settling into their winter camps. Had he not been so intent upon the welfare of his younger brother, and in such haste to reach him, Clay might have paused to ponder the significance of so much winter movement between the reservation and the camps of Sitting Bull and Crazy Horse. As it was, the sign served only to warn him to be cautious in the presence of so much Indian activity during the day. As a result, he had made better time at night, setting a steady, ground-eating pace that his surefooted Indian pony could maintain indefinitely.

Approaching the valley from the south pass just before sunup, he passed the burned-out remains of the Cochran place. As he rode silently by, the chilled night sky gradually began to fade away from the blackened corner posts of the cabin, leaving four eerie monuments to mourn what had happened there. Clay did not pause to reflect on the savage massacre of John and Ruth Cochran at the hands of a band of outlaws posing as Indians. He did not know the couple, but knew that they had been good people—this according to his old friend Monk Grissom. It seemed that Canyon Creek had suffered more than its share of tragedy. The thought served to increase his impatience to reach Katie Mashburn's cabin. With the Cochran place now behind him, he should reach the cabin well before noon.

Just as he figured, the sun was still climbing toward noon when he spotted the cabin that he and Jim had built for Katie. He pulled back on the reins sharply when he rounded the corner of the cornfield. Something was going on at Katie's. There were several wagons and saddle horses tied up before the cabin. As a natural habit, Clay paused to look the situation over before riding in. There was no sign of anyone outside the cabin. If it was a social gathering, there would be children running around outside playing. Looking toward the tiny corral, he spied the buckskin pony Jim had been riding when he last saw him. That was somewhat reassuring. Nudging the paint pony with his heels, he proceeded toward the cabin at a slow walk. As soon as he passed the new garden plot, he saw people gathered down near the river. He guided his horse in that direction.

He spotted Katie at almost the same time she turned to discover him. "Clay," she uttered under her breath. The sight of the tall, broad-shouldered scout very nearly brought a tear to the eye of the normally composed young woman, for she had prayed nightly for his return.

His gaze lingered for a moment, engaging hers, before he took notice of the others and realized what the gathering was. There was a fresh grave next to that of Katie's father. Clay was immediately alarmed. The others, aware of his presence now, turned to greet him. He stepped down from the saddle, accepting the quiet handshakes and greetings, all the while trying to question Katie with his eyes. Seeing the distress in his gaze, she made her way to him as quickly as she could. "It's Luke," she whispered.

He could not hide the relief he felt upon hearing the name, for he had feared it might be Jim. Relief immediately replaced by concern once more, he responded, "Luke? How?" He could see the pain in Katie's eyes as she pulled him aside to relate the tragedy of the past two days.

The news was not good. It was what he had feared he might hear. The cold-blooded bounty hunter had taken Jim, leaving an injured woman behind him and a young life snuffed out. Luke was a fine boy and one person whom Katie had depended upon. It was difficult to believe the brave young Shoshoni lad was no longer there for Katie to lean on. At least she still had Lettie, or so he thought until he took a closer look at the young girl.

The physical injuries were obvious. Lettie's face was still swollen with dark purple and yellow bruises. The poor girl's nose had been broken, but Katie felt sure Lettie would look like herself in a few more days. Undetectable were the internal injuries suffered at the massive hand of the savage bounty hunter. Clay had been somewhat surprised that Lettie had not come to greet him, since he and Jim had worked along with her and Katie to build the cabin. Instead she had remained seated on a stool beside the grave of Katie's father, smiling vacantly at him. He was stunned to learn that the young girl had never been the same since receiving the brutal blow from Slocum's fist. Katie very nearly lost her composure when she told Clay of the attack. He walked over to Lettie and bent down close to her. Lettie's smile faded and she looked at him with a vacant stare.

"Lettie," Clay said softly, "it's me, Clay." She continued to stare at him, giving no hint that she understood. "You know me, Lettie," he tried again. "Can't you talk to me?"

The girl gave no indication that she heard a word he said, nor any sign that she was even aware of his presence; her only response was to gaze into his face as if watching a sunset. Looking at Clay, Katie's eyes told him of her desperation as she stroked the frightened girl's hair. "Well," she said, "you see what she's become. She hasn't uttered a word since I found her lying on the ground by the washpot. I thought she was dead at first; she wasn't moving. Now it's like she isn't even here. I don't know what to do for her."

Clay shook his head in a gesture of helplessness. He had seen people knocked senseless before, but they usually either came out of it in a short time, or they died, depending on how hard they were hit. According to Katie, Lettie had been like this for two days. Judging by the marks on her face, it appeared that she had received more than the blow that broke her nose. It was his guess that the blow that left the bruises near her temple was the one that did the serious damage.

As he stood there, gazing at the injured girl, a quiet rage was boiling within him. So engrossed was he in thoughts of his brother, no doubt suffering at the hands of this same ruthless animal, that he was unaware of the people pressing close around him until Nate Wysong spoke.

"Clay, if you'll lead us, some of us men are ready to go after Jim."

"That's right, Clay," Reverend Lindstrom said. "We oughta be able to round up half a dozen for a posse."

Lost moments before in his unspoken fury, Clay brought his mind back to deal with the group of men assembled to bury Luke Kendall. Looking now from one face to the other, storekeeper and farmers, Clay's calm demeanor did not change as he considered their proposal. It seemed to him that the time for the men of Canyon Creek to form a posse would have been two days ago. "I reckon not," he finally stated.

The reverend's eyebrows rose in disbelief. "What?" he exclaimed. "You're not going after him?"

"I didn't say that. I'm going after him. I just ain't gonna lead a posse after him."

"You're plannin' to go alone?" Lindstrom still found it hard to believe. "You might not appreciate the evil beast you're going after," he insisted. "You're gonna need all the help you can get."

"That's where we differ, Reverend. I think I've got a pretty fair idea of the grizzly I'm trackin'. I appreciate you folks wantin' to help Jim, but I'd rather you stayed here and looked after your farms. If you want to make up a posse, I sure can't stop you. But I ain't gonna lead it, and I'd appreciate it if you'd stay the hell outta my way."

Lindstrom and Nate Wysong exchanged looks of surprise. Clay didn't wait for further discussion, turning on his heel and briskly walking toward his horse. Taking Katie by the arm, he pulled her along with him. When he got to his horse, he turned to face her, his voice low so the others could not hear. "I'm gonna need some food, if you can spare some bacon or something. I'll be leavin' after dark. I've got to rest my horse first. He's been rode pretty hard for the last few days." Katie nodded her understanding. She knew Clay could move faster and considerably more quietly without half a dozen of her neighbors tagging along.

"I've got to see my neighbors off," she said. "Unsaddle your horse and go on in the house. You can get some rest yourself before you start out after Jim."

He paused a moment while he studied her face. "Will you be all right?" She would be alone now, a thought that had not really struck him until that moment. She couldn't even count on Lettie as a helping hand.

"Hell, yes," she immediately replied. "Don't waste any time worrying about me. Just find Jim before that maniac kills him."

He nodded, holding her gaze a moment longer before she abruptly turned and went to see the funeral party off. Clay watched her as she walked away. Then he glanced again at Lettie, still seated by the grave, oblivious to the people milling around her. He knew then that something would have to be done to help Katie. She couldn't run this place by herself. But that would have to wait for another time. The job ahead had to occupy all his concentration now. Turning his attention to his horse, he threw the stirrup up and loosened the girth strap, his mind already working on the possible trails Slocum might have taken.

Katie stood in front of her cabin, thanking the neighbors as they climbed into their wagons and mounted their horses. She appreciated the support they had shown in mourning the death of the half-breed son of John Kendall. Like Katie herself, Luke had been somewhat of an enigma to the folks in the isolated little valley. In actuality, they knew very little about the boy, except the fact that he was more Shoshoni than white, and he was fiercely devoted to Katie. To some, their attendance at the funeral might have more likely been a memorial for Jim Culver, for there was general speculation among the settlers that Jim was as good as dead. It was with that thought in mind that Reverend Lindstrom lingered after the last wagon turned to leave. Fairly confident of what was on the preacher's mind, Katie turned to him and waited for him to speak.

Lindstrom favored her with a tired but benevolent smile, looking from Katie's iron-hard face to the empty face of her young friend, still gazing at some sunset that no one else could see. He shook his head sadly, as if summing up the hardships that had befallen them. "Have you thought about what you're gonna do?" Lindstrom asked. "You can't stay on here by yourself."

"Why not?" Katie replied in quiet defiance.

"Why . . . Why," Lindstrom said, flustered, "because you just can't. It's too much for a woman to handle without no help."

"I've got help," Katie said, and turned to smile at the childlike girl at her side.

Showing his impatience by sadly shaking his head again, he paused for a long moment before saying, "Lettie's mind is gone, Katie. It's hard to accept, and it sure don't seem fair, but the Lord does things for a reason. First your husband was taken, then your father, now Luke. It's plain to see that you need a husband to help you farm this place." He placed his hand on her shoulder and looked her straight in the eye. "This might be the Lord's way of telling you to find yourself a helpmate. Whitey Branch is a bachelor." He noticed the immediate raising of her eyebrows at the mention of the name. "I know Whitey ain't the smartest man in the valley, but he's a hard worker, and his heart's in the right place, and he's a God-fearin' man."

"Ha!" Katie exclaimed, unable to hold her reaction any longer. "Whitey Branch, huh? Why, Reverend, when did you get into the matchmaker business?'' She almost laughed in his face. ''You're right about one thing: Whitey sure ain't the brightest man in the valley. I've got chickens smarter than Whitey.''

Sufficiently chastised by her reaction to his suggestion, Lindstrom shifted nervously from one foot to the other. Like most of the men in Canyon Creek, he was hard-pressed to figure Katie Mashburn out. Deciding it useless to press his counsel, he offered weakly, ''Well, it was just something for you to think about.''

''I appreciate your concern,'' Katie said, ''but don't worry about me. I'll manage.'' She was perceptive enough to guess the reverend's real concern. His dream of Canyon Creek growing into a sizable settlement was always at the forefront of his thoughts. She figured he was worried that he might lose another of his flock if she decided to pull out and further decrease the population. The fact that he had suggested Whitey Branch as a possible suitor was evidence of his desperation to hold the community together. *Poor Whitey*, she thought as she stood back to watch Lindstrom climb aboard his wagon, *he hasn't got any more sense than Lettie does right now*. It would be a cold day in hell when Katie Mashburn took a husband for no other purpose than to provide a strong back.

The last of the funeral party gone, Katie walked back to the grave, took Lettie gently by the arm, and led her back to the cabin. She glanced toward the corral, where Clay's horse was eating hay beside Jim's buckskin pony. She almost thought she saw Luke sitting on the top rail near the corner post—her mind playing tricks on her, she guessed. He often sat there watching his horses. The thought hit her with thunderous impact and she realized how much she would miss the boy. A tear traced its way slowly down her cheek, and she quickly wiped it away, forcing herself to regain her self-control. Lettie gazed at her, the faint smile returning to her face. Katie smiled at the troubled girl. "Come on, honey; let's go inside."

At first she thought he was gone. Then, when she pushed the door shut, she saw Clay stretched out in a corner of the room, asleep on the floor, his bedroll between him and the dirt floor. She led Lettie to a stool by the fireplace and sat her down. Then she pulled a blanket off of her bed and gently laid it on the sleeping man. Kneeling beside him, she watched him sleep for a few moments. It pleased her to see him sleep so soundly. He was no doubt exhausted from riding day and night for a week. But she knew that if he were camped somewhere in the mountains or on the prairie, he would have been alert at the first little creak of the door opening. It told her that he felt secure in her home. It pleased her. *I'll fix something for you to eat when you wake up*, she thought as she got to her feet again.

Chapter 15

Jim Culver awoke before the first light of day sought out the dark valley floor. Sore and cramped, and stiff from the early-morning chill, he tried to ease his aching arms and legs. It was to no avail, for his bonds were too tight to permit much movement. Turning his head as far as he could manage, he strained to see the still-sleeping form of his captor. Close by the remaining coals of his campfire, snug under a heavy buffalo robe, Slocum presented the image of a huge mound, not unlike a sleeping buffalo bull. Having been afforded two days' worth of Slocum's hospitality, Jim knew that the core of that mound was pure, ruthless evil.

Even though his rational mind told him it was useless to struggle against the rawhide rope holding him fast to the trunk of the pine, still he strained to break his bonds. Ignoring the blood that seeped around the tough rawhide that held his wrists, he pulled with all the strength he could muster. It was not enough, for Slocum knew his business well. Finally, unable to summon another ounce of effort, Jim lay back, exhausted. In spite of the frost that glazed the toes of his Crow moccasins, he could feel the sweat from his exertion trickling down his brow. Shaking his head in an attempt to keep the sweat from his eyes, he winced as the motion caused the dried blood caked on the back of his head to crack. He could tell by the stinging sensation in his scalp that there was an open wound on the back of his head. But he seemed to be thinking clearly, so maybe the big son of a bitch hadn't cracked his skull after all. Cracked or not, however, it had taken a while for his head to stop spinning.

A grunt from the buffalo mound signaled that the brute was awake. As Jim watched, the mound began to move until, finally, the robe was thrown off and Slocum's massive head and shoulders emerged amid a series of snorting and coughing that rivaled a rutting elk. At once he turned to make sure his prisoner was secure. Seeing Jim leaning against the tree trunk brought a smile to his face, barely discernible under the heavy brush of beard.

Taking a stick of deadwood from the little pile he had gathered the night before, he poked around in the ashes of his fire to stir up the live coals. After he had resurrected a serious flame, he added firewood and watched it until he was sure it had a hold on new life. Content that his breakfast fire was established, he walked over to stand by his prisoner and nonchalantly emptied his bladder. "Ain't you even gonna say good mornin'?" he chided as he finished relieving himself. "What would you like for breakfast? How 'bout the same thing I fixed for you yesterday?" He chuckled at his own joke, since he had not seen fit to offer Jim any food. It was a long ride to Fort Lincoln, if in fact he decided to take his prisoner all the way back, and Slocum had no intention of keeping Jim's strength up. He would give him what he deemed enough to keep him alive, no more. Judging from his prisoner's size, and the width of his shoulders, he looked to be a match for most men. Slocum didn't include himself in that group. He had never met the man who was a match for him when it came to fighting. Still, it made no sense to nourish him.

When there was no response from Jim to his cajoling, Slocum returned to his fire to prepare his breakfast. He put a small coffeepot on the fire to boil while he fried some bacon, all the while glancing in Jim's direction to see if his prisoner was picking up the aroma of the cooking meat. "Damned if I ain't gonna have to fix me up some of them dried beans I got in my saddle pack tonight. It's a helluva long ride to Bismarck on an empty stomach." There was still no response from his prisoner, but Slocum was confident that Jim's belly had started growling a long time ago. He promised himself that Jim would be talking before it was over, begging for his own death. When the meat was done, Slocum poured himself a cup of coffee and came over to eat by Jim. Brushing a light film of snow from a rock, he sat down and made himself comfortable.

Looking Jim over while he ate, Slocum continued to taunt. "Looks like that place on the back of your head is bleedin' again. I sure hope I didn't crack your skull with the barrel of my rifle. That's a damn fine rifle, and I wouldn't wanna bend the barrel by bouncin' it off a hard head like yours." He knew Jim had already recognized the Winchester .73 as the rifle Johnny Malotte had stolen from him. "I had to slit the throat of the son of a bitch that took that rifle off of you. He thought he was gonna slit mine." He watched Jim closely, trying to determine whether he understood the message. Then he took a long gulp of his coffee. "Damn, that's good coffee. Don't nobody west of the Missouri make better coffee than me." Getting back on the subject, he said, "I mighta cracked the skull of that little bitch you was about to mount back there." He laughed when he recalled the incident. "She musta really thought you was somethin'—coming at me with that damn paddle like she did. I put my fist right through her face. I could feel the bones breakin'. You reckon you could hit somebody that hard?"

Determined to meet his captor's taunting with

silent defiance, Jim found he could not hold his tongue any longer. "Why don't you cut me loose, and we'll find out," he said.

This brought a grin to Slocum's face. "Now, that's a damn good idea. I'll tell you what: We'll wait till we git past the Belle Fourche, and then I'll cut you loose, and me and you'll have a go at it." He laughed when he thought of the shape Jim would be in after that many days without food. "Now, if you'll excuse me, it's time to break camp."

He walked back to the fire and picked up the coffeepot. Holding it up so that Jim could see, he then poured the remains of the coffee in the fire, grinning at his prisoner. Jim did not miss the smug grin of satisfaction parting the thick whiskers on Slocum's face. Slocum decided at that point that he would take Jim all the way back to Fort Lincoln. He was enjoying Jim's misery too much to kill him right away. He would give him enough water to make sure he was barely alive when he reached Bismarck. That, after all, was the only condition in his original agreement with Captain Boyd. He was not forgetting the fact that Boyd had told him the army was no longer interested in Culver. That didn't matter to Slocum anymore. He just wanted the satisfaction of dragging Jim's nearly dead body across the parade ground and dumping it on the captain's porch. Slocum *always* got his man; it was important to his sense of ego that Boyd understood this. If the army still insisted they wouldn't pay him, he'd simply slit Culver's throat right there.

Clay Culver stepped down from the saddle and led his horse to the ashes of a campfire. Only glancing at the remains of the fire at first, he looked around him to make sure he was alone. The early-morning sky was still gray, although it was getting lighter by the minute. Thinking of his horse first, he led the paint down to the stream to drink. Then he returned to take a closer look at the ashes. This was Slocum's first camp. The trail had been easy enough to follow. The big bounty hunter had made no efforts to hide his tracks. Probably satisfied that there was no one to follow him, Clay figured. Pulling a frost-covered stick from the ashes, he stirred them up, then felt them with his hand. *Stone cold*, he thought. This camp was probably two days old. Due to the frost and the light covering of snow on the ground, it was hard to tell for sure, but he was confident that he had made up some of the time between them.

The light snow that had fallen during the night had not been enough to completely cover the tracks, so Clay took a few minutes to study the campsite. Judging by the sign, he guessed that his brother had been tied to a tree. At least it was an indication that Jim was still alive. The tracks leading out of the camp were in a north-eastern direction, pointing toward a gap in the mountains some twenty-five or thirty miles away. According to Katie, the first time Slocum had shown up in Canyon Creek, he claimed he had come to take Jim back to Fort Lincoln. Assuming that was still the man's intention, Clay had to believe that Slocum intended to skirt the Wind River range and the Bighorns, and strike the Belle Fourche. It was a helluva dangerous way to go at this particular time, even if it was winter. He would be traveling in Indian country all the way.

Having ridden the paint hard during the night, Clay decided to rest there before taking up the chase again. *I could use some rest myself*, he thought. So he unsaddled his pony and hobbled him near the branches of a fir tree where the snow had not been thick enough to hide the grass. Then, using his saddle as a pillow, he crawled up under the lower branches and set his mind for two hours. In a few seconds he was sound asleep, knowing that if there were any danger, his pony would warn him.

In approximately two hours, Clay opened his eyes and immediately crawled out from under the branches. While watering his horse, he breakfasted on a cold biscuit that Katie had stuffed in his saddle pack. Wasting no time building a fire to cook the bacon she had provided, he saddled the paint and took to the trail again. Keeping his senses sharp, he kept his mind on the tracks he followed and avoided thinking about what might be happening to Jim.

Worrying wasn't going to help Jim any, but it could damn sure cause a man to get careless. *You just stay alive, little brother. I'll find you.*

Employing common sense as much as his skills as a tracker, Clay continued to gain ground on Slocum. For much of the way there were clear choices on the best way to cross a ridge or circle a mountain. So Clay didn't waste time doggedly following the tracks. As a precaution, however, he checked them periodically to make sure he was on the right trail. By use of this method, he was able to arrive at Slocum's next campsite before dark. The ruthless bounty hunter didn't appear to be in any particular hurry.

Testing the ashes, he found there was enough warmth in the ground beneath them for him to guess he was no more than possibly eight or ten hours behind. As he had done before, he scouted the campsite in order to get a clue as to Jim's condition. The sign indicated a similar scene to the night before, with Jim tied to a tree all night. Confident that Jim was still alive, Clay was in the saddle again, wasting very little time. There was a sense of urgency now, stronger than before, with the thought of overtaking Slocum in one more day's hard ride.

On the eastern side of the slopes that Clay was approaching, Slocum rode at a leisurely pace, his prisoner following along behind. The huge man glanced back frequently, pleased to notice that Jim, despite a defiant effort to fight it, was beginning to weaken. This would be his third day without food, and only the water he could get from eating snow. And judging by the back of his shirt, he had lost a lot of blood. Another day or so, and he would be too weak to cause any trouble, even if Slocum happened to get careless.

His arms aching from having his hands tied behind him for so long, Jim tried to keep his mind off of his discomfort. With thoughts of revenge the only nourishment available to him, he vowed to remain strong and feed off of those thoughts. Somewhere between these rocky ridges and Fort Lincoln, Slocum had to make a mistake. And when he did, Jim was determined to be ready to take advantage of it.

Trying to keep his mind occupied with thoughts other than the emptiness of his belly, Jim looked around him as they made their way along the rugged foothills of the Wind River Mountains. It was not far from here that Johnny Malotte had left him for dead, half floating in a tiny stream. If it had not been for the prompt arrival of Iron Bow, he would be dead now—and never have had the pleasure of meeting the surly beast on the horse leading his. The irony of it brought a faint smile to his face.

Just happening to glance back at his prisoner at that point, Slocum was puzzled to see what appeared to be a grin on Jim's face. It irritated him. "Time to rest these horses," he abruptly grunted, and stepped down from the saddle. Walking back to stand beside Jim, he demanded, "What the hell are you grinning about?" Then, grabbing him by the arm, he yanked Jim out of the saddle and sent him sprawling to the ground.

Landing on his shoulder, Jim could not help but grunt in pain when he fell to the ground. He tried to scramble to his feet, but with his arms tied behind his back he was barely able to get to his knees before Slocum knocked him to the ground again with the butt of his rifle.

Jim lay there a moment before struggling to gain a sitting position, a fresh trickle of blood running down his cheek. "You're a regular grizzly bear, ain't you?" Jim growled. "How are you against a man that ain't got his hands tied behind him?"

Delighted by the show of defiance from a man whose strength was close to running out, Slocum grinned as he looked down at Jim. "Now, that there's mighty brave talk from a man that shot my brother in the back. Here, let me help you up." He grabbed Jim's shirt and dragged him to his feet. "There, now we're standin' eye-to-eye."

"I didn't shoot that piece of shit in the back," Jim said evenly while trying to stand squarely on wobbly legs. "He jumped me and got what he deserved."

A spark of anger flashed in Slocum's eyes. "You lying bastard. The only way you coulda kilt Blackie was to get him in the back. You might as well own up to it."

Seeing how it incensed the surly giant, Jim couldn't resist taunting him. "Right in the chest—he was looking right at me. I pumped three slugs into the son of a bitch." The words were barely out when Slocum struck him. Jim tried to sidestep the punch, but it caught him beside his ear. Slocum grabbed his shirt to keep him from going down and then landed another punch flush in the face. Jim's legs collapsed under him and he crumpled to the ground.

"There, you had your chance to stand toe-to-toe. Next time I might even untie your hands, you lying bastard."

On a ridge overlooking the stream where Slocum had stopped to rest the horses, eight painted Indian ponies stood patiently while their masters watched the two white men below. Puzzled by the attack of one of the white men upon the other, the Crow warriors watched silently, their feathers fluttering in the steady breeze that swept the top of the ridge. Wolf Paw, son of Iron Bow, nudged his horse and moved farther down the ridge for a closer look. Something about the man whose hands were tied intensified his curiosity.

Seeing his friend's interest, Leads His Horse moved down beside Wolf Paw. "Do you think that is the man we have been following?" he asked. The war party had been trailing a solitary

set of tracks for over a week. They were searching for the man who killed Red Wing, their
medicine man. When Newt didn't return to
camp overnight, a search party had ridden out
to look for him the next morning. Near the
south end of the valley the stiffened body of the
old man was found where it had fallen in a
berry patch. His pony had been found grazing
near the bank of the river. Tracks of a shod
horse led away from the valley. The old man
was revered in the Crow camp, and while the
people grieved his death, Wolf Paw and seven
others mounted up immediately and rode out
to find the person who had killed him.

Wounded Leg had suggested that the war
party should withdraw to the top of the ridge
to watch the white men to make sure they were
not advance scouts for a larger party. When the
riders were close enough so that the Crows
could see one of the men was the prisoner of
the other, the warriors continued to watch in
simple curiosity.

Wolf Paw did not answer his friend at once,
but continued to stare at the white men. After a
few moments he turned to Leads His Horse.
"Look closely at the man who was struck
down," he said. "It is Dead Man."

Leads His Horse was taken aback. As Wolf
Paw suggested, he strained to get a better look
at the man lying on the ground. "You're right!"
he exclaimed. "It *is* Dead Man."

"He's not riding the pony Iron Bow gave him, or I would have recognized him sooner." Wolf Paw immediately turned and signaled for the others to join them. As soon as they were around him, he told them what he had discovered. "Dead Man is a captive of the big white man down there. I think the big one may be the man we have been following. Maybe Dead Man tried to kill him, but was unable to overpower him. We must rescue Dead Man," he added, his voice sharp with a sudden sense of urgency. There was immediate response to his urgent tone, for they all held Jim in the highest regard. A quick conference was held to decide the best plan of attack. Haste seemed to be imperative, since they weren't sure whether the big white man was going to kill Jim right away or not. At Wolf Paw's suggestion, it was decided to spread out and charge down the slope of the ridge, hoping to overpower Slocum before he had a chance to use his rifle.

Gradually Jim's head began to clear, and he struggled to turn over onto his side. The force of Slocum's blow had rattled his brain for a few moments, but he was now thinking clearly again. The pain in his shoulder told him that he had landed hard, and the rawhide binding his wrists was cutting into the skin. He turned his head, trying to find Slocum, and spotted him over by the stream, filling a canteen, his back to him. Maybe this was his chance! The brute evidently thought Jim would be unconscious for a few minutes.

It wasn't much of a chance, but he figured he might not get another one. So he struggled up onto his knees as quietly as he could, watching the back of the surly giant carefully. *So far, so good*, he thought, and got his feet under him to push up. Unsteady from lack of food and water, he almost went down again. He looked at his horse, some ten yards away. Toby looked back at him as if wondering what his master had in mind. Jim's gaze concentrated now on the stirrup, hanging impassively against Toby's belly. How could he step up in the stirrup without the use of his hands? His common sense told him he couldn't. But his defiant determination told him that he was going to try. One more quick glance back at Slocum, and he made the commitment. Doing his best to run on wobbly legs drained of energy, he headed straight for Toby. He saw right away that it was a foolish quest. He could not jump up in the saddle. His attempt was woefully short, and he slammed into the horse's side at the same time an explosion of rifle fire erupted behind him.

Thinking it somehow came from Slocum, he hit the ground and rolled under Toby's belly. As he did, he glimpsed Slocum sprinting for his horse, cocking his rifle as he ran. They were under attack, but Jim wasn't sure from whence it came. Rifle slugs were whining everywhere overhead, but he realized that none were close to him. Maybe they hadn't seen him roll under Toby's belly. At this point, he was in more danger of getting stomped under the horse's hooves as the nervous animal reacted to the gunshots. Looking up he saw Slocum, now in the saddle and returning fire, his grizzled face a mask of anger as he tried to get a steady shot off. Rolling over on his side, Jim looked in the direction Slocum was shooting and saw the Indians, half a dozen or more, storming down from the ridge.

There wasn't much he could do to protect himself, with his hands tied behind him. He resigned himself to accept his fate. *Hell*, he thought, *it's no worse getting killed by Indians than it is by this son of a bitch*. With that thought, he looked up again at Slocum, the huge man's horse pawing and sidestepping, straining against the reins as the bullets from the Indian war party kicked up dirt around its hooves. Forced to hold the horse from running with one hand on the reins, Slocum was trying to fire his rifle with the other. As Jim watched, Slocum angrily realized that he was overpowered and would have to make a run for it.

Amid the confusion of the attack, Jim would remember the mask of pure fury that was Slocum's face at that moment. Unwilling to abandon his prisoner, but with no time to get Jim on his horse, Slocum determined to kill Jim before he fled. Jim realized this only when Slocum suddenly turned his rifle to point directly at him and pulled the trigger. Jim's brain went numb for a second before he realized that the hammer had fallen on an empty chamber. In the time it took for Slocum to slide the rifle in the sling and pull his pistol, Jim rolled back under Toby. Still fighting his frightened horse, Slocum tried to wheel the animal around to get a clear shot at Jim. Each time he did, Jim rolled back to the other side, using Toby as a shield.

When the war party was within one hundred yards, Slocum found it too dangerous to linger. The bullets were ripping up dirt too close for his comfort. He was forced to abandon thoughts of executing Jim. "Damn you! It ain't over yet," he spat with one final glare of hatred before he turned the impatient horse and bolted toward the other end of the narrow valley at a gallop. Having dodged death from one quarter, Jim prepared to deal with the new threat.

The Indian warriors veered from their charge down the slope to pursue the man galloping away. *I guess they figure I ain't going anywhere,* Jim thought as he unconsciously strained at his bonds while he tried to think of some means of escape. The only chance he had was to somehow climb in the saddle and make a run for it while the war party occupied itself with Slocum. But the effort it had taken to avoid execution at the hands of Slocum had used up most of the little strength he had left.

He managed to get to his feet, only to find that the first seemingly simple step, to untie

Toby's reins from a willow limb, was going to be a challenge. Slocum had pulled the knot tight. Jim went to work on it with his teeth, even then wondering what he would do if he succeeded in untying it and Toby decided to run. "Easy, boy," he murmured, trying to calm the big Morgan stallion while he worked feverishly at the stubborn knot. Little by little, he managed to loosen the reins until he suddenly realized that the shooting had stopped. Taking a quick look back, he discovered that the war party had given up the chase and was now riding back toward him. "Well, shit," he mumbled in frustration. Looking over into the eyes of his horse, he confided, "I doubt I could have gotten in the saddle, anyway." He took a step away from Toby and stood defiantly to meet the war party.

As the riders approached, Jim suddenly realized they looked familiar. A few yards closer and he recognized faces. "Wolf Paw," he said softly. *This ain't my day to ride to the spirit world after all*, he told himself.

Wolf Paw's look of concern turned to one of joy when he saw Jim's smiling face. "Dead Man," he called out, his greeting echoed by the seven warriors with him. Soon Jim was surrounded by smiling, chattering faces, as his Crow friends expressed their joy in seeing him. Then seeing the dried blood matting Jim's hair and the back of his shirt, Leads His Horse was quick to pull his knife and cut the rawhide binding Jim's wrists. Jim winced with the pain that the movement of his arms caused after having been immobile for so long. Seeing that his friend was weak from hunger, Wolf Paw persuaded him to sit while he got some dried antelope meat from his parfleche. Jim greedily chewed the tough jerky while telling his Crow friends how he happened to be in the situation in which they had found him.

"I think that was the man we have been looking for," Wolf Paw said. "We have bad news to tell you." Then he told Jim of Newt Plummer's death, and how the war party happened to be this close to Shoshoni territory. "I think that if we look at the tracks of the horse we just chased, they will be the same as those we followed from the Bighorn valley."

It was hard for Jim to believe Newt Plummer was dead. How could that be? Jim had expected to be able to make many trips to the Crow camp to visit Newt in the old man's waning years. Knowing the old medicine man as well as he did, Jim supposed Newt would probably have said it was better to die the way he had, instead of dying gradually of old age by the campfire. Even so, it didn't keep the world from being worse off without the old trapper. Then thoughts of the ruthless villain who had just succeeded in escaping Wolf Paw's war party crowded into his mind. How could one man cause so much grief in the world? It wasn't right to let a man like that live.

Talk among the warriors returned to taking

up the trail again to go after Slocum. If he continued on the course he had ridden out on, he was more than likely heading for Fort Laramie. Jim was quick to stress that it would be a mistake to permit Slocum to gain a head start, and he insisted that he was strong enough to ride with the war party.

A couple of the warriors began to talk about the wisdom of continuing after Slocum in view of the direction he was now heading. The small war party had already ventured far from their village. And even though they approached Shoshoni country, they were willing to continue for a few more days. But now that the chase seemed to lead on a more southeasterly course, there were other things to consider. There were reports of many Sioux camps in that territory. And while the Shoshoni were not especially friendly with the Crows, they were not at war with anyone at present. The Sioux, on the other hand, were on the verge of war with just about everybody, and were sending out many raiding parties. This had to be given serious consideration by a Crow party numbering only eight. Further discussion was interrupted when one of the Crow warriors warned, "A rider comes!"

All eyes turned at once, searching in the direction indicated by the outstretched arm of the warrior. Descending a steep slope near the end of the same ridge the Crow war party had ridden down, the lone rider sat easily in the saddle, his body leaning back slightly to balance himself as the Indian paint pony carefully picked its way down the incline. Curious, the Crow warriors silently watched the unexpected rider. Had their attention not been captured by the broad-shouldered scout, dressed in buckskins, they might have noticed the wide smile on Jim's face. Wolf Paw was about to warn his warriors to be on their guard when Jim spoke. "It's my brother Clay," he said, and got to his feet to welcome him.

"Ah, Ghost Wind," Wolf Paw replied, a definite tone of respect in his voice. "I have heard my father talk about him."

Following Slocum's trail, Clay had heard the shots while still several miles away. There had been a pause after the first and second shots, causing him to fear they signaled the possible execution of his brother. But when those shots were followed by an almost continuous volley, he knew it more likely to be an ambush. Afraid of what he might find, he pushed his pony mercilessly until arriving on the ridge above the tiny valley. He saw Jim, his hands tied behind his back, stagger out to face the eight warriors, galloping hard toward him. Knowing he could not reach his brother in time, he had drawn his rifle from the saddle sling and quickly dismounted. Kneeling behind a small boulder, he had rested the rifle on it and lined his sights up on the leader of the war party. Waiting to let the warrior get a little closer, he had kept the sight on the Indian's chest. At the moment he was ready to squeeze the trigger, he had been astonished to see the warrior raise his arm in a friendly greeting. Glancing again at his brother, he had been surprised to see Jim taking a few steps to meet the riders. He had removed his finger from the trigger and looked at the warriors riding behind the leader. They were also greeting Jim. Clay watched the reunion below him by the stream for a few minutes more before he had put the rifle away and stepped up onto the paint.

Reaching the floor of the valley, Clay continued to slow-walk his horse toward Jim and the Crow warriors, who had all turned to watch him approach. Though his demeanor seemed casual, he was nevertheless keeping a cautious eye on the warriors, his rifle cradled across his arms, just in case the scene wasn't as it appeared. He relaxed in earnest, however, when Jim called out to him.

"Well, it's about time you showed up. I thought that ugly son of a bitch was gonna drag me all the way to Fort Lincoln." His grin filled his face. "Lucky for me Wolf Paw and his friends showed up when they did."

"Looks to me like you'da been a heap luckier if they'd showed up a little sooner," Clay replied, seeing the bloody evidence of his brother's wounds. It was not in his nature to express it, but he had been worried about Jim and was genuinely relieved to see him. "Looks like there was a catfight on your head."

"*Feels* like there was a catfight on my head," Jim returned.

Wolf Paw and the others stood back while the brothers clasped hands and greeted each other. He, especially, was in awe of the Ghost Wind, for he had heard stories of the mighty warrior from his father, Iron Bow. Seeing Clay in person, he was even more impressed and pleased to find the legendary scout as imposing a figure as Iron Bow had said.

After Clay had greeted each of the Crow warriors, Jim told him what had happened there by the stream, and the direction in which Slocum had fled. Then he asked the questions that had bothered him the most.

"Clay, what about Lettie? And Katie?" he quickly added. "Are they all right? I saw Luke go down. There wasn't anything I could do about it."

Clay's casual mood changed instantly as he was reminded of the grim mission that had led him here. "Katie's all right. Lettie got hurt pretty bad. There ain't much I can tell you about her except she's still in a bad way, but Katie's taking care of her."

Jim made no reply, obviously having hoped to hear better news. Searching his brother's face for indications of better news to follow, he finally asked, "But she's gonna be all right, isn't she?"

Clay frowned uncomfortably. "I don't know, Jim. She was hurt pretty bad. I'm not even sure she knows what happened to her. She ain't exactly in her right mind right now." He studied his brother's face, now stunned and devoid of expression. "I'm sorry," he said. Then, to change the subject as well as remind Jim that time was being wasted, he said, "The thing I've got to do right now is catch the animal that did it to her."

Jim nodded soberly, his mind still thinking about Lettie, silently blaming himself for his carelessness in not taking his rifle with him when he had walked down to the river with her. "We'd best get started," he said.

Clay gazed at him for a long moment, studying the determination in his younger brother's face. He decided that determination was the only real strength Jim had at the moment. He was obviously weak from his wounds, or starvation, or both. He looked in no shape to ride, at least as hard as Clay planned to. Slocum already had a good hour's start on him, and Clay had to move fast. "I think it best if you stay with your friends here and get your strength back."

"The hell you say," Jim was quick to respond. "That bastard has been hunting me all over the territory—knocked me in the head and damn near starved me to death. I reckon I'll be the one to settle up with him."

A quiet fury had been ignited within Clay Culver's soul when he had arrived in Canyon Creek too late to prevent the wanton murder of Luke and the vicious attack upon Lettie. Now that Jim was safe, the fury still smoldered, but was controlled by the calm and rational thinking that was typical of the tall mountain man. He understood Jim's passion for vengeance, but his brother was obviously still too weak to ride with him. Clay fully appreciated the danger involved in a confrontation with the ruthless Slocum. A well and physically fit Jim Culver was a match for any man, but Clay was afraid Jim's wrath would push him beyond reasonable caution. And with a man like Slocum, that might prove fatal. There was no doubt in Clay's mind that Slocum was a killer without conscience, like the wolf and the coyote, and like those killers, born with a cunning that testified to his survival. In short, Clay preferred to go after Slocum alone. He didn't want to worry about Jim's safety. His decision final, he said, "All right, get on your horse."

"I need a weapon," Jim said.

"Just get on your horse first," Clay replied stoically.

Wolf Paw and Leads His Horse stepped back to give Jim room, watching the brothers with great interest. Jim released the willow branch he had been using for support and took a few wobbly steps toward Toby. He started to reel, but stopped until he regained his balance. Wolf Paw looked at Clay and shook his head. With great determination, Jim steadied himself and started toward his horse again. With stumbling steps he reached Toby's side and grabbed the saddle horn for support. While Clay and the Crow warriors watched his efforts in silent fascination, Jim managed to get a foot in the stirrup, but could not summon the strength to step up into the saddle. After a couple of feeble attempts, he looked at his brother and said, "I might need a little help here."

"I reckon you'd best stay here," Clay said, his voice gentle but with a tone of finality. Jim was about to protest, but Clay turned away and directed a question toward Wolf Paw. "Can you take him to your village and tend to that cut on the back of his head?"

"You go after this man alone?" Wolf Paw asked. Clay nodded, and Wolf Paw said, "We will take care of him."

Jim was sick inside with the realization that Clay was right. He would be of little use to his brother, and might even be a hindrance. He couldn't even get up on his horse without help. Resigned to the way things had to be, he pulled his foot from the stirrup and remained standing there holding on to the saddle horn. "Be careful, Clay. The man's dangerous as hell."

"I know," Clay replied with a faint smile. Then, with a nod to Wolf Paw, he was off.

Chapter 16

Wolf Paw may have been right, Clay thought as he studied the tracks leading up a shallow draw toward a low line of hills to the south. It did appear that Slocum was heading for Fort Laramie. He had held consistently to that direction for the last several miles, never wavering. Clay considered the draw for a moment. *Nice place for an ambush*, he thought, scanning the sides of the draw, searching for any hint that the ruthless killer might have decided to lie in wait for any pursuers. The fact that Slocum was making no effort to hide his tracks was enough to cause Clay to exercise caution. If a man wanted to lead you into an ambush, he would make sure you could follow him. *Well, this looks like a good place for one*, Clay thought. *I think I'll go around, just to be safe*.

Guiding his pony up the left side, he crossed over to ride beneath the slope that defined the draw. With his rifle ready and his eyes focused on the rocks that dotted the sides of the draw, he walked his horse slowly, watching for the slightest movement. Even though he took no chances, he didn't expect to find anything until he came to the other end of the draw, where it opened out to the prairie. He felt sure that, if Slocum were lying in ambush, he would most likely be hiding behind one of the rocks near that end. If his hunch was right, Clay expected to spot Slocum's horse tied in the brush.

When he had circled the entire length of the shallow draw, he dismounted. Leaving his horse standing near a dry bramble patch, he made his way on foot up to the edge of the draw. There was no horse that he could see, and no sign of Slocum. Thinking his hunch had been wrong, he walked down to the mouth of the draw to look for Slocum's tracks.

There were no tracks leading out of the draw, a fact that puzzled Clay. From where he stood, he could see the far end of the draw. There was no place within the narrow passage where a man could hide a horse. Slocum had ridden in, but he never came out the other end, and if he was still in the draw, he must have dug a hole big enough to hide himself and his horse. Clay went back for his horse, then rode into the passage to find where Slocum had decided to change directions, evidently going over the side of the draw.

Where would I set up to ambush somebody? Clay asked himself as he rode along the bottom of the defile. Picking a waist-high rock with sage on either end, he guided the paint up to it. He and the man he followed were of the same mind, because there were plenty of tracks to show that this was the spot where Slocum had waited to see if the war party was still following him. Clay had guessed right about the horse, too, for he found hoofprints showing where Slocum had led it from the brush at the edge of the ravine. Following the tracks leading from the rock, Clay found that they led back toward the entrance of the draw. *He's going back!*

The discovery surprised Clay. He hadn't figured on that. He figured Slocum would keep riding until he reached Fort Laramie. Evidently as soon as he determined he was not being followed by the Crow warriors, he headed right back the way he had come. *Probably riding back up the draw at the same time I was circling around to the other end,* Clay thought. He was beginning to realize the man he tracked was not easily frightened. Clay quickly climbed into the saddle and gave the paint his heels. Now there was no time to waste. Jim and his Crow friends had no idea the tables had been turned and they might now be stalked. A man who enjoyed killing as much as Slocum could do a lot of damage with a rifle before the war party knew what hit them.

Slocum was still boiling with anger when he had come to the narrow draw. He was the hunter. He didn't like it when the roles were reversed, and he damn sure couldn't abide being chased out of the valley by a handful of Crow warriors. It was a surprise to him that a small party of Crows would be this far away from their home territory. It might have been that they were looking for him. Looking back as he had galloped out of the little valley, he had been able to spot only eight Indians. Eight of any kind of Indians weren't too many for Slocum to handle, as long as he could call the play. It galled him to think they had gotten the jump on him.

It had made him mad enough to decide to wait in ambush to trim the odds down. So he had waited, getting madder by each long minute that passed with no sign of Indians. In a short while he realized they weren't coming after him at all. That realization served only to add to his anger. Maybe, he had guessed, they had decided to satisfy themselves with rescuing Jim Culver. After all, he was supposed to be a friend of theirs, according to that Pascal fellow who tried to steal his horse back by the Belle Fourche. His anger coming to a slow boil then, he trembled with the thought that Jim had escaped him again. That thought had caused him to immediately fetch his horse and head back to see for himself. Culver was his to kill. No Indian had the right to take that pleasure from him, and he would kill every damn one of them if he had to. Without totally realizing it, Slocum had permitted his frustration with Jim Culver—and his hatred for him—to take over his every waking thought, crowding out concern for his own safety. Not until Jim was killed by his hand would Slocum have peace of mind.

His shoulders and arms still sore from having been immobile for so many hours, Jim nevertheless was already beginning to regain some of his strength. The small amount of dried meat that Wolf Paw had provided served to make him feel stronger as he rode more upright in the saddle. He knew it would take a few days' rest and some solid food before he could fully recover. His immediate concern was for his brother's welfare. He hoped that Clay fully respected the evil cunning of the man he trailed. To fail to do so could mean tragic consequences.

With Wolf Paw leading the way, the small party of Crow warriors and one white man were crossing through a stand of cottonwoods close by the river when Jim heard the first shot. He looked back in time to see the rearmost warrior, a young man called Otter, grunt as if hit in the back with a fist. Without another sound the warrior rolled off his pony's back, falling in a heap. Within seconds another shot rang out, and the man riding next to Otter yelped in pain before sliding helplessly off his horse. With no need for a command, the remaining riders kicked their horses hard, charging for the closest safety, which was the low riverbank, while more shots flew over their heads.

Without a weapon of any kind, Jim could only scramble for cover to escape the almost constant whine of bullets as Slocum fired as fast as he could in hopes of a lucky hit. The riverbank being only about waist-high, there was no protection for the horses, and already two of them had been hit. It wasn't the best spot to defend against a rifle on the high ground, but there were no other choices.

"We have to let the horses go," Jim yelled as Wolf Paw dropped beside him in the sand. Wolf Paw nodded his agreement, and released the reins on his pony, giving the animal a hard slap on the rump to chase him away. Jim didn't like the idea of releasing the horses, but to try to keep them there would surely mean slaughter. There was no doubt in his mind that Slocum was the one doing the shooting, and he would not be inclined to spare the horses. The relentless villain had somehow managed to double back on them. Jim only hoped that it had not been at the expense of Clay's life.

Once everyone was safely out of the line of fire, the six surviving warriors spread out along the riverbank. Each man with a rifle dug into the bank, carving out a slot to fire from. That left Jim with no weapon and two of the warriors with bows only. *He couldn't have picked a better spot to hit us,* Jim thought as he tried to spot a muzzle flash, training his eyes along the edge of the trees, his gaze darting from trunk to trunk. "I can't see him," he said to Wolf Paw.

"I think he is moving in the trees," Wolf Paw replied, never taking his eyes from the cotton-woods. They looked at each other helplessly, re-signed to the fact that Slocum had them pinned down proper. Wolf Paw looked up at the cloudy gray sky. "It is still several hours till nightfall. We have no choice but to wait until dark, and then we can move out against him." Unable to think of a better plan, Jim nodded agreement.

Approximately 150 yards away, Slocum crawled up to a large cottonwood and peered around the trunk. Keeping his eyes on the rim of the riverbank, he scanned it left to right and back again, slowly, so as not to miss the smallest of movements. He grinned when his gaze caught a tiny stirring in the leaves that had fallen near the bank, and he stared at the spot until the top of a head gradually rose above the rim. Taking careful aim, he thought, *Here I am, darlin'*, and squeezed the trigger. Almost in-stantly a puff of dust flew up no more than half a foot from the dark hair, causing it to disappear once more. "Damn," he swore. He had missed, but he was certain he had cured one Indian from sticking his head up. He crawled backward a few yards, then moved over to take up a posi-tion behind another tree. *No sense in taking a chance*, he thought. From his new position he carefully scanned the riverbank once more. He almost chuckled when he caught sight of most of a head and part of a shoulder through a notch in the bank. Taking aim quickly, he squeezed the trigger again. This time he didn't miss. "Ha!" He grunted involuntarily when he saw the head snap sideways and blood splash.

Behind the bank, Wolf Paw cried out when he saw his friend Leads His Horse crumple and slide down the bank. Instantly overcome with grief and rage, he would have charged up out of the bank were it not for Jim's restraining hand on his arm.

"No!" Jim commanded. "He'll just cut you down, too."

Wolf Paw corralled his emotions, but he was not to be dissuaded. "We cannot sit here until he finally picks us off one by one." He motioned for the others to crawl over near him. "We must decide what to do," he said, searching each face. "I say we should attack him. He can't get us all."

Before the others could offer their thoughts, Jim interrupted. "He might not get us all, but he'll get two, maybe three of us if we come stormin' over this bank. It's me he wants. Because of me you've already lost three of your warriors. I think if he gets me, he'll let the rest of you go."

His statement was met at once with strong objections from all of the Crow warriors. "We will not lie here like women and let you sacrifice yourself to save us. It is better to die in battle than to slink home as cowards."

"Before you decide," Jim insisted, "at least let me try to talk to him. He intends to take me back to Fort Lincoln. He won't kill me." He knew what he said was a lie. It was more than likely Slocum would shoot him down on the spot. He wasn't inclined to sacrifice his life for much he could think of. But it wasn't right for Wolf Paw and his friends to die because of him. If Slocum was distracted by him, maybe at least they might have a chance to escape.

Wolf Paw wasn't sure that what Jim said was true. "I don't think we can trust this man's word even if he agrees not to shoot you." He looked at the others for help, but they all looked to him to make the decision. "I don't like this," he finally said, looking back at Jim.

"Hell, let's see what he says," Jim said. "Hand me Leads His Horse's rifle." Not waiting for any more objections from Wolf Paw, he took the rifle. Looking around for something to use as a flag, he settled on a red bandanna one of the warriors wore. The warrior gave it to him, and he tied it around the rifle barrel. Without another word he held the rifle up and waved it back and forth. Almost instantly the snap of a bullet cracked overhead, followed by the sound of the shot.

"Slocum!" Jim yelled as loudly as he could. "Hold your fire, dammit!" He wasn't sure Slocum heard him, but there was not another shot. "Let's talk, Slocum. Whaddaya say?"

"I'm listenin'," Slocum's voice came back from the tree line.

"You got us pinned down. We can't get out

before dark. But you can't get to us without getting yourself shot either. So it's a draw until dark, and then we'll spread out all around you."

A deep chuckle came from the trees, followed by, "There ain't gonna be none of you left by dark."

"You don't have any reason to kill these Indians. It's me you want. I'll make a deal with you. If you'll give me your word you'll let them ride out of here, I'll give myself up. Whaddaya say?"

Slocum could hardly believe what he was hearing. Culver was asking for his word? He almost laughed out loud. "Shore," he yelled back. "I'll give you my word. Come on out, but leave that rifle there."

"All right, I'm unarmed," Jim called out as he untied the bandanna from the rifle barrel, then checked to see if the magazine was fully loaded. He knew Slocum's word wasn't worth a pinch of horseshit, so he cocked the rifle, pulling a shell into the chamber. During his negotiations with Slocum, the Crow warriors listened, dumbfounded by what seemed to them a foolhardy plan. Jim looked at Wolf Paw and smiled. "You and the others get ready to make for the water, and head downstream as fast as you can when the shooting starts."

"I think he will shoot you as soon as you step out," Wolf Paw said soberly.

"Maybe so," Jim replied, "but I'm coming out shooting, and if he gives me any target at all, and this rifle shoots halfway straight, I just might get him." Not waiting to give Wolf Paw time to try to talk him out of it, he crawled up to the edge of the bank. "Slocum," he yelled, "I'm coming out. Where are you?"

"I'm right here," Slocum answered, still unable to believe his luck. "Come on out."

"I'm unarmed," Jim called back. "I need to see you to make sure you ain't planning to shoot me."

From behind a large cottonwood trunk, Slocum waved his arm up and down. "I'm right here."

"All right," Jim called back. "I'll count to three and we'll both come out at the same time. Is that agreed?" He turned to Wolf Paw. "I see where he's hiding. He'll have to show himself to shoot, so I'll start shooting as soon as I come out of here. I'll keep him behind that tree. You and your warriors get ready to run."

While Jim was talking, Slocum, his face lit up with a grin, eased back from the tree he had waved from and crawled as fast as he could to another some fifteen yards away. Settling in behind the roots of the tree, he had a clear view of the riverbank. He pulled the Winchester .73, with the initials J.R.C. carved in the stock, up into position and waited for the fun to begin.

Jim fully expected treachery on Slocum's part, but he decided to count to three anyway, on the hope that the surly brute might actually step out into the open. It was time to see who could bluff the best. In a loud, clear voice, he counted out,

"One . . . two . . . three," and dived over the rim of the bank, rolling over onto his belly, the rifle in firing position. There was no sign of Slocum, but Jim didn't hesitate. He covered the tree trunk with a barrage of rifle fire as fast as he could cock it and pull the trigger. Cottonwood bark flew in ragged pieces from both sides of the tree Slocum had waved from. Totally exposed, Jim knew his only hope was to keep Slocum pinned down behind the trunk while he made a run for cover in the trees. Counting his shots as he fired, he saved one round as his ace in the hole in case Slocum stepped out into the open. Firing all but that shot, he scrambled to his feet and began to sprint for cover, waiting for the inevitable from Slocum. But there was no return fire. The thought flashed before his mind that one of his shots might have landed.

He found it hard to believe he was still alive, now no more than a dozen yards from the edge of the trees. Suddenly his legs turned to lead as the adrenaline that had fueled his attack seemed to run out and he returned to his weakened state. Now that dozen yards seemed to be ten times that distance, and he could feel his legs beginning to fail. Still there was no gunfire from the cottonwood he had shredded. Confused, he pushed his exhausted body on.

"That was about as crazy a stunt as I've ever seen. What were you trying to do? Commit suicide?" Clay Culver stepped out to meet his brother at the edge of the trees.

Startled, Jim stopped in his tracks, staring in disbelief at the broad-shouldered mountain man. Drained of all energy, he uttered, "Ghost Wind," and, unable to take another step, sank down heavily to sit on the ground. After a few moments, he asked, "Slocum?"

Clay indicated with a tilt of his head and said, "Over there, tied to a tree."

Too exhausted to be excited about it, Jim followed the direction Clay indicated with his eyes. There, no more than a few yards from them, the surly grizzly that was Slocum was seated at the base of a tree, his arms thrust behind his back and tied around the trunk.

"He was sighting down on you with that fancy rifle of yours," Clay said.

"Damn," was all Jim could respond for a moment, knowing he had come within a hair of losing on the bluff. "Is he dead?"

"No," Clay said, after hesitating. "He ain't dead, just got a knot on his head." He glanced down at the war ax he carried in his belt. He then moved out in the open to stand beside Jim. "We'd best let those Crow friends of yours see that we're all right."

In the excitement of the previous minutes, Jim had forgotten about Wolf Paw and the others. He had been concerned with trying to keep from getting shot and had assumed that the Crow warriors were making their break from the riverbank. Still sitting in the sand, he turned to see Wolf Paw coming toward them, the other four behind him. Instead of running, Wolf Paw had decided to do what to him was the more sensible thing. As long as Jim had insisted upon sacrificing himself as a target, Wolf Paw kept his warriors in place, waiting to get a shot at Slocum when he came out in the open.

After they all greeted one another, Jim climbed wearily to his feet, and they went to check on their prisoner. Coming out of his daze minutes before being confronted by his captors, Slocum scowled like a caged grizzly. He didn't say anything, just glowered menacingly, his eyes darting back and forth under frowning dark brows at the Indians staring curiously at him. Jim was still a little surprised that Clay had not simply shot the beast, but Wolf Paw did not find it surprising at all. The willful murderer of Newt Plummer and three of his warriors should not have been spared a slow, torturous death.

"Whaddaya wanna do with him?" Jim asked, uncertain what his brother had in mind.

Clay shrugged indifferently. "I thought you might have a notion on that, since you're the one he damn near killed." While Jim was thinking about it, Clay went on. "We can just shoot him right now, but shootin' might be too good for the likes of him. You might be thinkin' about taking him back to Laramie and turning him over to the army. But we sure as hell ain't lawmen or soldiers. The army would probably tell you they don't want him for anything. They ain't gonna hang him just because we say he oughta be hung." He glanced over at Wolf Paw. "I'm thinkin' we might wanna turn him over to the Crows. They sure as hell know how to take care of scum like him." Wolf Paw gave him a knowing glance and nodded.

Slocum had been sitting silently during the discussion of his fate, scowling as each warrior bent close to look at him. Clay's third option grabbed his attention sufficiently to cause him to speak. "Who the hell are you?" he demanded of Clay, still more than a little surprised that a man that size had been able to move up behind him and knock him in the head without making a sound.

Clay favored him with a patient smile, but ignored his demand. Instead he turned back to Jim. "Whaddaya say, little brother? Let Wolf Paw take him? I expect you'd want to deal with him yourself if you were in a little better shape, but maybe you'll be satisfied with a little Crow justice."

Jim stared at the man who had tormented him so, harmed the girl he loved, killed the man who nursed him back to health, and killed young Luke Kendall. Yesterday he had been kept alive almost entirely by the will to survive, just for an opportunity to strike back at the animal. Now he only felt tired, and didn't feel the need for personal satisfaction. He just wanted Slocum's life to end, to put a stop to a crazed killer. He turned to Wolf Paw. "You take him." A spontaneous war whoop rang out from one of the warriors, and Wolf Paw immediately directed his warriors to seize Slocum.

"You call yourselves men?" Slocum roared as two of the Crows jumped to the task. "By God, it's gonna take all of you bastards to kill me. Let me fight for my life. Any one of you man enough to face me?" He ranted and growled, even as the two warriors untied his wrists and, holding him by his arms, pulled him to his feet. "By God, I'll fight any *two* of you." He glowered directly at Clay. "You're the big stud here. I claim my right to fight for my life. It's Injun law."

Clay smiled at the belligerent bully. "Now, who the hell ever told you that? There ain't no rules in the game you've been playing."

Slocum's eyes narrowed as he was led past Clay. "I'd break your back for you," he growled.

Ignoring him, Clay turned his back, concerned now with his brother. "We'd best get you to Canyon Creek and rest you up a spell." He had just gotten the words out when he heard a warrior cry out behind him. He turned to discover Slocum charging him like a crazed grizzly. The warrior who had cried out in pain was lying on the ground, his arm broken and hanging at a crazy angle. The other warrior had been slammed into Wolf Paw and the others, knocking them backward. Clay saw the flash of the knife Slocum had pulled out of the Crow warrior's belt as the desperate bully attacked. With no time to think about it, Clay dropped to his knee, meeting Slocum's charge with a shoulder placed solidly beneath his rib cage. He narrowly missed feeling the bite of the skinning knife as Slocum took a wild swing and missed. Then, like a huge cat, Clay thrust his shoulder upward, lifting the huge man off his feet and tumbling him head over heels. Slocum landed on his back, knocking the wind from his lungs. Still like a great cat, Clay turned to face his adversary again, crouching, ready to spring, while Slocum strained to get his breath. Clay watched him carefully as Slocum recovered and picked up the knife now lying on the ground beside him. With an enraged roar, the brutal bounty hunter sprang to his feet. With the knife raised to strike, he set himself to charge.

The shot that split the air startled both participants. Slocum looked stunned, and suddenly stopped. He dropped to his knees, staring but not seeing, as a trickle of blood began from the small dark hole in his forehead and ran down his nose. On his knees for only a moment, he finally fell, face-first, to the ground with a heavy and final impact.

"You took your time about it," Clay remarked nonchalantly, still looking at the belligerent monster at his feet.

"You looked like you were enjoying it," Jim replied with equal casualness. "I didn't wanna spoil your fun."

Chapter 17

Since Iron Bow's village was closer than Canyon Creek, Clay decided it would be best to go with Wolf Paw so that Jim could regain his strength before going back. They reached the camp late on a snowy afternoon, leading the horses carrying the bodies of the three slain warriors. It was not a joyous reception because of the loss of the three young men. But Jim and Clay were welcomed warmly. Iron Bow was especially glad to see Jim again, but he could not help but express his amazement that once again his young white friend was recovering after cheating death. "Dead Man," he called him. "I think you cannot die because you are already dead and you choose to walk among the living."

Slocum's scalp was displayed on a lance that was placed before Newt Plummer's lodge. The lodge itself had been moved to the edge of the camp and the entrance flap sewn up with the old white man's body inside.

In two days' time, with nourishing food prepared by Iron Bow's wife, Jim was fully recovered and ready to start out for Canyon Creek. Clay had resisted most of his brother's inquiries about Lettie, not wishing to give Jim more to worry about. He figured there was plenty of time to deal with that. Jim, however, was not that patient, and pressed Clay to tell him the full extent of Lettie's injuries. On the day that the brothers took their leave of Iron Bow's village, Clay finally relented.

"Jim, there's no way of tellin' how much worse or better Lettie is since I left there. We'll just have to wait and see. But you might as well resign yourself to the fact that Lettie might not ever be right again, at least the way you used to know her. I don't know what you'll find when we get back. She was hurt pretty bad. It looked to me like that bastard broke her nose when he hit her with his fist. I reckon there's been time by now for most of the swellin' and bruises to go away. But that ain't the part that worries me." He paused, seeing the hurt in Jim's eyes. "I'm sorry to be the one to have to tell you about this, but it looks like she got hit pretty hard beside the temple. And I guess that's the one that did the most damage. When I saw her she would just sit there, staring off somewhere. She doesn't say a word. She acts like you ain't even there. It's gonna be hard for you, Jim. I don't know what else to tell you. It's just that the Lettie you knew ain't there anymore."

It was with those sobering thoughts that Jim bade farewell to Wolf Paw, promising to come back in the summer to hunt with him. They left the Crow village, leaving tracks in new snow that had fallen during the night. There was a hollow feeling in Jim's heart and a sadness at leaving his Crow friends. He was riding Toby, a fact that brought some comfort. And as he followed Clay's paint up from the river, he reached down and rubbed his fingers over the initials carved in the stock of the Winchester. At least some things were back to where they were before his whole world had turned upside down.

Katie Mashburn straightened up and rubbed the small of her back. At times like these she missed the hell out of Luke. He used to do most of the woodcutting. She paused to think about the boy for a moment. He had been almost like a son to her. *God*, she thought, *I could sure use his help around here now*. Laying her ax aside, she gazed out across the stark white expanse of pasture. Something had caught her eye. Her hand automatically dropped to rest on her pistol as she strained to focus on two dark objects against the snowy background of the far ridge.

As she continued to watch, the objects took definite shape, and she said a silent prayer that it might be whom she hoped for. It took forever, it seemed, before the two riders were close enough for her to make the decision whether or not she should go back to the cabin and get the rifle. She looked back then at the cabin, thinking of the girl inside. Lettie had taken a turn for the worse. For the past few days she had been more and more lethargic. And two nights ago she went to bed and failed to wake up the next morning. Distressed, Katie had pressed her ear to the young girl's chest. There was still a heart-beat, but the breathing became fainter on the following day. Katie didn't know what to do for her. The girl couldn't go on without food and water. It could only be a matter of time.

Her eyes constantly on the two riders now, she began to feel an excitement inside and a rac-ing of her pulse, as she realized that it *was* whom she most wanted to see at that moment. There was no mistaking the imposing figure on the lead horse. Tall and straight, Clay Culver always looked at home on a horse, riding with an easy motion that seemed in tune with the animal's every move. It was a sight that Katie had become familiar with over the past few years, and one that she secretly admired. It gave her a sense of peace. Behind him, in almost identical fashion, his younger brother rode. At a distance, most folks would find it hard to distinguish one brother from the other. But Katie could tell them apart, even almost five hundred yards away. She immediately turned and started toward the cabin. They would be hungry.

Inside, she pulled the quilt aside that served as a room divider and looked in on the sleeping girl. Bending close over her, she whispered, "Jim and Clay are back, Lettie. Don't you want to wake up and see Jim?" There was no response from the young girl, and Katie bent closer to make sure Lettie was still breathing. Feeling helpless, she shook her head sadly, thinking of the moment when Jim would first see her. She straightened up and said, "It's all right, honey, wherever your poor mind is right now." With a long sigh she closed the quilt again and went to the stove.

Taking the dipper, she filled the coffeepot with water from the water bucket and set it on the stove to heat while she ground fresh coffee beans. Looking around to see what else she could provide in a hurry for two hungry men, her eyes settled on the pan of biscuits she had baked that morning. When she had baked them she had intended for them to last for two or three days. *They'll have to do*, she thought. *I can fry some bacon to go with 'em.* Satisfied that it would suffice, she went back outside to greet the brothers.

As soon as she emerged from the cabin, Jim held up his arm and waved. She waved back, thinking, *Would it break your arm to wave, Clay Culver?* As was his nature, Clay displayed no emotion beyond the faint hint of a smile as he and Jim rode past the corral and pulled up before Katie. He took his time dismounting. Jim, on the other hand, jumped down quickly and gave Katie a friendly hug. "Well, I came back from the dead," he said, smiling.

She gave his arm an extra squeeze. "I wasn't sure I'd ever see you again." Then she turned to face Clay.

"Katie," was Clay's simple greeting.

"Clay," she returned, determined to match his detached air. She met his gaze and couldn't help but feel his eyes had so much more to say to her. "I put some coffee on as soon as I saw you," she said.

"Much obliged," he said. Then his eyes glanced toward the cabin door. "Lettie?"

In answer, she shook her head slowly. Turning to Jim, she took his arm again. "Jim, I wish I could tell you some good news, but I can't. Lettie's alive, but she's gone from this world. You just have to accept it. That bastard's killed her just as sure as he took a gun and shot her."

Jim didn't speak for a moment, his emotions prohibiting vocal response. He nodded his head to indicate he understood, then said, "I need to see her."

She released his arm and stepped back to stand beside Clay. "I'll take care of the horses," Clay said softly. Katie took Toby's reins and walked with Clay to the corral so Jim could be alone with Lettie.

Seeing the bruised face of the young girl stunned him for a brief moment as he stood over her bed. In spite of Clay's efforts to prepare him, Jim was shocked by the deathlike scene he now witnessed. The shock lasted for only an instant before giving way to grief-stricken compassion. He caught a dry sob in his throat as he gazed at the fragile lines of her sweet young face, still showing faint scars from the blows delivered by the evil Slocum. The sight of it filled his heart anew with the anger he had experienced on that day, when he was helpless to protect her. Looking at her now, he saw that she seemed to be in a deep sleep, far away from this rough frontier cabin, perhaps too far to ever return.

"I'm so sorry," he whispered, feeling the guilt of failing to protect her from Slocum's vicious attack. He knew at that moment that he wanted her to live more than anything he had ever wanted in his life. He could not bear the thought of losing her. He took her hand in his and whispered, "Lettie, honey, it's me, Jim." It was more than he could bear. Kneeling down beside her, he buried his face in her limp hand, wishing that he could cry. There were so many things he should have told her. He cursed himself for his fear of being tied down. He should have told her he loved her when he had the chance. Now it was too late. He had been a fool.

"Jim?" The voice was weak, barely above a whisper.

Not sure he hadn't imagined it, he raised his head to look at her. He *had* imagined it, he thought, and his heart sank again. But then her eyelids flickered slightly and opened. "Jim?" she repeated.

"Yes, I'm here," he said, unable to control the emotion in his voice. "I'm here, honey."

Her voice faint, barely above a whisper, she said something, but it was too weak for him to understand. He bent low over her, his ear close to her mouth. "I knew you'd come back to me," she whispered.

"Nothing could have stopped me," he said tenderly. "I love you."

Her face relaxed in a gentle smile. "I know," she whispered contentedly. "I've always known." She closed her eyes then. "I'm very tired."

"You need to rest. You've been through a real bad time. I'll be here when you wake up." He kissed her lightly on her lips and stepped away to look at her while she went to sleep. Hearing Clay and Katie come in then, he turned and motioned for them to be quiet. "She's gonna be all right. She woke up and talked to me."

With a look of great relief transforming her face, Katie beamed at Clay, then hurried to check on Lettie herself. There was a change in the young girl's face, one that seemed to indicate an inner peace. But she was so still that Katie bent low to listen to her breathing. At once alarmed, she pressed an ear to Lettie's heart. It confirmed what she feared. Lettie was gone.

The settlers of Canyon Creek gathered on a snowy winter afternoon for yet another funeral at Katie Mashburn's farm. This time it was to say good-bye to one who had not been long among them, but had already firmly established herself as one who belonged. As Reverend Lindstrom offered the final prayer, Clay Culver turned and gazed toward the mountains beyond the north pass. There, on a distant ridge, he could just make out the outline of a solitary figure on horseback, standing motionless for a few moments before turning and disappearing slowly into the tall pines. Clay understood. His brother could not bear to watch Lettie being lowered into the frozen ground. Jim would come back and say his final farewell over Lettie's grave when the two of them could be alone. Right now Jim could find the solace he desperately needed only in the high, rocky bosom of the mountains.

SIGNET

Charles G. West
HERO'S STAND

Up in the Montana mountains, Canyon Creek is the perfect little town for Simon Fry and his men to hole up for the winter. The folks are friendly enough to open their homes to eight perfect strangers—and gullible enough to believe that Fry's gang is a militia sent to protect them from hostile Indians.

Jim Culver is new in town, but he knows something isn't right about Simon Fry's "militia." They seem more interested in intimidating people than helping them. Anyone who questions them ends up dead or driven out. Someone has to step forward to protect the people of Canyon Creek from their new "protectors."

That someone is Jim Culver. And this sleepy town is about to wake up with a bang

0-451-20822-6

Available wherever books are sold, or
to order call: 1-800-788-6262

No other series has this much historical action!

THE TRAILSMAN

Available wherever books are sold, or
to order call: 1-800-788-6262

S310